A DANGEROUS DESIRE . . .

Longarm knelt beside her on the grass. She moved close to him and began talking in a low, overheated whisper . . .

He wanted to warn her once more that they might be throwing away their only chance to escape—their chance to get out of this alive. Wasting time and precious energy like this could be hazardous to their health.

But she needed loving. And besides, she'd already said it: God had yet to invent a better way to die . . .

Also in the **LONGARM** series
from Jove

TABOR EVANS

LONGARM

ON THE HUMBOLDT

A JOVE BOOK

First Jove edition published January 1981

10 9 8 7 6 5 4 3 2 1

Printed in the United States of America

Jove books are published by Jove Publications, Inc.,
200 Madison Avenue, New York, NY 10016

Chapter 1

The first time Longarm saw her, he felt as if someone had tied a wicked half hitch in the taut nerves deep in his belly.

Until now, the long stage ride north to Denver had been tiring, tedious, boring, and monotonously uncomfortable. At Devil's Gorge station, things looked up. Way up. All the way up.

" 'Board. All aboard." The driver came out of the way-station cafe, still chewing his steak and potatoes.

She stood near the brink of the platform, regal, yet somehow helpless, as if she were used to people jumping to wait on her. She wore—and it wasn't so much *what* she wore as the *way* she wore it—a tan traveling suit that appeared, from Longarm's vantage point inside the shadowed coach, to have been more sculpted than tailored to her stunning form. Though her fur-trimmed jacket was severely plain, her ruffled white shirt pinned primly at the base of her throat, and the hem of her pleated skirt revealing no more than the color and shape of her high-button shoes, the total effect was devastating. A man looked at her and thought, between sweet anguish and bitter delight, "Oh, damn."

She didn't move. Obviously she was waiting for someone to stow her bag and hand her inside the coach, which was already crowded with two middle-aged men, Longarm, and a sour-faced woman in her forties. The gal on the platform didn't have to worry about being ignored. She stood there and stopped traffic in every direction. Men bumped into each other and into uprights and baggage, ogling her.

Longarm grinned. He didn't blame them. She was somewhere in her twenties; hard to tell exactly about women's ages these days. Anyway, it was difficult to determine because you couldn't see her eyes. She wore dark brown smoked glasses, almost as if she were hiding something, or hiding from somebody. And with a shape like hers, that wasn't easy. She was tall for a woman, and every inch was stacked like silver in a poke. It was mostly an essence of beauty—some aura emanating from inside her. Someone had told her once that she was beautiful, and she'd never forgotten it. By now, nobody around her could forget it.

Her hair was blonde, piled fine-spun and pleated and twisted in a rich old-gold color, and caught in a thick bun at the nape of her slender neck. Her lips were perfect, like chiseled red shards of precious jewels, and her skin was as smooth as molten gold. She was slim, but her high-standing breasts bulged elegantly, her waist was flat and trim, and her hips plunged to long legs that wouldn't stop, outlined under that restraining outer garment. Looking at her, Longarm got the intoxicating feeling that she wasn't wearing *anything* under that traveling suit. Or maybe he just hoped she wasn't. He wondered what color those eyes were, and why she hid them.

The driver caught the rest-iron to swing himself up on the boot from the raised platform. He stopped as if poleaxed, gawking at the slim, trim-waisted woman. There were few women in the West, and almost none who grabbed your eyes and held them until they burned and hurt.

"You going on this coach, miss?"

"Yes." Her voice was as lovely as her appearance, modulated and throaty. A voice meant to whisper caresses. "Would you take care of my bag?"

"Yes, ma'am. Where you going?"

"Denver. This is the stage to Denver, isn't it?"

"Sure is." The driver spoke as though these were the proudest words he knew and he was happy to be able to speak them. He might have lied to please her.

He secured the bag and then stood grinning, ox-like, at her.

She favored him with a dazzling smile and lifted her arm. "If you'll help me, please?"

He leaped to obey, forgetting to chew, suspending respiration. Who could blame him? How many times did a rough, horse-smelling fellow like him get invited to touch such a beauty?

He held open the door and she stepped into the cab. She caught her shoe on the step and stumbled slightly, but he grabbed her adroitly with both hands. "You're all right, miss," he assured her.

"Of course I am."

Longarm grinned faintly. She would have gotten three votes on how all right she was from within the coach. The elderly woman, with that evil instinct sometimes native to aging females, got up and plopped herself into the seat facing to the rear beside Longarm, making room for the girl at the window, beside the two older men. Longarm could see them mentally burning candles to the old biddy.

The driver and the two male passengers beside the girl made her as comfortable as possible. The driver grinned helplessly at her, totally enchanted. "Nothing else I can do, miss?"

Her smile was rarer gratuity than a gold piece. "No. I'm fine, driver, thank you."

Reluctantly the stout, bearded driver slammed the cab door and swung up on the boot. He pushed off the hand brake and cracked the whip, and with a jostling, camel-like motion, a creaking of metal and the scream of thoroughbraces, the four-span coach headed northward through the pine forests toward Denver.

The stage swayed and rocked worse than a boat battered in a gale. The woman beside Longarm went deathly pale and bit back bile gorging up into her throat, already sick to her stomach.

The beautiful blonde remained cool, self-possessed, regal, and serene. Dust clouded past the windows, but she ignored it, glancing warmly at the people inside the

7

cab. "My name is Alicia Payson," she announced as she turned, dazzling the man beside her with a smile.

He introduced himself in turn, shaking her hand and giving her a thumbnail sketch of his life until this moment. The fat man was next. He told her his name and where he was from and how long he'd been selling leather goods in this territory.

"I'm sure it's very exciting," Alicia Payson said. "You both sound as if you lead stimulating lives. I envy both of you."

"I'm Emma Frye," the woman beside Longarm said. "I'm not usually this morose, but I've been ill since this terrible contraption took off from the station. Does that man have to drive so fast?"

"I imagine he has a schedule he has to keep," Alicia said. She reached across and patted Emma Frye's hand. But her head was tilted, her nostrils flared slightly, as if she were studying Longarm minutely.

Longarm remained slouched in the corner of the cab. He kept his snuff-brown Stetson tilted low on his forehead, shadowing his eyes, his face in repose, an unlit nickel cheroot clenched between his teeth. His features appeared hewn from stone in his deeply tanned face.

He was a tall man, exceptionally tall when the average height for American males was five feet, six inches. He towered almost ten inches above that, lean, muscular, and rock-hard, his body conditioned by the demands of his profession. He was just on the downhill side of thirty, but there remained nothing youthful in his rugged face. It was braised and cured to a saddle-leather brown, and she could not see his gunmetal-blue eyes in the deep shadow of his flat hatbrim. He touched at his carefully trimmed and waxed longhorn mustache and returned her gaze with a faint, teasing smile, but he did not speak.

He supposed he didn't appear too prepossessing to Alicia Payson, and figured it was just as well. There was something of the pampered aristocrat about her. She had the thrilling beauty of a well-made fantasy, but there was about her the sort of scrubbed purity that warned that the trail into her bedroom led past the altar, and Longarm was not at that place in his life where he could get involved in cottage talk.

He sighed and sank deeper into the uncomfortable seat, aware that Emma Frye was getting paler and sicker by the mile. He stretched out his tweed-clad legs and wriggled his toes inside his low-heeled cavalry stovepipe boots. These, he'd discovered, were far more suited for running than for riding, which was just what he wanted. He spent at least as much time out of the saddle as in it, and in these boots he could outrun almost any pursuer, except maybe the rare bad dreams that chased him in the night.

He shifted his cross-draw gunbelt, moving the double-action Colt Model T .44-40 to give the ailing Mrs. Frye more room.

He sweated under his brown frock coat and gray flannel shirt. He wanted to loosen the string tie at his throat, but did not. His sweating didn't make sense, because every roll of the stage carried them higher into the afternoon mountain chill. He decided he was uncomfortably hot either because that girl was lovely beyond compare or because she stared at him, smilingly yet intensely, across the narrow space.

"Don't you want to tell us who you are?" Alicia Payson said. "It makes traveling together so much more enjoyable if we know each other."

Longarm grinned at Alicia tautly, thinking, *You know damned good and well, lady, you don't care who I am—a rough and ordinary lawman who smells like horse sweat, cheap cigars, and rye whiskey.*

"I'm Custis Long," Longarm said. "They call me Longarm."

"I'll bet they do," Alicia said. She gave him a faint, wry smile. "Do you want to say why?"

Longarm shrugged. "Everybody's got to be called something, and I figure anything beats Custis."

She smiled, as if pleased about something. "Don't they, though?" Her head tilted slightly. "Could it be because you are somehow involved with the law? Oh, not against it. In it. Do they call you the Longarm of the Law?"

He laughed. "How did you know that?"

But she did not smile. "I have special—powers—like that," she said. "For instance, I could have told Mr. Beale he was a leather salesman before he told me. And I knew Mr. Jacob was a clothing representative."

"Ladies lines," Mr. Jacob said.

"And Mrs. Frye," Alicia began, and then she stopped, a look of alarm in her face. She leaned forward, taking Emma Frye's hands in her own. "Are you all right, Mrs. Frye?"

Emma Frye tried to smile, but failed. "If I were on the ocean, I'd know what was wrong with me—I'd know I was seasick."

"I do think it's riding backwards," Alicia Payson said, her voice gentle and throaty with concern. "Sometimes riding facing the wrong way can be very upsetting. Wouldn't you like to trade places with me?"

Emma Frye thanked her gratefully, and they exchanged places in the bouncing cab. Both Jacob and Beale were so busy supporting Alicia that they were unable to lend any assistance at all to Mrs. Frye. Emma sagged her head against the window sill, sucking in fresh air. Alicia Payson fell hard against Longarm, and for a long moment the full insulation of her spectacular breasts pressed against him. She sank back in the seat, smiling. "There. Isn't that better now?"

Alicia asked him the usual casual traveler's questions, and he gave her polite answers. He'd been born in West-by-God-Virginia, had lived through the troubled times leading up to the late War, had suffered during its battles, and had grown up in the tragic Reconstruction years that followed. He'd drifted west a long time ago. In his time he'd been a soldier, a cowboy, a railroader, a hard-rock miner, and, for the past eight or ten years, a lawman.

As for Alicia, she'd lost her father tragically when she was six years old. She'd been in Texas most recently, and was traveling alone from necessity, though this was almost unheard of for a woman. It had to be done. It was urgent that she get in touch with a certain man in Denver.

10

"Maybe I can help you find him," Longarm offered idly, being polite, not really meaning it, chatter passed between strangers.

"Maybe you can." The way she spoke, with steel ribbing underlining each word, charged through Longarm. Even when she smiled, this girl was serious. Deadly serious.

As the westering sun set behind the Colorado foothills in the long climb to the Mile-High City, a bone-chilling cold permeated the coach. At the next way station, the driver thrust three heavy buffalo robes through a window. "You folks snuggle down under these," he said. "You'll think you're a-settin' before a roaring fire at the Ritz."

Darkness smoked down upon them, and the horses settled to a steady pace. The blonde remained sitting straight, but she shared one huge robe with Longarm. Its lining was pleasant against his hands. He heard her teeth chatter, but she said nothing. But before they'd traveled five miles, she'd shifted until her trim thigh and shapely leg rested hotly against Longarm.

Longarm kept his flat-brimmed hat lowered and straight on his head, cavalry-style, and said nothing. The darkness flooded the interior of the cab, making a stygian grotto of it with the oil-cloth curtains secured at the windows. Emma Frye, slightly recovered, was the first to surrender to sleep, snoring loudly. Soon Jacob had sunk against her, almost pulling the shared robe off Mr. Beale. But this worthy gentleman was obviously sleeping quietly too, for he did not even protest, blowing tiny bubbles between parted lips.

Longarm was tired, but knew he was not going to sleep this side of Denver, and maybe never again as long as this heavenly body jostled so intimately against him. He found his mind and senses totally preoccupied by this blonde beside him. She sagged more and more upon him, her head bobbing tiredly. He felt his heartbeat speed up as the faint, clean-scrubbed scent of her body attacked his nostrils.

When finally she let her head fall upon his shoulder, he reckoned she was asleep and pulled the heavy buffalo robe up closer around her. In doing so, his hand brushed the upthrust resiliency of one of her breasts. He moved his hand away quickly. Rather than retreating, the blonde turned a little more toward him. He allowed her to snuggle her head into the less bony area between his shoulder blade and his neck. She pressed down into its softness as if it were a pillow.

Now Longarm was in trouble. Her rich, spun-gold blonde hair lay within inches of his nostrils. The strange, warm musk of her hair assaulted and intoxicated him and, believing her asleep, he let his cheek rest against the fragrant crown of her head, and drank in the rich incense of her.

Across the dark well of the tonneau, the other three passengers slept soundly, bouncing and tumbling with the sway of the coach. Longarm felt as if he were neither fully awake nor completely asleep, but rocking in sweet discomfort in some netherworld.

He grinned tautly. Even had he created this fantasy, it was unlikely he would have peopled it with such an incredibly lovely creature. She pressed closer and her lips brushed his throat, a touch as light and random as the flitting of a butterfly, but as hot as sparks of hellfire. His heart thudded raggedly. Was she nuzzling his throat in her sleep? Was it entirely accidental or on purpose that she raked his sensitive skin with her perfect lips?

She did not move for a long time, and just when he decided she was asleep, she slid her arm across his chest. Now her breasts, like gentle lances, impaled him, and he wondered if she felt the fusillading thunder of his heart.

Slowly, almost imperceptibly, her hand loosed its tenuous grip on the upper pocket of his vest. Her fingers shifted downward, with the terrible slowness of an ice floe, to the gold chain that linked his watch in one vest pocket to the double-barreled .44-caliber derringer in the other. She shifted her hip, bumping the Colt .44-40 in its holster. He grinned tautly. By now, these were not the only guns loaded and primed for action under that buffalo robe.

12

He began to sweat, but he would not have moved the robe even if he melted down. That slowly drooping arm was driving him loco, and he waited with bated breath to find where it would finally settle. Every time they struck a bump or a pothole, or rounded a curve in the darkness, that hand lost a little of its battle against gravity. It rested now against the heavy brass of his belt buckle.

When he was certain she must be asleep, he was sorely tempted to place her errant hand gently where it would be warmest and do the most good. She spoke suddenly in a throaty whisper, and he started, literally shocked.

"Do you mind if I move closer, Mr. Longarm? I . . . want to have a . . . private . . . talk with you."

Longarm tried to keep his voice level, but his heart pounded so that he felt breathless. With that throbbing eminence poised just below his belt buckle and her straying hand, he could not see how there could be any mistaking her meaning in using that word *private*.

"Talk," he invited. "I'll lie and say I'm all ears."

Instead of speaking, Alicia let her hand move down over the buckle. Unable to believe what was happening, he felt her fighting the buttons on the fly of his skin-tight, brown tweed pants.

He wondered if he was asleep, lost in the kind of fantasy that attacks every man traveling alone. Had he fallen asleep hours earlier? Was he doomed to awaken any minute, throbbing and in pain—and alone?

He bit down hard on his underlip. This blonde knew what she was doing, with a wisdom as old as womankind. She knew what she wanted. She had far less trouble loosening his buttons than he'd had cursing them closed.

He sucked in a deep breath, feeling her clasp his throbbing erection in her fist, and he was rewarded by hearing her delighted and shocked intake of breath.

"I had—no idea," she whispered, awed, against his chest. Her head was well under the robe now. He

13

moved only enough to slip his hand beneath the fiery heat of her upper arm.

Her hand moved faster on him, and he could feel the fire of her rasping breath. Closing his eyes and praying that he would never wake up, he let his seeking hand cover the fevered rise of her breasts. She let him force her head down to the flat plane of his stomach with his kisses against her sweetly fragrant hair.

To preserve his sanity as long as possible, he tried to keep his mind from directly considering what she was doing to him under that robe. She was fierce about it, dedicated to pleasing him right out of his skull. He didn't know if she wanted it all, but he did know that any minute, unless she moved quickly, she was going to get it.

With one hand, he gripped her head as if in a vise. She sent him spiraling mindlessly out of himself. He was aware of unbuttoning her blouse, fondling and caressing the smooth, burning flesh. He even pulled her skirt up around her hips and verified what he'd suspected to be true. She was absolutely naked under that elegant tan traveling suit!

"Mr. Long?"

Longarm straightened, trembling, as if someone had ambushed him.

He jerked his head up. Disoriented for a moment, he gazed at Emma Frye, sitting forward in the seat across from him. He knew what was happening to him, but he almost didn't know where he was. "Ma'am?"

Mrs. Frye nodded. "Just woke up. Is little Miss Payson all right?"

"Oh, she's . . . just fine." He lowered his voice, feeling Alicia's frantic caresses under that robe. "I think she's trying to get . . . some sleep."

"I do hope she feels all right."

"She feels real good, ma'am. How are you feeling?"

His heart pounding raggedly, Longarm fought to keep his voice normal, because he was a hundred miles from feeling normal or sane, trying to carry on this conversation with the aging woman while Alicia drove him out of his mind.

14

"Much better," Mrs. Frye said. "Oh, I feel much better. I guess riding backwards did upset me. I hope it won't make poor little Miss Payson ill. How long before we come into Denver?"

Longarm pretended to consider her question. "We ought to be coming in . . . pretty soon, ma'am."

"Well, I'll just try to get a little more sleep."

"Yes, ma'am. You do that."

Suddenly he reached the point of no return, that sweetly agonizing place where he could hold back no longer. He felt her close her arms about him in a fierce embrace, and for an eternal moment in time the bouncing, jostling, rocking coach was as still as a swan in a warm sea. The world didn't move; it stood still somewhere between heaven and earth. . . .

When the stagecoach pulled into the brightly lighted station at Denver, Alicia sat up primly and patted her hair. She looked untouched, untouchable. She said goodbye to the other travelers, who yawned and pressed her hand. She whispered to Longarm. "Stay where you are. I've something I must say to you."

He shrugged and nodded, pleased to oblige. He watched the others walk away. He turned back, feeling the blunt muzzle of his own derringer biting into his neck, just under his left ear.

He sighed. "Well, you got my gun in more ways than one, didn't you?"

"Nothing is ever free, Mr. Longarm."

"A sad fact of life, Miss Payson."

"You do as I say and you won't be hurt."

"I'm already deeply hurt."

"I want you to take me to the Windsor Hotel."

"Hell, I'd have been glad to do that without a show of firearms."

"You'll find I'm deadly serious, Mr. Longarm. There's more to it than merely delivering me to the Windsor Hotel."

"I'd be sick if there wasn't."

"Any cab could do that. You'll accompany me to the Windsor Hotel. You'll register me as your wife."

15

"I'd yell for the law. Except I am the law."

"When we're in the hotel, I'll tell you why I was looking for you . . . why I was on my way to Denver to find you."

His lips sagged open. "You? Looking for me? How'd you ever even hear of me?"

"From a Texas Ranger. He couldn't help me, but he said you were the best lawman he'd ever met. He said you can find any man, if anybody could. He also told me that you are a federal marshal, but you might work for me—even part-time—if I could get your attention. Well, I've tried to get your attention, Mr. Longarm."

He laughed, shaking his head. "Holy mother."

"My grandfather used to say, Mr. Longarm, that a mule would work well for you—but you had to get the mule's attention first. My grandfather always used a club."

"Crude, but effective, I'm sure," he commented wryly.

"I met you and decided what sort of man you were and what would get your attention in the quickest possible manner."

"I can tell. Price is no object with a girl like you."

She thrust the gun into his neck. "Maybe you'll believe, at least, how serious I am."

"I am convinced, Miss Payson."

"Then let's go."

"After you," he said.

"You'll have to help me," she said. She whipped off the smoked glasses.

A sick horror spread through Longarm like a debilitating illness. Her eyes were almost colorless—empty, staring, a faint milky blue under thick, upcurled lashes.

No wonder she wore those concealing glasses. Alicia Payson was as blind as true love.

16

Chapter 2

Waist-deep in hot water—and he recognized that this was figuratively true as well as literally—Longarm shared with Alicia Payson an ornately carved brass tub for two, in the dressing alcove off the bedroom on the second floor of the Windsor Hotel.

They sat facing each other, legs entangled intimately, and heavily coated with soap suds with which they took turns scrubbing each other vigorously and lingeringly. Longarm found especially alluring the prolonged soaping of Alicia's full breasts and the flat planes of her waist. They had spent a great deal of bath-time wrapped in a fevered embrace because the steaming suds, the intimacy, the shared massages, Alicia's ethereal beauty —everything—aroused them.

"You're incredible," she whispered. "I never suspected that men—any man—after the first time, could . . . could . . ."

"Rise to battle again?"

"That often. I thought once . . . and it was over for hours."

Longarm shrugged, then realized that the gesture couldn't be seen by Alicia, so he said, "Don't know that I could, always, but I reckon when I got a pretty enough reason . . ."

Alicia laughed and blushed, soaping him intimately. Waves of pleasure percolated upward, exploding at the crown of his skull like Roman candles. "Do I look pretty to you?" she asked.

He placed her hand upon his rising eminence. "Can't you tell?"

She nodded, but her expression became serious.

"Sometimes I can feel, even across a room, the . . . vibrations of some men toward me."

"I'll bet you can."

She smiled again, fleetingly. "You have lovely vibrations." She placed her warm, soft palm against his cheek, and went on, "It's important that you believe I have this highly developed . . . power . . . to pick up vibrations from others. If you don't, you may not believe all I have to tell you. And you must believe me; I do have this power. I'm sure it's because I'm blind. My other senses are keener than most people's— that's not unusual—but there's something else. I just *know* things about the way people feel toward me, the same way I can sense obstacles in my path, which is how I can get around as well as I do, without help. But I need help now, Longarm. *Your* help."

She withdrew her hands from his body and shook her lovely pale blonde hair, then stood up suddenly, spilling water and glistening in the light.

Longarm reached out to support her, but Alicia stepped from the tub as a sighted woman might. She hesitated a fraction of a moment, then took up one of the folded bath-sized hotel towels and shook it out.

Feeling the stirring of renewed desire kindled by the sight of her naked, long-stemmed, slender body, the way her breasts tautened when she lifted her arms over her head, the warm cream color of her smooth flesh, Longarm sat in the suddenly cooling tub of water and watched her hungrily.

Alicia made her way uncertainly, but without hesitation, to her suitcase. Now confident, she dug inside the bag and brought out something, then turned, holding it. "Look at this, Longarm," she said.

"That's like ordering a starving man to keep his eye on a pot of beef stew—or telling a fox to guard a hen house," Longarm said.

"No. Not me, this." She held out the object in both her hands.

Longarm's mouth sagged slightly. Puzzled, he gazed at the Arbuckle Coffee can—an old one, surely one of the first the company made. "It's a coffee-can bank,"

18

Alicia said. "My daddy made it for me when I was a little girl. It's all I have left of him. Daddy and his partner, Mr. Floyd Gunnison, used to put pennies and dimes and coins from the Denver Mint in this bank for me. That's how close they were—Mr. Gunnison treated me as if I were his own little girl. Twenty years ago, the first mint here in Denver coined gold pieces with one percent more gold than United States coins. Daddy and Mr. Gunnison used to save them for me, even after the government took over the Denver Mint. They told me I'd be as rich as a princess." She drew a deep breath, her throaty voice developing a steel-like edge. "Mr. Gunnison is the man I must find, Longarm. The man you must find for me."

Longarm got out of the tub. He scrubbed himself prickly dry with a thick towel, conscious of the persistent ache of desire contracting the nerves in his groin, even as he tried to listen, like a professional lawman should, to Alicia's story.

She stunned him by saying, "I'm sorry you're so excited . . . and so hard."

He frowned, truly impressed. "How can you tell from way over there?"

Her head tilted. "I told you. You must believe me, Longarm. I can *sense* many things, even things that people with normal vision aren't aware of. My senses really are more developed than—"

"Your senses ain't the only well-developed things about you—"

"Poor Longarm."

"No. I'll make it. But you're going to have to put some clothes on so I can hear what you're saying."

She smiled and came across the cluttered floor to him, then took his hand and led him gently to the bed. She set the Arbuckle Coffee can on the bedside table and drew her nails along his skin as a playful kitten might. "I can talk," she said in a most matter-of-fact way, "with you on top of me."

He caught his breath. "But can I listen?"

"I'll talk slowly." She drew him down upon her.

19

"There. Isn't that nice? We've tried every other way. Now this . . . with you on top."

"Maybe we've discovered a new way," he chuckled.

Longarm sprawled exhausted beside Alicia across the rumpled mattress and listened to her strange story. Sounds of the world beyond the window reached them only remotely.

"When I was six years old," Alicia was saying, "my father and Floyd Gunnison had a terrible fight. Over money. A great deal of money. Maybe as much as a million. Or more, I don't know. Mr. Gunnison shot my father and killed him. I ran to where my daddy lay dead. I fell beside him, crying hysterically. Since I was the only witness—I wasn't blind yet then—Floyd decided he couldn't let me live, either. He shot me in the head as I lay there."

Alicia drew Longarm's hand along a ridge of scar tissue on her right temple, concealed by her thick hair.

"He shot me and ran away, taking all the money and mining rights they'd been fighting over. They had jointly owned a silver mine. I learned much later that they had sold it. I don't know how much money there was. I do know that all I had left was the coffee-can bank of coins.

"I don't know what happened to Floyd Gunnison. I was blinded. The bullet caused damage to my optic nerves that couldn't be repaired. I grew up in hospitals, in orphanages, in foster homes. This coffee can is all I have left . . . it and the nightmares that never set me free."

"Didn't the law ever find Gunnison?"

"Yes. I heard about it much later. He was shocked and heartbroken that somebody had killed his beloved partner and lovely little girl. He convinced the sheriff there must have been a robbery. He said he came in and found me and my father dead. The police accepted his story. It wasn't until they got me to the morgue that they found out I was still breathing, still alive.

"I was hysterical. Out of my mind. And blind. I heard that a couple of years after he killed my father,

20

Floyd Gunnison left Denver. And then I heard that he had been killed. I thought that ended it. A family took me to Texas and I grew up there."

Longarm frowned, puzzled. "Why have you decided after all these years to look for Gunnison again—twenty years later—and after you'd heard he was dead?"

"Because I don't think he's dead. I *know* he isn't dead. Somehow I never did believe he was dead. It was that feeling in me. I knew he was alive. I knew Floyd Gunnison was too evil and too treacherous to die. Only the good die young, Longarm."

"I've got to quit being so good, or you'll kill me well before my time."

Alicia stroked his face gently, but did not smile. "I know he's alive. I came back to Denver recently to see a famous specialist. There was some slight hope for my sight. But he said no, I'd never see again. There was no hope for that. The nerves were irreparably damaged. But while I was here in Denver—in this same hotel, the Windsor—I *saw* Floyd Gunnison."

"You *saw* him?"

"I know it's hard to believe, but that was what it was like. I sensed him. I *smelled* him."

"After twenty years?"

"I remembered his smell from when he used to hold me on his lap when I was a little girl and he was Daddy's best friend. As I grew up hating him, I remembered that smell. Oh, I never forgot it. And all people have their own scents. They all smell differently. And when I was in the room with Floyd Gunnison—after twenty years—I felt those terrible vibrations. It was Floyd Gunnison. I knew then; I know now."

"Twenty years seems like a long time to be so certain."

"I *am* certain. My senses—smell, especially—have truly been sharpened. And my hatred kept him alive. And people *do* have different odors. I can even tell their occupations by smell. Remember the people on the stagecoach? I told you all about them, didn't I? What their occupations were?"

21

He shook his head. "But they'd already *told* you, fortune-telling lady. I'm not being rough on you, but we have to go slow here."

"I told you about *you,* didn't I? And I can tell you about Emma Frye. You check and see if I'm right. She's a housekeeper. Out of work. She was on her way to Denver to find work. And she likes to work for widowers or bachelors."

"Why?"

"Because she likes widowers and bachelors."

"Sounds simple enough to be true. But how would you know that?"

"The tensions around her. She was afraid—didn't know if she'd find work in Denver or not."

"That tension could have come from her being sick to her stomach."

"She was sick to her stomach, all right—from the tension."

"You've got all the answers."

"All except the one I've got to have. I must find Floyd Gunnison. I can never rest until I find him—and testify against him for killing my father and blinding me."

Longarm sighed. "Well, if Gunnison is alive, there's no statute of limitations on murder." He caught her face in his hands. "And if you do find him? You're not thinking of taking the law in your own hands? You don't figure to kill him?"

Something flickered in the blind girl's face. Longarm felt a chill in the pit of his stomach.

He could not believe it when full morning sunlight flooded their hotel room. The suite looked like a battle area, cluttered with hastily discarded clothing. The ornate brass tub of cold, soapy water sat gray and abandoned in the alcove, and Alicia lay beside him, awake, taut.

"My God," he said. "We've talked all night."

"We stayed awake. We didn't do that much talking."

He reached for his vest and pulled his Ingersoll

watch from its pocket "My God, I've got to be at Marshal Vail's office in an hour."

"You'll make it."

"I've got to stop at the barbershop for a shave."

"I'll shave you."

"You? You can't see to shave me. It's the only throat I've got."

She smiled. "Would I harm a hair on your wonderful head? There is one thing, for your own safety. Before I start to shave you, you must swear that you believe me, everything I told you. You must believe that Floyd Gunnison is alive. And you will find him for me."

Longarm smiled broadly, and said, "I make it a point always to take the word of a beautiful naked lady holding a straight razor."

Clean-shaven and feeling renewed and invigorated, Longarm left the Windsor Hotel and headed across the business and shopping section that had sprung up in the angle formed by the confluence of Cherry Creek and the South Platte.

The morning was dazzlingly bright, the atmosphere incredibly clear; he'd found out there were fewer than sixty days a year when the sun didn't shine on this high plateau.

He breathed deeply, striding along the wide, shady street. Buildings of brick and stone gave the town a clean, solid look. Stone and brick were used almost exclusively in Denver construction because of the fearful lesson the town had learned in 1863 when a fire wiped out every frame structure. In places he could still discern faint signs of the latest devastating flooding of Cherry Creek, in 1878. The golden dome of the Capitol glittered in the crystal clarity of the morning sunlight.

Reaching the U.S. Mint at Cherokee and Colfax, Longarm turned the corner, heading for the Federal Building. He climbed scrubbed white marble stairs and strode wide corridors, boot heels echoing, to a big door with gold-leaf lettering. *United States Marshal, First District Court of Colorado.*

Longarm entered the spartan, frugally furnished office of the chief marshal. Government offices were permitted luxuries and lavish extras based solely on salary grade. Marshal Billy Vail rated a desk, three chairs—only one of which was comfortable, a red morocco armchair—and two filing cabinets. If he'd been two grades higher, he'd have rated carpeting. His floor was highly polished. A window opened upon a sunlit rectangle of the plaza. A small American flag, proudly exhibiting its thirty-eight stars, and a banjo clock, along with a map of the western half of the country and a photograph of the President, graced the walls. Longarm sank into the morocco leather chair, across the desk from his boss.

Marshal Billy Vail looked up from the paperwork stacked on his desk, and shook his head. "Don't know why I put up with it. Twenty pounds of useless reports —in triplicate—every day, with copies to Washington."

"Maybe because it's safer in here than shooting it out with the Comancheros or long-loopers," Longarm suggested in a mildly taunting way.

Vail sucked in an outraged breath and leaned back in his squealing swivel chair. About fifteen years older than Longarm, he wore scars from forgotten ambushes on long-dimmed back trails. He was deskbound, bald, and going to lard in belly and jowls, but in his mind he remained as young and efficient as ever, and sometimes the need to be back in the field almost overcame his native prudence.

"I could do a job out there, Longarm," he said. "Don't you ever think I couldn't do a job out there right alongside you. Maybe outlast you, if you come right down to it."

Longarm grinned. "Don't think you'd like it anymore, Billy. They're using real bullets these days."

"Yeah?" Vail jumped up from his chair and jerked his shirt open. "Where you think I got this?" He drew his hand along an ill-healed bullet wound.

"Fooling around some Mexican hacienda?"

Vail glared out from under his bushy black eyebrows, then shrugged, rebuttoned his stiffly starched

24

shirt, and stuffed the tails under his belt. He sat down. His voice was cold and businesslike. "Your next assignment," he said. He took up some papers, read them, then checked the railroad timetable pinned on the wall behind him. "Damn it, you've missed the Denver-Pacific train north. Won't be another train to Cheyenne till noon tomorrow."

"What am I supposed to do in Cheyenne?"

"You're not to go near Cheyenne. You'll change trains at a place called . . ." He ran his finger along the Central Pacific Railroad map. "Place called Clump."

"Clump?"

"That's right. You change to Central Pacific at Clump. You ever hear of a town called Claim Jump?"

"No."

"Nobody else ever did until they had a hell of a silver strike out there. Suddenly the town's as big as Leadville, with temporary tents, lean-tos, and jerry-builts dropped down like it was done with all the forethought of a mule with diarrhea." He reread the letter from Washington. "Somebody out there has been cutting the Western Union telegraph wires just about as fast as the line riders can find the cuts and repair them."

"The government working for Western Union now?" Longarm inquired.

Vail was shifting papers around on his desk. He looked up, eyes chilly. "Yours is not to reason why, Mr. Long. And no, Western Union is a private enterprise. But, for your information, it holds a federal franchise in interstate communications, and that makes it our business. Government services are dangerously curtailed when telegraph wires are cut. Your job is to find out who is cutting those wires and bring the culprit to trial. It's a federal offense, worth ten to twenty, plus all kinds of fines. But mostly it's a headache to our people in Washington, and they want it stopped. Pronto."

Longarm merely nodded. Vail found what he wanted among his papers. He spread out an enlarged rendering of a map of the Great Basin country of Nevada, showing the wastes between Elko to the east and the Humboldt Sink to the west. He smoothed the map on top of the official communiques and reports littering his desktop, and drew his finger along the east-west course of the Humboldt River. "The wire-cutting's going on in here," he said, and repeated with a wolfish grin, "all in here."

"You're talking about an area of at least 165 miles east to west and ninety miles north to south."

"Roughly." Vail nodded in satisfaction. "Big job for a big man, Mr. Long. And you'll find it the roughest, driest, deadliest, emptiest, most godforsaken plat of real estate between Chicago and Frisco. But, Longarm, there's one bit of good news."

"Yeah?"

"Yeah. I think there's two spots of shade between Ruby Lake and Reno. I never saw 'em, never met anybody who did, but somebody said there was."

Small red dots marred the enlarged map. Longarm said, "What are these red spots? You been eating cherry pie?"

"They're the spots where the cuts have been made. We're keeping a record, trying to find a pattern for you."

"Looks like all the cuts are between the Humboldt Sink and the town of Claim Jump."

"Yeah." Vail grinned savagely, pleased with himself. "Except this one. Like I say, there's no pattern yet." He touched a red dot just west of Elko. "That cutting just took place a couple days ago. Could be coincidence. Could've been done by the same wide-ranging knave."

Longarm exhaled. "Nothing is ever easy."

"If it was easy, mister, would they pay us a hundred a month and found?"

"Speaking of which, I'll need expense money."

"We've figured out a very fair allowance for you."

"You fellows have got to stop figuring ten cents a day for breakfast. And have you ever slept in a one-dollar room?"

"When I could afford it."

Longarm laughed. "Always ready with the answers. No wonder they promoted you out of the line of fire, Billy."

Vail chewed away any traces of a flattered smile. He ran his fingers back and forth on the twisting course of the Humboldt.

"The Central Pacific rail lines follow the river. So did the old wagon trails west. If there was ever any water anywhere, it was in the bed of the Humboldt, though even its bed was bone-dry in places. The Western Union people took a straighter path mostly between Pine Valley and the Bear Paw Mountains—"

"I don't see any Bear Paw Mountains on this map."

"Well, they're there, like a claw swiping north and south along the Basin. Hell, I don't know what they're called officially—maybe just foothills. People out that way used to call 'em the Bear Paws."

"I'll find 'em."

"Sure you will. No maps made these days of that wild country out there show everything. Some of that back land I doubt even the Mountain Men hunted. You ever seen a Paiute Indian?"

The question was rhetorical; Vail knew very well that Longarm had not only seen Paiute, but had tangled with one or two particularly ornery examples. He continued, without waiting for an answer, "Well, you got a treat in store for you, old son. Maybe it's them, cutting those wires. They wander a lot. Got a kind of central village, like a prairie dog town, and they roam out from it. They don't like the army to know too much about their movements."

"Right," Longarm agreed, taking out a cheroot and sticking it between his front teeth. "And it seems to me I heard tell of some reformed Mormons living in the Basin. They broke away from the main bunch, and still practice plural marriage. Can't say I'm rarin' to run afoul of any renegade Mormons soon again."

Vail smiled slightly. "Can't say as I blame you. You're still a mite salty from your run-in with those Avenging Angels a while back."

27

Longarm struck a sulfur match on his thumbnail, touched it to his cheroot, and returned his gaze to the map of the wasteland. "Is anybody suspected except Paiutes?"

"There's all kinds of characters out in that boom-town of Claim Jump. Thieves, murderers, cutthroats, fugitives. Plenty of bad men who wouldn't want certain messages sent fast east or west. And ranchers. Honest as hell, some of them. Honest as they have to be, all of them. But those open-range ranch owners hate bobwire. And they might take a dislike to high-strung wire just as much. Whoever is cutting those lines, they've got to be stopped—fast and permanent."

Longarm walked out of the Federal Building into the blaze of sunlight. It was provident that he had until noon tomorrow before he caught a train for the long ride to the wilds of the Humboldt country. There was time to repay Alicia Payson for her overwhelming kind-nesses to him, time to find proof on the man she sought. Maybe he could settle the matter and send her off home by noon tomorrow.

He decided to check county vital statistics first. He'd learned in eight years that solving mysteries or finding missing persons was mostly a matter of dull digging into dull statistics. The sooner he got started . . .

Chapter 3

"No! No! No!" Alicia Payson wailed. "No! He's not dead! Floyd Gunnison is not dead! I don't care what you found out. That's what he wants you to believe. He wants the world to believe Floyd Gunnison is dead. But he's not dead. He's alive and you've got to find him for me. You promised. You swore."

Longarm caught her about the waist and held her tightly against him, trying to talk into her ear. She fought him furiously.

"Listen to me, Alicia."

"No. You think I lied." Her voice rose to a scream.

"Good Lord, they're going to throw us out of here. They're going to arrest me for wife-beating."

"I'm not your wife!"

"I know that. You know that. But on the register—"

"You didn't find him. You found the same old stuff. Now you want to stop looking for him." Alicia fought him fiercely.

"All right, honey. I've had enough of this. I wanted to find your man Gunnison. I believed your story, most of it. As much as I could—"

"You think I lied to you!" she wailed.

He threw her across the bed and fell on top of her. She tried to bring her knee up into his crotch, but he caught her and pinned her down. "Let me go or I'll kill you," she raged.

Laughing in exasperation, Longarm checked to be sure his derringer was still safely in his vest pocket. She caught his motion and spoke between bared lips. "I don't need a gun to kill you, Longarm. There are a lot of other ways to kill a man."

"Honey, you know the best one. So stick to that and stop fighting me."

"I hate you."

"Sure you do. And as soon as you hear me out, you can get up from here and walk out and you'll never have to see me again."

"You'd like that, wouldn't you?" she panted, her pale eyes fixed on the ceiling.

"The very idea is a fate worse than death. Hell, I could have lied to you, put you off, maybe made you wait until I got back from my assignment. But I didn't, Alicia. I did everything I could."

"No. You've done what everybody has done. And now you want to stop——"

"A twenty-year-old grave in an almost abandoned cemetery seems a pretty good stopping place. But you hear me out. If you can think of anything more I can do——I'll do it. After you hear me out."

She shrugged and lay coldly quiescent beside him on the bed. She was like a stranger, remote and withdrawn. More than a stranger——she had loved him fiercely and now she hated him deeply.

He gave her an account of his actions in her behalf; it was far more complete and detailed than the reports he turned in to Billy Vail in triplicate.

He had gone into the county statistics office. It had been easy. There it was. Floyd Gunnison——died February 9, 1860.

He collected all the data possible, but he knew Alicia Payson would not be satisfied. He returned to the government stables behind the Federal Building, and checked out a single-seat rig and horse. He drove across town to the old city of Auraria, one of the towns that had incorporated as Denver. He finally located the Auraria cemetery. All he was really thinking was that here he was chasing down a dead man while he could be making love to a live lady. But he persisted.

The cemetery was old, almost abandoned. The narrow lane between the plots was potholed, rutted, and overgrown. But he had found the plot where lay Floyd Gunnison. He had found the grave and the marble

30

headstone. The tablet was moldy, discolored, and ancient, but the letters had been chiseled by a craftsman and were still legible. *FLOYD GUNNISON. B—1835. D—1860.*

That was the end of it—a knave, maybe a murderer, his own life snuffed out in his twenty-fifth year.

Longarm hunkered over the abandoned gravesite. Under all ordinary conditions he would have called off the pursuit. He had found Floyd Gunnison's final resting place; the chase was over. But then he exhaled heavily. Alicia Payson still wouldn't be satisfied with his efforts.

From the Auraria Cemetery he drove back to 17th Street and downtown to the publishing-printing offices of the Denver *Republican.*

The extremely successful young publisher—he was in his early forties, but getting as wealthy as Croesus from his chain of newspapers across the West, and if a man amasses a fortune as Plitt Shawlene had, he remained young in the public eye well past his middle years—met him as he entered the foyer.

"Longarm! You looking for me? You got another story more exciting than the Ned Buntline fairy stories about Bill Cody?"

Longarm laughed. "There ain't any stories wilder than the Buntline fairy tales. What's the good word, Plitt?"

"Buy silver!" the publisher said loudly, laughing. "Silver is going to plate the world, Longarm, and the man who owns silver will own his share of this old globe."

"Afraid I can't buy very much on government pay," Longarm said. "But I enjoy watching a man like you pile it up, Plitt. You've got use for millions. I haven't. I wouldn't know what to do with them."

"It's like oysters. Or snails. It's an acquired taste. You start piling it up, and pretty soon piling up money is more fun than anything else."

"Lord, I hope I never get that old," Longarm said. "So what can I do for you?"

"You keep newspaper files as far as twenty years back?"

"Sure do. Got our files from volume one, number one. You go down this hall to a door marked 'Morgue.' Don't let that stop you. It's our filing room. You tell the fellow on duty that old Plitt said to give you whatever you wanted."

Longarm grinned and shook hands with the publisher. Plitt was above medium height, slender in a tailored suit and highly polished riding boots. His hair was wheat-colored, as was his thick, coffee-strainer mustache. He slapped Longarm on the shoulder and invited him back when he had a new adventure to sell, then he strode out into the sun-blasted street.

Longarm entered the filing room, a rectangular shell with cheap pine shelves in seemingly endless rows, stacked to the ceiling with old newspapers. Staring at the newspapers, Longarm felt his heart sink. Digging back was going to be a tedious task, when he should be at the hotel entertaining Alicia Payson. On the other hand, there was no sense going back there without having every detail covered from every angle. He grinned wryly and asked for the file of newspapers for February 1860.

The clerk moved to get the papers, then stopped. "You know the name of the person or event you're looking for?"

"Yes."

"I can save you some time. You give me the name, and I'll bring you his file in an envelope."

Longarm exhaled, laughing. "You got it. Floyd Gunnison."

The clerk dug through some musty filing cabinets marked "G," and returned with a manila envelope. He grinned proudly. "We got cross-files, Mr. Longarm. Just like the big newspapers in New York City."

Longarm sat at a bare pine table and spilled out the clippings on Floyd Gunnison. There were several, but only two interested him.

He read the brief obituary three times to be sure he had digested it all, without missing the least pertinent detail. It seemed clear enough—and final enough. The sudden death of twenty-five-year-old Floyd Gunnison, a six-year resident of Denver, was reported. No cause of death was listed, but this was not unusual since next-of-kin often protested violently—and sometimes with bullets—when the truth about the cause of death was printed in a newspaper. Hanging ropes and guns and barroom brawls didn't make pleasant reading for a corpse's survivors.

The story stated that Gunnison's funeral had been private, open only to close friends and immediate family. Services had been conducted over a closed casket, at graveside, in the Auraria Cemetery, Reverend Duggan Duggan officiating.

Longarm got a sheet of newsprint from the clerk and copied the story precisely, with dates and names. Then he turned his attention to a story with larger headlines, one that must have made the front page of the Denver *Republican*.

This story reported on the robbery-murder of silver miner Bry Payson. Obviously this story had been written before the coroner had learned at the morgue that Alicia Payson, six years old, had survived the deadly assault. As Alicia had told him, Floyd Gunnison had "discovered" the grisly crime and summoned the police. Gunnison had been almost too hysterical to talk, and had gone up into the mountains for a month to recuperate from the violent shock of his dearest friend's death. As Alicia had told him, by the time Gunnison returned to Denver, Alicia was in another state with her first foster parents.

Alicia had told Longarm that she did not know how long Gunnison had searched for her, or if he had searched at all. He was told by the hospital that she was clinging to life by a slender thread, and was not expected to live; she was blind, and her mind, too, may have been affected by the gunshot wound. He had felt safe for a while, and then, abruptly, the newspaper had reported that Floyd Gunnison, too, was dead . . .

Patiently, Longarm copied out these stories on the assault, robbery, and murder at the Payson home.

He sighed, satisfied. He had followed the string to its end. He had done all he could. Armed with his evidence, which he accepted unquestioningly, he returned horse and rig to the government stables and hurried to the Windsor Hotel and Alicia.

Finally, Alicia grew quiet. But her silence was far less than reassuring. There was a chilled resignation in her submission. He had failed her, as everyone else had.

He tried to kiss her. Alicia turned her lips away from him. "You mean I'm paid off?" he inquired.

"Damn you. Paid off for what? You haven't done anything."

He stared at her. "Alicia, what do you want of me? I found the man's vital statistics record. He's dead. I found an abandoned grave in an old cemetery. He's buried. I followed it as far as I can."

She turned her head away. Her throaty voice was empty with defeat. "All right. Go on. Get out."

"Just like that?"

"What do you want?"

"You might thank me."

"For what?"

"For trying. I tried, Alicia. I told you I was a lawman, not a magician."

She shrugged. "Then thanks . . . for nothing."

He stood up and gazed down at her. A deep sadness washed through him. "I won't see you again?"

"Why should you?"

"What will you do?"

"What do you care? I'll find Floyd Gunnison. I haven't stopped looking just because you believe the lies he wants everybody to believe. He's alive—and I'll find him."

He turned away. He heard her draw in a deep breath and hold it. When he turned, she was crying silently. He went back to her.

"Don't touch me," she said. "I'm all right. I'm just tired. I cry sometimes when I'm tired. Don't let it stop you. Get on with your job, *lawman*, and God help the people who depend on you."

34

He drew a deep breath. "You hit hard, don't you?"

"You don't have to stay here and listen."

"That's true. And I wish I could say I don't know why I stay. But I *do* know. I don't want to fail you, Alicia. I don't think I have, but you do, and that's the same thing."

"You've done all you can. Goodbye, Longarm."

He sat down beside her on the bed. She dropped her arm across her eyes. "What do you want now?" she said. "You want to crawl on top of me again."

"It's not a bad position. No, Miss Payson. I found out a long time ago—to want a woman is nice, but if *she* wants you, it's heaven. I prefer it heavenly. No, I'm not going to touch you. But I've got until noon tomorrow. You tell me one thing I haven't done, one more rock I can turn over, and I'll do it, whatever it is, no matter how insane I might think it is. I'll do it."

She crept closer to him and slipped her arms about him.

At seven-thirty that night, Longarm walked into the Windsor Hotel dining room with Alicia Payson on his arm. He had thought she was lovely before, but he had never seen anyone as beautiful as she was in a beige, form-fitting evening dress that melted downward over her lithe curves from shoulder straps to beige slippers, the toes winking from the hem of her gown. Except for the dark glasses, she was incredibly perfect. She carried herself regally, walking like a princess, and Longarm was certain no one guessed she was blind.

They waited for the maitre d' to seat them. The room was crowded, and without exception, every diner stopped eating and stared at them.

Alicia smiled. "You must look lovely, Longarm. People are staring at us."

"I never looked prettier," Longarm told her.

She laughed and squeezed his arm. When the maitre d' motioned them forward, Longarm moved before he realized that Alicia had not been alerted. She stumbled slightly and he caught her elbow.

"Sorry," he apologized.

"It was my fault. I wasn't alert. I don't want anyone feeling sorry for me."

"They won't. Trust me."

"I do trust you." Her hand remained lightly on his arm. "Totally."

"Why, suddenly?"

"Because." She smiled and drew in a deep, satisfied breath. "You smell good." She laughed. "You *taste* good, too."

Longarm felt the blood flush upward across his cheeks. She could make him blush. She laughed as if she could actually *see* his discomfiture.

The maitre d' held a chair for Alicia. She sat down in it smoothly and gave him a dazzling smile.

Before Longarm could sit down, somebody gripped his arm fiercely. He turned and gazed into the laughing face of the publisher of the Denver *Republican.*

Plitt Shawlene accompanied a gaudily lovely woman, highly rouged and powdered, busty, full in the hips, with long legs outlined against the sequined fabric of her bright red dress.

"What good are my millions, Longarm, if a deputy U.S. marshal can show up with a girl that takes the play from my expensive lady? This is Trixie Mondale. Trixie is appearing in a musical comedy at the Denver Opera House this month. Biggest crowds they ever had. She's expensive to know. I expect all eyes to turn when we walk in." He bowed toward Alicia. "Why in the world is an aristocratic beauty like you slumming with a critter like Longarm, ma'am?"

Longarm laughed and introduced Alicia. "You said it, Plitt. You were busy tonight—with Miss Trixie Mondale. What else could Alicia do? There are only two of us in town, you know."

"It's a pleasure to make your acquaintance, Miss Payson," Shawlene said. "I do hope I'll see more of you."

Alicia acknowledged his compliment with a non-committal smile. She told Trixie how lovely she was, and Trixie said in her famous New York accent, "You ain't exactly chopped liver yourself, kiddo."

"I'd insist you join us at our table," Shawlene said, "but I don't know if Denver is ready for this much beauty concentrated in one small area."

"Some other time," Alicia said. Going taut, Longarm sensed that Alicia was becoming impatient, nervous. He anticipated an outburst. He sighed with relief when Shawlene said good night and walked away with his arm tightly about his musical comedy star. But when he reached his own table, he turned and gazed for a long moment toward Alicia.

"What's the matter?" Longarm whispered to Alicia as soon as they were alone.

"I've thought of it," Alicia said. "What you can do. The one more stone you can turn. Come on, let's get out of here."

"I'm hungry."

Her throaty voice had the ring of steel. "We've no time to eat, Longarm. You're working for me now, not Uncle Sam."

Silently, doubting his own sanity, and not believing that it was happening, Longarm drove the single-seat rig, with Alicia beside him, into the Auraria Cemetery just after ten o'clock that night.

"You're going to be satisfied when I show you the grave?" he asked again.

She shrugged. "I don't satisfy easily, Longarm."

He laughed in agreement, then stopped the horse, fired a sulfur match, and lit a lantern. Then he gave Alicia the reins and leaped down from the boot to the ground.

Holding the horse by the checkreins and lifting the lantern above his head, he moved slowly forward along the narrow, rutted lanes. No matter what anyone said, no matter how sophisticated a man became, there was an eeriness about a graveyard at night, a silence deeper and thicker than anywhere else, a chilled sense of eternity.

The pines, elders, and oaks hurled thick canopies over the still land. The lantern light struck aged headstones and bounced oddly, or hurled shapeless shadows into still deeper shadows.

He pulled the horse to the place where he had stopped earlier in the day. "All right," he said. "Here we are."

Alicia nodded and put out her arms. He swung her down to the ground. The wind sighed around them. An owl cried and, distantly, a coyote bayed at the thin sliver of moon.

Holding the lantern high, Longarm led Alicia to the Gunnison gravesite. The leaning headstone, lichen-covered and dark, seemed older and more forgotten than ever in the lamplight.

He knelt beside the tilted headstone and drew Alicia down beside him.

"You want to read it?" he said.

Alicia nodded, without speaking, and knelt beside him. He took her hand and drew it over the face of the tablet. She nodded again and withdrew her hand from his.

He hunkered beside her and watched her trace each letter and figure with her fingers. She repeated it several times. He began to feel better. She had admitted at last that she had finally reached the end of the trail. This was the gravestone of her father's killer. It was over.

He held his breath, watching her, giving her time to absorb it and accept it.

"I want you to dig it up," she said.

He nearly dropped the lantern. "What?"

"You promised. Anything I wanted. I didn't want to *visit* his grave. I could have done that anytime. I want it dug up."

"You *are* loco, you know that?"

"What's that got to do with it? Suppose I am insane? If so, I have been ever since Floyd Gunnison killed my father and blinded me. You prove to me he's down there, Longarm, and we're quits. I swear it."

"This is ghoulish. Digging up a grave in an abandoned cemetery in the middle of the night—"

"A twenty-year-old grave."

"That, too. And has it ever occurred to you that I might get arrested for this?"

"Who'd arrest you?"

"Who knows? It's going to look great in tomorrow's *Republican*: 'Federal Marshal Arrested as Grave Robber.'"

"I'll bake you a cake. Just dig."

Shaking his head, Longarm walked to the buggy. He took a shovel from the rear bed of the vehicle and tossed his coat across the seat. Raging inwardly, he walked back to the gravesite.

"Aren't you going to take off your guns?" Alicia taunted him. She sat comfortably on the nearest squared headstone.

"I may need them."

"For what?"

"Who knows? I may kill myself if I come to my senses."

She sighed in deep satisfaction, and sat in her sleek evening gown covered with a jacket. The night was chilly, and it grew colder as he worked, but she seemed totally unaware of the cold or the cutting wind.

Setting the lantern on a nearby marble stone, Longarm dug, putting his rage into his work, laying aside the raw clumps of earth.

They did not talk. She kept her head poised, tilted, turned in his direction, as if she could watch his movements as the earth piled up beside the Gunnison headstone and he sank deeper into the long, narrow slit.

He did not know how long he worked. He was almost in the grave up to his shoulders when his shovel bit into the aged casket. "It's here," he said. "The casket is here. Is that what you wanted to know?"

Alicia got to her feet, quivering with excitement. Her face seemed strangely pale and wild in the lantern light.

"It is really down there?" she said, her voice quivering with repressed excitement.

He struck the casket again with the shovel blade. The noise rang from the hole.

"What kind of casket is it?" she said.

"Looks like plain pine."

"It should be easy to open, then."

"Now, Alicia, don't you think this has gone far enough?"

Without speaking, she walked carefully to where the lantern rested on a grave marker. She returned with it and held it out over the hole. "Open it," she said.

Swearing, Longarm used the shovel as a battering tool. The casket ruptured, broke. He bent down and ripped away the top.

"Give me that lantern," he said, his voice hollow.

She handed it to him. He held it over the casket. "Name of God," he whispered. "It's empty."

"Of course it is," she said from above him. "It always has been."

Chapter 4

Longarm awoke, troubled and sweating, at daybreak the next morning.

Alicia Payson sprawled naked on the rumpled bed beside him. She slept on her stomach, her arms up beside her head, her rich hair spilling like cream across the pillow.

The town outside the second-floor window of the Windsor Hotel bedroom lay in the stunned dawn silence. Remotely, a cock crowed, and from a still greater distance, another answered. The silence flowed in on the sweet, fresh breezes of early day.

He gazed for a long moment at the lithe symmetry of Alicia's body. He longed to reach out and caress her, to run his hands through her hair, to fondle her, but flaring like a red danger signal across this need was an uneasy premonition. He felt a fluttering of butterflies in his belly, a warning of trouble that he couldn't pin down or explain.

He lay for one more moment, staring at the wanly brightening ceiling. His sense of something wrong brought him as certainly back to Alicia as did the stunning lines and planes and curves of her pliant body. Alicia had come away from that cemetery last night entirely too calmly, too submissively. Maybe she didn't realize it, but an excess of silence in her was as much a warning signal as one of her violent tantrums, and now he'd experienced both.

"You're something special, little lady," he told her silently, under his breath. "Like no other female I ever met."

Holding his breath, he eased off the bed and padded

across the carpeting like a cat burglar. He checked his holster and vest first. Some of his premonition of wrong was being played out; both of his guns were gone.

He shook his head, grinning ruefully. No wonder that little hellion slept so soundly and peacefully. She figured she held all the aces; if her body wouldn't keep him away from his assignment, she believed his own guns would—when turned against him.

He stood for a moment, checking the room. Using his pocket knife, he sliced the cords from the drapes. Carrying them and holding his breath, he tiptoed back to the bed.

Carefully he lifted one of Alicia's wrists and knotted the cord about it, securely, yet not tightly enough to disturb her sleep.

He waited some moments before he went around the bed and secured Alicia's other wrist. Then he tied the cords to the ornamental peaks of the headboard. The cord was slightly slack, but Miss Payson was securely spread-eagled on the bed.

He consumed less than three minutes in finding his guns. His Colt was in her suitcase, and the derringer reposed under odds and ends in her handbag.

When he turned, Alicia was awake. Her face was set in pale fury.

"Good morning," he said.

"Let me go—and I'll kill you."

"That's why I tied you up, honey. I'm too young to die."

"You're too *mean* to die. You're going to run out on me, aren't you?"

"I work for Uncle Sam, honey. I told you. I'll see you when I get back."

"I *will* kill you." She rolled her head back and forth, jerking on the cords like a wild mare.

"I ought to warn you," he said, "I just took half hitches in those cords. The harder you tug on them, the tighter they get."

"You bastard."

"I'm just sick that I couldn't quietly let you shoot me this morning when you finally woke up, Miss Payson.

42

I know you'd handle it tastefully, but look at it from my side. Think of the scandal. 'Federal Marshal Shot in Windsor Hotel Love Nest.' How would that look on my record?"

"Damn you. You think you're so smart. Hold all the aces, don't you? You don't care that I was right last night. That grave was empty—and always has been. And I knew it. And Floyd Gunnison is alive—and you could find him for me."

"Sweetheart, I told you. I believe you. I am sold on you in every way a man could be. But I've got a train to catch at noon. I've got an urgent assignment. When it's over—"

"When might that be, you bullhead?"

"I have no idea. I only know that when I come back, I'll have a few days—or I'll *take* a few days. I'll be all yours. If Floyd Gunnison lives—"

"*If*? Aren't you convinced yet, you miserable jackass?"

"All right. Wherever Mr. Gunnison has chosen to hole up, we'll flush him out. When I get back."

"What am I supposed to do until then?"

"Take some lessons in niceness. It wouldn't hurt. Listen to me, Wild Bill. Gunnison has been around for twenty years. He's somewhere. You're sure you . . . smelled him. Okay. I'll find him for you. In the meantime, I've got my job. And it won't wait."

"What makes you think Floyd Gunnison will wait?"

He washed his face and hands at the washstand, then dried with a face towel and dropped it on the floor. He began to dress, taking his time, watching her with deep appreciation and sharp longing. Although she could not see him, he was aware that Alicia knew he was gazing across the planes of her lovely body, and this infuriated her. Her face flushed red to the golden roots of her blonde hair.

"I swear to you," he said, "that if Floyd Gunnison lives, I'll find him."

"Why don't you find him now, before you go?"

"Have you ever worked for Uncle Sam?"

43

"They'd give you time off, if you asked. But you won't ask. Why are you running away, you coward?"

He laughed, fighting his fly closed. "How any filly, so sweet and loving in bed, can be so shrewish—"

"Why don't you take me with you?"

"Have you any notion where I'm going?"

"No."

"Neither have I. But I know it's no place for a woman."

"Oh, hell, I can go anywhere you can go."

"*Going* ain't the trick, sweetheart. It's coming back alive that counts. Now I've got a job to do, Alicia, you might as well get it through that thick skull of yours. And I can't take you with me."

"You *won't*."

He slipped on his vest, buttoned it, and arranged his watch, chain, and derringer across it. He took up his coat and shoved his arms into its sleeves. "That's right, I won't."

"But you're just going to come back—someday—and find me?"

"Where will I get in touch with you?"

"Never mind. I'll find you," she said.

He laughed. "I was afraid you'd say that."

"Oh, Longarm. I'm desperate. All these years I've searched for that evil man. We've almost got him. And you're my only hope. And now you're running out on me."

She lay as if she were watching him set his flat-brimmed hat low over his eyes and straight on his head.

"Go ahead, coward," she said. "Run away from me. I'll find you, damn you. You can't run fast enough or far enough that I won't find you."

"Damn it, wait here."

"Oh, no. You won't get away from me that easily. I'll get free and I'm coming after you. I'll stick to your tail like a burr until you finish your job for me."

He walked to the door and stood grinning back at her, feeling a deep sense of emptiness that he hid in laughter. "I'll promise myself that, on cold nights beside

44

lonely campfires. I'll promise myself that you're behind me somewhere—looking for me."

"You can stake your life on it, damn you!" she yelled as he quietly closed the door behind him.

Longarm walked out of the Windsor Hotel into glittering sunlight. He glanced toward the cafe, but rejected the idea of breakfast. He'd eat later. His stomach was empty, but he wasn't really hungry.

He cut across a cinder pathway to the Colfax Avenue bridge. The streets were still almost vacant at this early hour. Two cowpokes lazed their mounts along the shaded avenue.

He ran his fingers along his stubbled jawline. He'd have to buy a shave this morning. Ten cents for George Masters, who wasn't pretty and couldn't handle a straight razor half as well as the blind girl. He winced, trying to thrust Alicia from his mind. He knew better. She was going to trail after him for a long time.

George Masters was just opening his barbershop for the day, sweeping out and chocking his front door open.

George was a stout, balding man, somewhere in his forties. He smelled of talcum powder, bay rum, and, faintly, of last night's gin. He wore a white apron over the spreading expanse of his belly, and arm garters on the biceps of his striped shirt.

"Mornin', Marshal. Sit right down. My first customer of the day." George shook out a fresh barber's cloth and spread it over Longarm and pinned it at the nape of his neck. "Gettin' a little ragged over the collar, Marshal."

"Just shave me, if your hands are steady enough this early. A shave, a little bay rum, and a lot of silence, George."

"What's eatin' you this mornin', Marshal?"

"A broken heart, George. What's it to you?"

"Not pryin', Marshal. You just lay back and be comfortable."

As the steam soaked into his pores, Longarm, behind his closed eyes, could see Alicia's image, clearly etched in his mind. He let the image linger there—as though he had a choice.

George removed the towel and began to brush hot lather across Longarm's jaw. Suddenly he stopped and inhaled sharply.

Several things happened at once. Longarm sat up, opening his eyes and drawing his Colt under the barber's cloth. George sidestepped, lunging away from his barber's chair. Through the front window, Longarm saw two men, guns drawn, running toward the barbershop.

George dropped to the floor and crawled through the door to his rear room, where he kept his betting tickets, moonshine, first-aid kit, barber's supplies, and brooms and mops. He was curled up tightly in a corner when the first shot rang out.

The shot neatly removed the brass ball on top of George's barber pole.

Watching the assailants closing in on him, Longarm recognized them. He'd seen these jaspers before, and recently. They'd been easing their horses along the street. Now he knew, they'd been waiting for him, staking him out.

One of the gunslingers ran across the sunlit grass and shielded himself behind the bole of a cottonwood. He braced his gun against the rough bark, took careful aim, and fired. His bullet bored a ragged hole through the barbershop window.

As quickly as he fired, the gunslinger went around the tree and ran at an angle toward the barbershop, just out of range of the open doorway. As the fellow crossed the walk, Longarm fired from beneath the barber's cloth. His bullet caught the gunman in the shoulder and spun him around. He howled like a scalded hound and dropped his gun, which bounded at least a yard away from him.

He staggered and fell to his knees. Bracing himself on his hands, he stayed there. His partner ran toward the barbershop from the other side.

Longarm leaped up from the chair and framed himself in the shadowed doorway.

The gunman saw him there, and hesitated. He glanced toward his fallen partner and some of the enthusiasm for this caper abruptly and permanently left him. He jerked up his gun and fired once, halfheartedly, toward the man standing in the doorway. But something about that big, immovable target unmanned him and he didn't even wait to see if he'd been lucky. He wheeled around suddenly and ran, then threw himself behind a low retainer wall and kept scrambling along it, without looking back.

Longarm fired after him once, just to spur him on. When he turned, the other owlhoot had leaped up and was running toward the nearest alley, his arm hanging like a bird's broken wing. He didn't even stop to take his gun.

When the quiet from the front of his shop persisted for some moments, promising at least a temporary halt in hostilities, George came hesitantly from the rear room. "I went in there to get my gun," he explained.

Longarm was calmly shaving himself, standing before the wide mirror. George Masters stared around at the shattered glass, the broken barber pole. He looked ready to weep. "Oh, Good Lord, Marshal, don't you know any other shop in Denver where you could get shaves?"

"Not as close as I get in here, George." Longarm washed off the last remaining traces of lather, dried his face, and splashed on bay rum. He spoke over his shoulder. "Send a bill to the marshal's office, George. You'll get reimbursed for this damage. Sooner or later. Probably later. Lots of red tape."

"Who were those men?"

"Who knows? Maybe they weren't after me at all. Maybe they wanted you, George. You've been getting mighty careless with your shaves lately. A man pays ten cents for a shave, he wants a good one."

Longarm walked through the crowd of curious onlookers gathered outside George Masters' barbershop. Even in a frontier town, gunfire in the morning attracted a gawking crowd.

Longarm headed toward the railroad station. He was

more puzzled about that stupid, halfhearted attack on him than he was troubled or upset. Gunmen had a way of hating lawmen, but he couldn't place those two jaspers. They'd looked young, and there was nothing professional about the way they had carried out the assault. Still, guns in the hands even of amateurs could be deadly, and there had to be some reason behind it. The whole thing seemed pointless.

Suddenly he stopped in the middle of the street as if he'd been struck viciously in the solar plexus. There was one fearful reason why somebody might have sent hired killers looking for him. He and Alicia had been probing into the alleged death of Floyd Gunnison. Last night they'd unearthed a twenty-year-old empty coffin.

Alicia! The man she'd hated and had been seeking for twenty years. Feeling a terrible sickness roiling in his belly, Longarm swung around and walked in long, ground-eating strides.

He entered the Federal Building, hurried along the wide corridors, and threw open the door marked *United States Marshal, First District Court of Colorado.*

The pimply-faced young bureaucrat, crouched behind the clattering upright typewriter, looked up, shaking his head. "What do you want?"

Longarm only shook his head at the clerk, dismissing him, and headed toward the inner office. He knocked once and then slapped the door open. The clerk was shouting behind him, "Marshal Vail is busy. You can't barge in—"

But Longarm already had barged into the chief's office. Vail jerked his head up, scowling. He recognized Longarm, but didn't moderate his annoyance. "What do you mean, barging in here?" He glanced toward the banjo clock on his wall. "Why aren't you at the train station?"

Longarm shook his head, brushing aside those details. "I was on my way, Billy. I've still got time. I won't miss that train."

"You sure as hell better not. This assignment is Washington priority."

"But I need your help."

Those five words almost mollified the chief marshal. "My help? Longarm needs help? From me? Never thought I'd hear that."

"Will you help me?" Longarm's impatient voice rattled the room.

Vail's voice matched his deputy's. "I don't promise nobody help, Longarm, until I know what they want."

"Two gunmen shot at me in the barbershop."

"Hell, is that all? That goes with the territory, you know that."

"That's not all. Will you listen to me? We may not have much time." He gave Vail a sanitized version of his meeting Alicia on the stagecoach to Denver, but was forced to admit he had registered as Mr. and Mrs. Custis Long at the Windsor Hotel.

"You ain't putting the Windsor Hotel on your expense account," Vail said.

Longarm told him the story Alicia had given him. He saw that Vail didn't believe him, and he admitted his own skepticism, but everything she'd said had proved out. He'd found the twenty-year-old grave, and he'd found it empty, as it always had been.

"So what do you want from me?"

"I want protection for that girl—'round-the-clock protection—until I can get back here."

"I can't do that."

"You better do it. And you put a good deputy on it. Maybe Wallace. I'm holding this office responsible for her. There's fraud and murder and maybe theft of government silver involved. You can write her down as a witness. But you've got to protect her."

"Where is she now?"

Longarm strode into the lobby of the Windsor Hotel with Chief Marshal Vail at his heels. On the way over, he had filled in all the details and loose ends. Vail agreed. "There is no statute on murder. If the man's alive, he can be indicted."

Longarm crossed the busy foyer, heading toward the stairs. The desk clerk spied him and called, "Sir! Just a moment, sir. Where are you going?"

Vail hesitated long enough to flash his U.S. marshal's badge. "Official business, son," he said.

They mounted the stairs two at a time. Longarm spoke over his shoulder, "I left her tied up—"

"You *what*?"

"It would take too long to explain, Billy. I realize now I shouldn't have done it. Hell, I didn't realize she was in danger. She may be pretty naked—"

"I'll try to bear up," Vail said. "Blind women don't clean my shovel."

Longarm came out on the second floor. "I don't have a key," he said. "If she's still tied up, we may have to kick the door in."

He reached the door of the room he'd shared for the past two nights with Alicia Payson. He rapped on the facing. "Alicia? Are you in there? It's me, Alicia. It's Longarm. Open up, we've got to—"

The door was jerked open by a stout woman in a gray negligee, her hair tied in cloth curlers. Behind her, a fat-bellied man stood in his undershirt, staring at Longarm.

"Where is she?" Longarm muttered. "Where's Alicia?"

"There's no Alicia in here," the woman said. "I don't even know the hussy. Nobody here but my husband and me."

"Herbert Deerling and wife," the man said. "From Colby. Over in Kansas."

"We just got in this morning," the woman said. "If you don't get away from my door, I'll call the law."

Shaken, Longarm retreated. The woman slammed the door. They heard her lock it.

Vail said, "You sure this is the right room, Longarm?"

"It's the right room. I'll never forget that room." Longarm turned and strode along the corridor, down the stairs, and across the lobby to the desk. He faced the clerk. "My room—" he began.

"I'm sorry, Mr. Long. We thought you had checked out of your room. We rented it to another couple. That's what I tried to tell you as you raced across—"

"All right, all right. Where is she?"

"Where is who, Mr. Long?"

"Alicia. Alicia. My wife."

"Your wife, Mr. Long? I don't understand."

"The hell you don't. Two nights ago, I registered here with my wife. Nobody who saw her will ever forget, and I know you ogled her like a pinto with the itch."

"I beg your pardon, sir."

"All right, I'm sorry. I'm upset. There was a young woman. A young blind girl. Blonde. She was in that room with me—for two nights. Just tell me where she's gone and we're quits."

"I'm sorry, Mr. Long. I don't know of any such young woman as you describe. She certainly does sound unusual. Beautiful. Blonde. Blind. Hardly a woman one would forget in a hurry."

"You know damned well you haven't forgotten her. Now listen to me." He flashed his deputy marshal's badge. "This may be a matter of life and death. I've got to know where she is."

"I'm sorry, sir. I've never seen such a woman."

"I registered her here."

The clerk remained unperturbed. "You registered here two nights ago, Mr. Long. I dislike saying it, but you were . . . quite drunk. You were also—and definitely—alone."

Vail moved to the desk and turned the registry book around facing him. He thumbed back two nights, and ran his finger along the registrations. He spoke softly, warningly. "Longarm. You better take a look at this."

Longarm stared down at the entries. There was his own signature, Custis Long, scrawled in what may well have been his own handwriting.

He turned the pages in both directions, and came up with nothing. There was no sign that a page had been removed. He kept coming back to that signature, which looked as if he may have written it when he was carrying a load.

He shook his head. "This has been changed, chief." But there was no conviction in his own voice.

"Longarm," Vail said, "you've got less than an hour to make the Denver-Pacific train north. You make it, or you turn in your badge."

"Billy, she was here. In that room. I don't know what they've done, but I do know she's blind and she needs help."

"Longarm. It's clear that you've been drinking. I don't know what else you've been doing. But I know this: you do me a creditable job on the Humboldt, and maybe I'll leave this whole business out of your personnel report to Washington."

Longarm's gunmetal-blue eyes impaled the desk clerk murderously.

He stared about the quiet lobby, the normal world. Business as usual. He felt the rage boiling up inside him. He jerked his head around and faced Chief Vail. "Screw Washington," he said.

Vail shrugged. "That's up to you. You screw anybody you like. Curtail your drinking to hours off duty. I don't care. You just be on that train north at noon."

Chapter 5

Longarm rode north in the day coach of the Denver-Pacific railroad, seething with rage. At that moment he hated the world and everybody in it—almost as much as he hated himself. He was a lawman, supposed to be a professional, considered good at his job. He should have had sense enough to know he and Alicia Payson couldn't nose around digging into a secret, even one cold and dead for twenty years, that somebody obviously didn't want exposed to daylight, without drawing attention to themselves. His instincts should have told him. Alicia Payson was right about everything else. She was right about needing protection—*his* protection. But, oh, no! He was too smart. He could put her on a back burner. Whoever it was had struck faster than a sidewinder—and as treacherously as one. And he had made it easy for them, leaving Alicia spread-eagled and helpless on that hotel bed.

He bent down and opened the light canvas bag he traveled with—a change of underwear and a fresh shirt —and pulled out the coffee-can bank. The jaspers who had nabbed Alicia had been smart and fast—but not perfect.

Hoorahing cowboys staggered, stumbled, jostled, and wrestled their way up and down the aisle of the speeding train. The motion of the swaying cars sent them bumping against seated passengers, and their own orneriness had them staring down those they met in passing. Their eyes dared any man to protest. They were itching for a fight.

Longarm ignored them, though he was struck vigorously several times in the shoulder. He didn't bother to

53

look up. His mind was turned in on itself, on his own inner rages.

He had found the Arbuckle Coffee can in the garbage behind the Windsor Hotel. This at least had convinced Billy Vail that Alicia Payson wasn't just a figment of his wet dreams.

His mouth stretched in a wolfish grin. There was no deep mystery about what had happened. Whoever had come into the Windsor looking for Alicia had come armed with cash. It was not a big deal to bribe underpaid hotel clerks, bellboys, and cleaning people. Earlier, in the train's dining car, a simple experiment he remembered from boyhood proved how easily—using milk, lemon, and vinegar—ink could be lifted and blotted off paper. Scrawling what would pass for a drunken man's signature required no great skill.

The cleaning people had removed all traces of Alicia from that second-floor bedroom. Renting it out to the first couple to show up was a lead-pipe cinch and just rounded off their stupid little charade. And it was stupid, because the coffee-can bank meant nothing to them, and they'd swept it out with the other clutter. It was all the proof he needed that Alicia had been in that hotel and had been forcibly removed.

"All right, Longarm." Billy Vail had nodded his head in agreement. "I buy it. She was in there, and somebody took her away, and they want me—or anybody else—to believe she never was there."

"I'll find her."

"No. You'll get on that train. I know how you feel, Longarm. But I also know how Washington feels. This is top priority. You get out there and stop that critter, or critters, from chopping Western Union wire, I'll give you the time you need to track down Alicia Payson."

"She could be dead by then."

"That's something you got to face, Longarm. She might be dead right now. We're betting she's not. She poked her nose in where she shouldn't, and somebody has punched it in. I'll put a deputy on the case until you get back."

"Who? Wallace?"

Vail shook his head. "Wallace is on a case. I've got Gene Avery Eberhardt. He's a good man. He never takes no for an answer. He's recuperating from bullet wounds in his belly. When I explain what's happened, he'll take on the assignment. So I swear to you, old son, we'll be working on it while you're gone."

Longarm nodded bleakly, because there was nothing else he could do. He checked his pocket watch and they headed fast for the train station. Longarm was silent. They could send a boy into the country, but they couldn't keep him out of town forever. He'd be back, and fast. He was about to set a new record for apprehending and indicting a criminal, or criminals, on this job—complete with a one-paragraph report for Billy Vail. In triplicate, of course.

Sitting with that coffee-can bank in his fist, Longarm stared at it and muttered a solemn vow deep inside his mind, where no one could hear. If anything happened to Alicia Payson, he hoped God would have mercy on her abductors, because he would not.

Exhaling heavily, he replaced the coffee can in the collapsed canvas bag and buckled it closed. As he looked up, his gaze struck a familiar face. For a moment he couldn't place the woman. Then, remembering, he jumped to his feet and touched her arm as she passed. "Mrs. Frye?" he said. "Emma Frye?"

Emma Frye's eyes widened and her mouth sagged open. She looked startled, shocked, even frightened—anything but pleased. At first she attempted to ignore him and to move on down the crowded aisle through the milling, yelling cowpokes. Then she bit down on her underlip and glanced both ways warily before she answered him. "Oh, yes. Imagine. Meeting you here. Hello, Mr. Custis . . ."

"Long. Custis Long."

"That's right. Mr. Long. Longarm, wasn't it?"

"It certainly was, Mrs. Frye," he said. "Still is."

"Well, I am surprised to meet you again. So soon and all."

"Yes. It's a small train, isn't it? You heading out of Denver already?"

Nervously, Emma Frye glanced both ways before answering quickly, "I've found a wonderful new job, Mr. Custis—Mr. Longarm. A caretaker, housekeeper."

Score another one for the blind lady and her predictions. "Bachelor or widower?" Longarm inquired, remembering Alicia's analysis.

Emma frowned faintly. "What? Oh, widower. A real fine gentleman. Lives out in western Nevada. I'm sorry, I must go. I wouldn't want him to be . . . upset, if he saw me talking to you. I told him I didn't know anyone in Denver, and you know how easily older men can get jealous."

"And no wonder," Longarm said gallantly.

Emma was already hurrying away. She paused and glanced back over her shoulder, giving him a wan smile, and then she was lost in a crowd of shouting and shoving cowmen.

Two brief, unequal battles broke out along the aisles. The conductor and the porter pushed their way through, pleading for peace.

The porter stopped beside Longarm and shook his head. "Reckon they don't mean no harm. Just letting off steam. On their way home. The Snake Head Ranch. Ever hear of it?"

"No." Longarm was staring at a cowpuncher at the end of the day coach. His right arm was in a sling, his shoulder bandaged as if his collarbone may have been smashed by a bullet. It was probably a coincidence that he had shot that assailant this morning in the shoulder. The way these jaspers carried on, they invited big trouble anywhere they gathered. Plenty of honorable men would stand in line to shoot one of these obnoxious cowboys in the shoulder.

"Big spread. They don't know how far across because they say crows can't fly that far."

Longarm grinned at the porter without really hearing him. He had not taken his gaze from that broken-shouldered jasper. It would be a hell of a coincidence, but he couldn't afford to let it go without checking it out.

Longarm stood up. It was easy to keep the wounded

youth in sight because Longarm was at least a head taller than most of the men in the aisle. He sidled along the swaying, crowded corridor, begging pardon and smiling as he moved forward.

Suddenly he struck something immovable. A young cowpoke stood braced, daring him to walk over him. Puzzled, Longarm stopped and looked down at the youth, whose ten-gallon Stetson, from the most expensive hat shop in Denver, was pushed back on wheat-colored hair. His eyebrows were like straightened caterpillars over faded blue eyes that snagged Longarm's attention, held it, and sent a chill along the nape of his neck.

He could not remember having ever looked into such deadly, vicious eyes. All he could think of was that unless one had seen the eyes of a dead rattler, there was no way to explain what was in the eyes of this youngster. It was hard to believe eyes could curdle into such evil in no more than eighteen or nineteen years.

"Hold it," the boy said. "What you mean, pop, gettin' in my way?"

The other cowpunchers fell quiet, watching the slender, dapperly attired youth.

Longarm shrugged. "Sorry, friend."

"I ain't no friend of yours. I don't even know you." The youngster's voice was high-pitched, made even more so by his rage.

Longarm tried to step aside to let the boy pass but, perversely, as Longarm had known he would, the youth moved in step with him, grinning savagely, still barring his way. "You asking for trouble, mister?"

"Looks like it," Longarm said. "If you'll accept my apology, old son, I'll get on——" He looked over the belligerent kid's shoulder. The bandaged cowpoke was gone. Longarm's anger flared. He kept himself under taut rein. "There's been some mistake, but let's forget this little altercation before one of us gets hurt so bad it'll take you six months to recuperate."

The kid whooped with savage, snarling laughter. "Hey! Look at this. Pop's threatening me."

The other cowpunchers, some of them smarter than

the boy, only watched, edging back. The other riders craned their necks to see better, their faces troubled.

Longarm's eyes glinted coldly. He spoke in a low, savage tone. "Get out of my way, you little loud-mouthed punk, or I'll break you apart."

"Why don't you start now, pop?" the boy shouted at him, voice quaking with rage. "Start now, or start backing up. And keep backing up until I tell you to stop."

Longarm stared down at the gun that had appeared in the boy's fist.

He spoke softly, but in a deadly tone that had instilled caution in wiser men. "You better learn, boy. Never pull a gun on a grown man unless you mean to use it—or you just may never grow up."

"Back up, goddamn you!" the boy screamed, his voice rattling through the car.

Before Longarm could move, the door behind the boy was shoved open. The conductor rushed in, followed by a huge man somewhere in his forties.

The man's voice was full, a basso profundo that stood up against mountain gales and was heard over rushing torrents and on windy ranges. "All right, you galoots. Settle down. Or answer to me. I mean that thing. Get back to your own cars. And stay there." He addressed the people in the chairs, his craggy face pulled into something resembling a smile. "Folks, I'm sorry for any inconvenience or pain or trouble these wild men might have caused you. There ain't no excuse for it. But I reckon they think they got a reason to raise a little hell. It's been a long year on my ranges. We've recently come off a roundup. We've delivered our cows to the stockyards in Denver. These saddle tramps been hoo-rahin' Denver for a couple, three days. Reckon they think their party ain't over yet. Think they can keep on hell-raising all the way home. Anyone—*anyone* —of you folks, man, woman, or child, has one minute of trouble with any of my men from this moment, don't even answer him. You just come straight to me. The conductor will bring you to me. My door's open. You tell me your complaint—and that puncher will regret the day he was whelped." He smiled again and doffed his big hat. "Just relax now, folks, the party is over. I hope you'll all have a pleasant trip."

Longarm glanced toward the boy. The gun had magically disappeared. He grinned coldly and stepped aside for the youth to pass. Instead, the kid stood there one moment longer. He whispered tautly, "This ain't no way over, mister. We'll meet again."

"Sure." Longarm grinned blandly. "If I'm ever under your rock, I'll look you up."

"Don't push it, mister. Don't push it." The boy heeled around and walked away, following the other chastened, silenced cowpokes from the day coach.

Longarm turned and retreated to his seat. The Mexican slumped by the window had been asleep when Longarm entered the car. He was still asleep. Longarm grinned. He had slept through the fracas, and even through the big rancher's stentorian address. Some people were just born lucky.

The porter paused beside Longarm's seat. "Sorry about that flare-up with that kid."

Longarm shrugged. "Yeah. He was feisty."

"That Mr. Job Blackwelder quieted them fellows down fast, huh? Huh? Mr. Job Blackwelder. Only see him on the train couple times a year, but you don't forget him, huh? He's some big hombre."

"Yeah." Longarm nodded abstractedly. He was thinking about the youth with the bandaged shoulder, and the kid with the dead-hawk eyes. He was reaching, but they could have been the two jaspers who had tried to bushwhack him at the barbershop. He decided to take a walk through the train and see if he could find the boy. He wouldn't need a confession; he'd know the truth from what he read in the youth's face. He'd seen a lot of guilt in a lot of faces in the past few years. Sometimes he thought he could *smell* guilt on a man. This thought brought Alicia rushing back into his mind, and he winced. "Man seems four-square, all right."

The porter laughed, shaking his head. "Mr. Blackwelder seems like he'd be a fine friend, but not a man I'd want for an enemy."

59

Longarm stood up. "Think I'll stretch my legs," he said.

He walked away, going through the car. He pushed open the door and was slammed in the face by a torrent of rushing wind and clattering of wheels on rails. He staggered across the coupling area and entered the vestibule of the next car. Blackwelder had done his job competently and thoroughly. He had put the fear of God—spelled Blackwelder—in his men. This car was quiet, with people sleeping awkwardly in the green-plush-covered chairs.

He lumbered his way, swaying with the racing train, to the observation platform at the rear. The platform was vacant at the moment and he lit a cheroot and watched the night-streaked hills and clumps of trees racing past. A lake with the moon like a flower in its lapel slipped by on the wind. The smoke whipped in gray, cold gusts around him, and he smelled the burnt cinders.

He pushed open the door and reentered the car. A girl sat alone in a chair beside the window. She looked up, met his eyes, and smiled faintly before she lowered her gaze.

Longarm hesitated, tempted. He might have stopped, but she was a blonde. A blonde to remind him of Alicia Payson. The last thing he needed.

He made his way through the quiet cars. The gas lamps had been dimmed, the lights lowered. In one chair a young woman sprawled in exhausted sleep. A child sat precariously in her lap, bawling.

His own day coach was quieter than ever now; most of its occupants were asleep or silently staring at the lights reflected against the night in the windows. His Mexican seat partner seemed not to have stirred.

Longarm was restless, too stirred up to sit still. He prowled forward, going slowly through each car. The dining car was empty, and the waiters sat at a white-linen-covered table playing five-card stud poker, nothing wild, no limit. They grinned at him, but Longarm shook his head and walked on through the car.

Mr. George Pullman's sleeping cars were made up,

the dark curtains drawn. Longarm sidled his way through, hearing odd and intriguing sounds as he passed some of the berths. He grinned and kept walking.

He pushed open a forward door; the intensified roar of the engine and coal car was loud on the gale wind that struck him. The conductor stood just beyond the door. He smiled, but shook his head. "Sorry, sir. This is as far as you can go."

"What's wrong?"

"Nothing wrong at all, sir. Blackwelder's private cars, the next two. You got to understand how rich a man can be to understand how Mr. Job Blackwelder travels. His own private cars, including his own private diner."

Longarm grinned. "I try to imagine being that rich, but then I keep seeing my expense account that never quite covers expenses, you know. You ever live like that?"

"Doesn't everybody?" the conductor said.

Longarm laughed. "Everybody but Mr. Job Blackwelder."

"Mr. Blackwelder's a fine man. He's probably what God would be like if He had money."

Longarm said good night, turned, and retraced his steps through the cars. The dining-car poker game had become deadly serious. The players forgot to smoke. Some of them forgot to breathe. They did not look up as Longarm passed.

Sighing, troubled, drawn taut, Longarm sank into his chair, wishing he had some of the disposition of the sleeping Mexican. To sleep. Yet, he dreaded sleeping. If he slept, he would dream about Alicia. It was bad enough thinking about her consciously. Your unconscious mind could play you some hellish tricks.

He tipped his flat-brimmed hat over his eyes, bit down hard on his cheroot, and closed his eyes. The clicking of wheels over rail joints set up a rhythm in his mind. *Alicia. Alicia. Alicia.*

His fists clenched. He wanted to talk to that boy with the shattered collarbone. He sweated, uncomfortable, unable to sleep . . .

Someone was shaking his shoulder, gently but persistently.

"Mr. Long, sir. Mr. Long, you awake?"

He thumbed up the brim of his hat and peered at the porter.

"Sorry, sir, didn't mean to wake you."

"It's all right, I had to get up anyway. Somebody was calling me."

"I'm sorry, sir, but it may be important . . . you are a U.S. marshal, aren't you?"

Longarm nodded.

"You know a young fellow named Curly Tom Lane?"

"Not that I know of."

"He's one of Mr. Job Blackwelder's cowhands, Mr. Long. I don't know if you saw him. He's got a broken shoulder. Said a horse pitched him."

"I saw him."

"He come into the sleeper where I was layin' down for a little while. You grab sleep where you can on this run, Mr. Long. He asked me to give you a message. Says he wants to talk to you. Something important, he said. He asked me to tell you to go out on the rear platform and wait for him. He was pretty nervous. He said he would get there as soon as he got a chance and for you to wait."

"Thanks."

"I don't know anything but that. If you go or not, that's up to you. Them ranch fellows are tricky. Never can tell what they're up to. You can just forget it if you want to. I thought I ought to tell you."

"Thanks. I'd tip you, but it's not on my per diem. I tip you and go without breakfast for two days."

The porter smiled. "That's all right, Marshal. Mr. Curly Tom Lane, he gave me a half eagle—just for delivering his message."

"It sounds more urgent by the minute."

"Maybe. But like I say, them boys are full of hell."

When the porter was gone, crabbing his way forward against the sway of the racing train, Longarm sighed. He took out a fresh cheroot, bit off its tip, and clamped it between his teeth. For a minute he watched his reflection in the night-dark window glass, the forest streaking dimly past beyond.

His heart pounded raggedly in anticipation of meeting Curly Tom Lane. There was a chance, no matter how slim, that he might learn something about Alicia's disappearance. On the other hand, the kid with the dead-hawk eyes and Curly Tom might have something tricky planned. He didn't know about Curly Tom Lane, but the only games the evil-eyed youth knew were deadly. There was a chance it was a trap, but that didn't deter him; it was a chance he had to take. Deadly traps went with the territory. If there was the least possibility that he might wrest one scrap of information about Alicia, it was an opportunity that outweighed all risks.

He got up, exhaling heavily. He set his hat straight on his head, shrugged his jacket up on his shoulders, pulled his inseam down from his crotch, and walked slowly but determinedly through the swaying, silent cars to the observation platform.

He stepped out on the darkened enclosure. The train was racing across the northern Colorado High Plains country. Once in a while a nester's lamp winked like an earthbound star in the blackness.

He'd been on the platform for some moments before he realized he was not alone.

He retreated to the darkest wall and set himself against it. Across the platform in a lounge chair he saw what at first looked like a huge croker sack all tied together. Then he saw that it was two people, wrapped in each other's arms. After another moment he became aware that the female was the blonde who had smiled invitingly at him earlier. Her companion wore the loud, striped suit and yellow shoes that proclaimed him a drummer. The salesman was pawing the girl, kissing her loudly, gasping for breath in his excitement.

Longarm saw that the blonde was aware he was there. She seemed to take a vengeful, perverse pleasure in openly demonstrating what pleasures might have been his, had he been smart enough to avail himself of the opportunity.

With a faint smile, he even saw that the girl was going to permit far more liberties to be taken with her person because he *was* there to witness. He knew that decorum dictated that he retire to an inner car. But on the other hand, unless he followed Curly Tom Lane's instructions to the letter, the skittish cowboy might not show up.

Longarm stayed where he was. He tried not to watch the couple sharing the lounge chair, but it was difficult not to glance toward them. The girl's dress was open at the bodice now, and her full breasts were bared to the salesman's anguished eyes as well as to Longarm's.

Moaning in sweet anguish, the drummer pressed his face to the blonde's generous bosom and nuzzled, suckling louder than a starving infant. Over his head, the blonde watched Longarm's face. She was coolly defiant, wriggling her hips. Longarm found himself responding in spite of himself. His trouble was, he was human. He was more than that. He was human as hell.

He ached, checking his watch, staring across the open plains country, trying to look everywhere except at the girl who had now permitted her dress to be raised above her lithe hips and the drummer's hand to massage her furiously and intimately.

"Oh, God," the girl gasped aloud, writhing in the drummer's lap, her gaze fixed on Longarm's face. "Oh, God. Oh, my God."

"Yes it is," Longarm said. "A lovely evening. Yes. It is."

An hour passed, and Longarm sweated, ached, and stared, unwillingly but openly. He didn't believe what he was seeing, but he had the agonized knowledge that most of it was being done for his benefit.

He backed away, opened the door, and retreated back inside. He'd have to watch for Curly Tom Lane in here. What was going on out on that platform was more than he could endure without actively participating.

He removed the cheroot from his mouth, and found it chomped to shreds. He threw it from him. Behind him, the conductor approached. The man was calling out, "Clump. Clump, Wyoming. We're coming into Clump."

He got up, raging inwardly. Curly Tom Lane had sent him on a wild-goose chase. Cowpokes spent a lot of time on open ranges. They got some weird ideas of what was funny.

As he reached the door of the last car, it was thrown open and the porter staggered in. He braced himself against a chair rest and gazed at Longarm, wild-eyed. He looked as if he might cry. "Oh, God, Marshal. My God, we got trouble."

"Lot of that going around," Longarm said.

"You don't understand. It's that Lane boy. The kid that asked to see you."

"Well, he didn't show up."

"That's it, Marshal. He's dead. We got railroad detectives waiting at the station in Clump. Somebody threw Curly Tom Lane off the train. He's dead. Broke his neck."

Chapter 6

Longarm stood beside the tracks, his shoulders hunched forward against a north wind. Barbed wire was the only windbreak between the arctic tundra and this desolate plains country. He shivered, chilled to his toes at the junction of the north-south and east-west northern routes of the Central Pacific.

He watched rail workers run back and forth, swinging lanterns and yelling at each other in the darkness. Once in a while a yard engine struggled forward a few yards and sat puffing from the exertion, until it was reversed to its original position. Longarm supposed it was the late hour, somewhere between midnight and terminal pneumonia, but there was a weird atmosphere of nightmare about this place and everything that was happening.

The railyard at Clump, Wyoming, was lighted like a carnival. The line junction bustled with activity, and yet it seemed to Longarm that not very much—nothing, in fact—was being accomplished.

He saw that his Mexican friend was squatted leeward to the wind beside a depot building that looked like a hen house. His head was sunk forward between fat shoulders, fast asleep.

For over an hour he had watched the passengers being herded in pairs from the northbound car and questioned by railroad detectives in the ten-by-ten waiting room. All this time, the westbound CP Special dozed on the main line a short distance away.

Somebody, teeth chattering from cold, said, "Can't us passengers changing west here board the Central Pacific?"

The railroad detective made a downward-slashing gesture of refusal. "Nobody leaves this area until our investigation is over."

Finally one of the railroad detectives opened the waiting-room door and shouted, "Is there a Custis Long out here?"

Longarm hobbled on freezing toes to the waiting room. Inside, a potbellied stove burned cow chips. The iron vessel glowed red. After the night wind, the small room was like an oven. There were wooden benches along the wall, and a window connecting the tiny crib with the ticket agent's office.

"Why won't you let people wait where they can be warm?" Longarm said.

One of the detectives jerked his head up. "We're conducting this investigation, mister." He motioned toward a chair. "Sit down. We'll ask the questions." He was in his thirties, broad-shouldered, but going to lard in the belly. His boots hurt him and he kept shifting his weight from one foot to the other. His face was flushed, sun-seared, his faded eyes tired. Even his mustache drooped on both sides of his downturned mouth. "Your name Custis Long?"

Longarm nodded. The other detective was a banty rooster of a man, restless, unable to sit down, his string tie loose and shirt opened at his collar. He said, "You mind saying where you're going, Mr. Long?"

"West," Longarm said.

They peered at him, unsmiling. "West covers a lot of ground, Mr. Long. You mind narrowing it down? Name us a town."

"Choose one," Longarm said.

"You better cooperate."

"I'm willing to tell you. But I can't. I'm a deputy U.S. marshal, on assignment. That'll have to cover it."

"Look, Mr. Long, I don't know who you think you're dealing with. We're not hick operators. We know about you. We know you are a government marshal. But let me tell you something as funny as hell. Government marshals sometimes get themselves in trouble, just like ordinary people."

"Happens all the time," Longarm agreed.

"We're dealing with a very brutal murder here. It looks like there's something behind it. Not just a fight between two cowpokes. Not jealousy, or theft, or drinking—your usual causes of killing on railways. Now, we happen to know that this boy Curly Tom Lane was mixed up in something that had nothing to do with his job as a line rider for the Snake Head Ranch."

The little man nodded tautly. "We also know that he sent you a message to meet him on the rear observation platform. It couldn't have been anything to do with your hush-hush assignment, Mr. Long. The train porter tells us you were surprised and a little worried when he delivered the message."

Longarm shrugged. "I went out on the rear platform. I waited for this kid Lane. He never showed up."

"Can you swear to that?"

"I swore *about* it at the time. I can swear *to* it."

"Somebody threw Curly Tom Lane off that speeding train, Mr. Long. Broke his neck. Killed him instantly."

"I heard that. But I never saw Lane after I got his message. I waited almost two hours. That's all I can tell you. I don't know him. I never knew him."

"And he didn't meet you secretly on that rear platform?"

Longarm drew a deep breath. "There were two people out on that platform with me. The whole time. They were still there when I finally left. Why don't you ask them if they saw me throw anybody off that train?"

The little man grinned coldly at him. "We've already asked them."

Longarm stood near the day-coach entrance of the westbound Central Pacific. He had been almost the last person interrogated by the railroad detectives, but the people transferring were asked to wait. The long and tedious business of uncoupling the three private Blackwelder cars from the Cheyenne-bound short line began. The cars were unhooked from the rest of the train, then the northbound pulled across the juncture lines and sat puffing intermittent smoke balls while a yard engine shoved the three Blackwelder cars onto a siding. While these cars sat in the farthest reaches of the brilliantly illumined yard, the work engine reversed, hooked up to the second section of the northbound, and shoved it onto a siding. The yard engine then steamed and rattled its way to a third siding, which brought it around to the rear of the northbound.

Longarm shook his head, exasperated. "Maybe by Christmas," he thought.

As if reading his mind, someone spoke warmly in a rich voice. "Takes a while to get us shifted around. But once we're hooked to Central Pacific and start west, we get full priority. Full priority, sir. No sidings for the Special from here to California. My name is Job Blackwelder, sir, and I'm pleased to make your acquaintance, and I deeply regret any inconvenience we might be causing you."

Job Blackwelder crunched along the cinders of the right-of-way to where Longarm stood. He was a colossus of a man, big and expansive and outgoing, laughing and smelling of Scotch whiskey from the depth of a great sheepskin-lined jacket with fat fleece collar, cuffs, and hem. Longarm had met a lot of ranchers; they were a breed apart, but he'd never met one quite like Job Blackwelder before.

The rancher was cactus-rough, flint-hard like the sun-seared Nevada basin land where he ranched. But he was rich—rich as few ranchers ever are, even the biggest—and wealth had mellowed him. His voice battered things, commanding and thunderous, but it was warm. He shouted orders on wind-driven ranges, but the wind never tore *his* voice apart; his orders were heard, and they were obeyed.

Longarm studied him, fascinated. Blackwelder was middle-aged and fighting against time relentlessly, wearing diamond rings and two-hundred-dollar, hand-tooled, calf-leather boots with two-inch heels. Those heels elevated him above the eye level of most men, but he had to look up at Longarm, and he seemed to relish the experience. Little men jumped to his tune, and big men

69

shrunk down to his size, sooner or later. This was what his wide smile seemed to say.

He hadn't yet reached his fifties, but he was gray; his beard and mustache were gray, as were his thick eyebrows and the fat flesh of his eye sockets. His eyes were gray. His neck was thick and his jowls were heavy and his cheeks were flushed, steak-fed, and diluted with expensive whiskies. If he couldn't stand getting old, he paid some money and bought something fancy, and this kept him young. He hated aging above all things, this was clear. He was a man who loved the power he wielded, the way he dominated everything and everybody he met. He always had, and he always meant to. But in the secret storeroom of his mind, he admitted this was a young man's world, and to control it, a man had to stay young. And he meant to command it all, until the day he died or discovered a way to pay some money and hang on.

"I'm a rancher, sir. Out in the Bear Paw country."

He extended his callused hand and Longarm shook it. He grinned when, for a moment, Blackwelder made the handshake a test of strength.

Longarm said, "My name is Long. Custis Long. Folks call me Longarm."

"They do? Why? You built special?" The big man nudged him and guffawed.

"Never made many comparisons."

Blackwelder enjoyed this. He drew in on his dollar cigar and exhaled expensive halos of gray smoke. Longarm continued to chew on his dead five-cent cheroot. He decided that if Blackwelder offered him a hand-rolled stogie, nothing in government regulations would require him to refuse it. A good cigar was hardly a bribe, even a dollar cigar. Longarm inhaled deeply.

"Have a cigar." Blackwelder extended one of the fat, dark brown smokes. For the second time it was as if he read Longarm's thoughts. "Sure don't see how you fellows can stand them cheroots."

"If you work for the government, you get used to anything," Longarm said.

Blackwelder fired a long match and held it cupped

70

in his hand while Longarm sucked in fire blissfully. When the cigar was lit, he drew in deeply, filling his lungs and all the crevices of his mind with the rich, warm taste. He forgot the deadly north wind, the waiting, the dark. He smiled.

"Heard you were a government man, Longarm."

"Oh?"

"Not prying, sir. I never pry. But I see a man that interests me, I like to know about him. Knowing about people, about things, keeps a man young. You don't get old as long as you're interested in people and what's going on around you, huh?"

"I reckon not."

"Man like you. Big. Tall. Stand out in any crowd. Always think of government men as furtive little fellows sneaking around."

"I sneak around a lot."

Blackwelder laughed. "It can't be easy."

"If it was easy, Mr. Blackwelder, would Uncle Sam pay us a hundred a month and found?"

Blackwelder rocked with laughter. "I like you, Longarm. Does a man good to be around you. Laughter's the best medicine. And you're a man with a real good, dry sense of humor."

"I wish I could laugh at a hundred a month."

"And found!" Blackwelder slapped him on the back. "Man, that wouldn't keep me in cigars."

"You'd grow a taste for cheroots." Longarm drew deeply on the cigar, making that statement a self-taunting lie.

"I can't understand it. Don't mean no offense, sir. But you take a smart, young, intelligent fellow like you. You could chop yourself a rich hunk of this country. Yet you work for the government. Stand around in freezing cold, smoking five-cent cigars. I always wonder why."

"I can't tell you. Probably, if I thought about it, I'd kill myself. But not until I finish this cigar."

"If you thought about it, Longarm, you could do what you want to do."

"You know, that might just be the answer, Mr. Blackwelder. Maybe this *is* what I want to do."

"I reckon. Yeah. Makes sense. You ain't getting rich. But you get a lot of action. Live around. Meet some strange people, I reckon. Yeah. Keeps you young. Heading out into my country, are you?"

"I'm going into Nevada, yes."

"Looking into trouble out our way, are you?"

Longarm grinned. "You got a guilty conscience, Mr. Blackwelder?"

Blackwelder threw his big head back, roaring with laughter. "Hell, man, anybody who's made as much money as I have has got himself a guilty conscience. Few men get dirty-rich and stay clean-honest. You make a choice. I made mine, Mr. Longarm. A long time ago. No . . . it's this damned government. They keep reaching out. All the time sticking their hands in your pocket, putting their noses in your business. We got one hell of a lot more government coming out of Washington, Mr. Longarm, than we got any need for. I can tell you. I don't need no government men prying around the Bear Paw country, telling me how to run the Snake Head Ranch."

"You can relax, Mr. Blackwelder. I can tell you right now, if this train ever starts up, I'm headed for the Winnemucca Indian Agency. You know the place?"

"Know it well. So well, I wouldn't head there for a million dollars. Not on purpose."

"When you're making a hundred and found, you go where they send you."

Blackwelder stopped smiling. He shook his head. "Tell you the truth, Longarm, I was a mite concerned about you. We got ourselves a little trouble. Like I say, nothing we can't handle, and we don't need government interference, but because you don't *need* the government to interfere ain't ever stopped 'em yet. Eh? You know, the boy that got himself killed, thrown off that train coming north, he was one of my hands. A line rider named Curly Tom Lane."

"Yes. I know."

"Now, I want you to understand. Clear and plain

72

and right off the top of the deck. Whatever trouble Curly Tom got into, it had nothing to do with my spread. This kid Lane fancied himself a gun handler. He was looking to make himself extra money, hiring out." He shook his head. "I tell you, Longarm, kids like that get to shooting coffee cans and bottles and ducks and rabbits on the prairies, just to relieve the boredom. You know. Next thing, they're fast-drawing, filing down the hammer, seeing themselves as fast draws, gunslicks."

"Lot of that going around, all right."

"I don't know what Tom Lane got himself into in Denver. Hired out to moonlight—with his gun. I know that much. And very little more. Got into something. Something over his head. Got shot—his collarbone smashed. And now somebody's pushed him off the train. Broke his neck. I'm sorry. He was a good kid. Kind of wild. Worked hard. Now he's dead. I tell you, when I heard you were a marshal, I was afraid you were following us. I didn't need that. And I was mighty full of rage at that kid for getting us under government surveillance with his damn fool gun fever." He laughed. "Well, I feel a lot better, knowin' you got other fish to fry, Mr. Longarm."

Someone shouted Blackwelder's name from along the tracks. "Pa! Hey, Pa! They got our cars hooked up now. Say we can get aboard."

The blond youth with the expensive Stetson and the quick gun and the dead-hawk eyes ran to where they stood. Something flickered in his face when he saw Longarm and he hesitated, then strode forward, face set and shoulders back, defiant.

"Longarm, want you to meet my son. My pride. My life. He's what it's all about, Longarm. You get a son you're proud of, you build your whole life around him, and everything you amass up, it's for him. Meet my son Logan. Logan Blackwelder. Logan was his mother's name. He looks more like his mother than me. Thank God, eh?"

"Good to meet you, Logan." Longarm extended his hand.

73

The youth hesitated, then wiped his palm along his trouser leg and extended his own hand tentatively.

"Shake hands," Blackwelder ordered, laughing. "Hell, I heard you two men had a little altercation. I think you were a fool, Logan. And by God, I didn't think I raised a fool for a son. But maybe if you shake hands, you can forget any past trouble and start new."

"Sounds fair to me," Longarm said.

"It's forgotten," Logan Blackwelder said. But looking into those dead-hawk eyes, Longarm read the truth. It was not forgotten, not by Logan Blackwelder. It never would be forgotten.

The day coach of the Central Pacific Special was warm and luxuriant. It was like walking into a new and pleasant world. These cars were the smartest and most comfortable passenger trains built to date. They glistened and smelled new. Seat padding was deep, the covers smooth and bright. Small pillows in white cases, and itchy blankets one size too small for a growing midget, were stacked in closed overhead compartments.

When Longarm entered the heated day coach, his blood began to circulate again and his feet gradually warmed. He could wriggle his toes without being afraid they'd crack like icicles. He saw that the Mexican had appropriated two small pillows and two blankets and was curled up, sleeping like a fat burro.

Longarm grinned and found an empty seat. He sagged into it and stretched out his legs. He finished off the cigar, luxuriating, prolonging it, savoring it. He tipped his hat over his eyes and leaned back.

Though his hatbrim covered most of his face, he could glimpse the forms and shapes of the people who swayed past in the late-night aisles. Most of the passengers slept. Many of them had not awakened during the interminable wait and coupling of Blackwelder's private cars.

Something troubled him, the prickling premonition of danger. The Snake Head Ranch cowpokes were prowling again. They were no longer rowdy; there was no more hoorahing. They were mannerly, quiet, step-

74

ping aside for men as well as ladies in the aisles. That was one of the things that troubled him. They were too quiet.

The second thing that bothered him was how often the same jaspers passed his chair, pausing, then moving on, as if playing some kind of deadly game. He opened one eye under the brim of his hat.

Three or four of the Snake Head Ranch cowboys walked past his chair several times within the next half-hour. One of them was Logan Blackwelder, Job Blackwelder's pride and joy.

They said nothing, made no overt moves. They merely slowed, eyeing him, as if committing him to memory or trying to snag his attention, prod him into doing or saying something. It could have been just the restless cowpokes relieving boredom. Somehow he kept thinking of coyotes sniffing, circling, nosing.

He couldn't say why, but he felt his hackles rise. A hot feeling of rage flickered in him too. Maybe it was the same rage that had first simmered when Logan Blackwelder pulled his gun on him and tried to back him down. For whatever reason—logic or hatred—he kept melding young Blackwelder and that second bushwhacker running toward George Masters's barbershop in Denver. Logan. Bushwhacker. Logan. Bushwhacker.

He hadn't gotten a good enough look at the ambusher for any kind of positive identification. A man seen at the wrong end of a gun barrel was seldom clearly etched in a man's memory. But there was a thin thread, a connecting link. Curly Tom Lane was allegedly a wild kid who fancied himself a gunslick, a fast draw, a hircd gun. If Curly Tom had been one of the bushwhackers, couldn't Logan Blackwelder have been the other?

One thing young Blackwelder had proved by drawing on him was that Curly Tom Lane wasn't the only hot-headed, gun-fevered punk raised on Snake Head land.

Hell, this could even provide a motive for young Blackwelder's drawing on him under the guise of hoorahing a train car. Maybe Logan had been daring

75

him, pushing him, prodding him to draw, looking for an excuse to squeeze that trigger and yell self-defense. With his money, he could make it stick. And as Job Blackwelder had said, a man's guilty conscience can lead him down strange paths.

Still, it was an idea as full of holes as a hen-house alibi. It grew more out of cold hatred than logic. Logan Blackwelder had all the money in the world; he didn't need to hire out as a gunslick. Still, Curly Tom Lane had hired out, for laughs. The youth Longarm had winged had had a gun-wielding partner, and there was no doubting the implacable hatred smoldering in the Blackwelder kid's dead, flat eyes.

If these young hellions had planned some kind of deadly game with him as the butt, he wanted to get out of range. He had too much on his mind: a top-priority assignment and a date in Denver with Alicia Payson's abductors. He had no proof that Job Blackwelder's malevolent, spoiled, and sinister offspring was involved in that Denver bushwhacking; he couldn't swear that Curly Tom Lane was the kid he'd winged. He had no time for their stupid games. Hell, if Logan kept poking at him until he struck back and hurt the young bastard, old Job would be on his trail till doomsday. He wanted no part of any of it.

When the conductor came through the car, Longarm stopped him. "Nearest town to the Winnemucca Indian Agency is Winnemucca, right?"

"Winnemucca, Nevada. Coming in there tomorrow sometime."

"Is there a stop this side of the town—that's still near the agency?"

The conductor laughed, shaking his head. "The agency is across the plains from a water stop. You don't want that, mister. Distances in the Great Basin ain't like they are anywhere else in the world. That plain's the emptiest place on God's earth. With nothing but shank's mare, you'd be lucky to make it to the fort. Take my advice, friend. You get off this train at the Winnemucca depot and hire yourself a horse and rig— and a five-gallon can of water."

Longarm settled back in the seat. It made sense to take the conductor's advice. The trick was to keep his head, keep his temper controlled, no matter what the coyotes from Snake Head Ranch did.

At that precise instant, the fat Mexican toppled along the aisle, bleeding, battered, and sobbing incoherently.

Longarm leaped up. He caught the Mexican's arm. "What's the matter? What happened to you?"

The Mexican, bleeding profusely from the side of the head and along his throat, only gurgled something unintelligible and swung his arm forward toward the front of the train.

Longarm eased the fat man down into his chair, rang for the conductor, and ran through the car. He went cautiously out of the door, but found nothing between the cars. The next car forward was quiet, strangely quiet. Even those people who were awake did not look up as Longarm strode past.

He pushed open the next door, waited, then stepped out into the noisy linking space. He found it empty.

He entered the first Pullman car. The curtains were drawn, the bunks made up, the occupants sleeping. He reached the end of the car and had just touched the door when he heard something behind him.

As he turned, a knife slashed past his head and embedded itself in the door framing. Raging, he jerked the knife from the wall and wheeled around, running. Ahead of him, the door opened and closed.

As he went through the first day coach, he knew he'd lost his assailant. The car was quiet. He studied the people in the chairs, but found nothing and no one suspicious.

When he reached his own car, the conductor and the porter were working over the Mexican with a basin of water and a first-aid kit. They had him almost cleaned up and bandaged.

The conductor said, "Somebody beat him up. In the privy. Cut him pretty bad. We're putting him off at Elko and sending him to a doctor."

Longarm handed the conductor the long-bladed,

77

glittering knife. "Give this to your railroad detectives. If they find the man who owns it, they've got the coyote that worked our friend over. They might even have the killer who threw Curly Tom Lane off the Cheyenne train."

Chapter 7

When the train stopped for water, Longarm tossed his canvas bag to the ground and swung down after it. He called to the conductor, "Which way you say the agency is?"

The conductor grinned wolfishly and swung his arm in a direction that seemed generally westerly. One could see the bleached bed of the Humboldt River, the cracked alkali banks, the flat basin land scraggly with clumps of sage. "Yonder," he said and waved, shaking his head. He saw it and he still didn't believe it.

"May all your daughters marry Republicans," Longarm called and stalked downslope, heading west.

He exhaled. The conductor rated him among the imbeciles of this world, and maybe he was. It must be hard to believe that a sane man would leave a fast-moving train for a chance to walk—in the middle of nowhere. It looked as if the sun set between this watering tower and the first outskirts of civilization.

To hell with it. This was a decision coldly reached. He wanted to leave that train under his own power, not wearing a knife or nursing a bullet. Also, he didn't want to be prodded into taking young Blackwelder apart. That way led to trouble that would never end as long as there was a Blackwelder. The hell with the whole arrogant clan.

It was barely daylight. He had moved out before even his enemies were astir. He'd sat, sleepless all night, watching every shadow twist out of deeper shadow.

He got up, prepared to debark. The passengers lolled in stunned early morning sleep. He'd made his de-

79

cision, and he hoped he could live with it. He was going to leave the Central Pacific Special before he had further confrontations with the knife-thrower or Logan Blackwelder. Somebody wanted him dead, as they had desired the demise of Curly Tom Lane, and maybe for a related reason in somebody's guilty mind.

One motive occurred to him immediately. They wanted to keep headstrong Job Blackwelder from learning the truth about his beloved son: that Logan was in the same trouble, with the same people, which had led to Curly Tom Lane's death. If Logan Blackwelder had been partnered with Curly Tom in Denver, moonlighting as gunslicks, he wanted to talk with him. But he'd have to walk over Job Blackwelder—dead or alive—to get at young Logan, the apple of a doting father's eye. At the moment, such a battle wasn't worth it. He'd settle for a quick escape, a whole skin, and a later date with the insolent kid. Oh, he'd meet Logan Blackwelder again. He felt that with the same certainty as he believed the basin sun was going to broil him before he ever reached the Winnemucca Indian Agency. There was no doubt. He and Logan would meet again.

After the train pulled away from the water tower, Longarm paused. As it picked up speed, he saw Logan Blackwelder and two or three Snake Head cowmen standing on the rear platform, staring across the bleak ground at him. Looking at them, all Longarm could think of was a pack of coyotes, teeth bared, sniffing, nosing at the wind, frustrated for the moment . . .

He watched the train until it was gone in the blue-hazed distance and the empty glittering rails merged to a point in the sun-dazzled valley.

A shudder wormed down between his shoulder blades. "There's lonesome," he mused aloud, "and then there's this place."

He glanced back. A water tower and a windmill. Two phallic symbols of man's progress in the wilderness.

He walked a few yards, then spoke seriously, addressing himself. "No sense talking to me, old son. I'm not going to answer you. Talking to yourself. That's not too bad. But *answering* yourself—that means an empty attic for sure. Anyway, that's what Grandma always said."

He found not even a hawk against the bleached sky. Ahead, the monotonously level basin, dingily scabbed with buffalo grass and low, bushy greasewood, stretched across the endless haze to a flat, pink horizon, or climbed into dim foothills to the north.

He kept walking steadily, not pushing himself, across the barren prairie, until in the distance he discerned a scribbled line of smoke, thin against the pastel earth. Dark clouds rolled from distant gray hills down across the empty sump of the basin. The clouds were broken now and then by a few sickly rays of tarnished sunlight that intensified the stormy darkness, rather than lightening the threatened earth. Rising wind drove grains of sand like grapeshot, which prickled like needles and burned his eyes. Raindrops fell like spittle blown on the wind.

The distant smoke thickened as he approached it, and he found signs of life in the remote valley. On the banks of the shallow, sluggish Humboldt River, outlined by elder and cottonwood trees that sucked sustenance from the stream bed, a ten-foot wall, made of pinyon logs hauled in from God knew where, enclosed a cluster of clapboard and adobe buildings of an army stockade.

He didn't know the name of the fort. By that year, hundreds of these jerry-built army posts were flung across the windswept plains, on lonely mountain passes or desolate hillsides, beside raging rivers and in the shadows of snow-capped mountains, as well as upon the hellfire rims of sun-stunned deserts.

The Winnemucca Indian Agency occupied the largest log-and-frame building near the outer stockade gates. Across from it, in the negligible shadow of a sagging American flag, was the trading post, or the canteen, as the pony soldiers called it. The log walls of the post had been erected high and sturdy and fast by troop labor, but inside those walls, the fort appeared raw and forever unfinished.

The officer's line quarters reared on the morning side of the parade grounds. These cottages, of clapboard or adobe brick, varied from single-room, junior-officer apartments to three- or four-room houses for senior officers and the almost imposing, detached, two-storied frame quarters of the commandant. Across the rectangular, red-clay parade area, which was hard and bald as cement, stood the enlisted men's barracks. These were several long, low, single-storied log buildings with narrow porches running along their fronts. Behind these were the mess halls, supply sheds, quartermaster stores, and the iron-barred guardhouse. Administrative offices were grouped near the big, wide-swinging front gate under the garrison pennant. Blocking out the stockade's rear, and standing apart, was the flat-roofed hospital. Near the meagerly shaded Humboldt were arranged the lean-to feed sheds, the stables and corrals, the wagon barns and smithy. Across the river stood a few tents and single-room shacks, quarters of married enlisted men.

A sign at the front gate gave the name of the place as Fort Bloody Run.

Longarm shook his head. A gloomy, tedious, and isolated sun sore on the belly of the basin. "You'd soon be answering yourself back in this Eden, wouldn't you?" he said.

He made no reply.

Captain Felder Kennecut was a martinet. The officer could have posed as a model for the word. Not even Louis XIV's stern drillmaster, General Martinet himself, could better have exemplified the unbending strict disciplinarian and nitpicker.

Longarm hid a faint grin behind the upturned points of his mustache. Someone had once said that a true martinet never thinks he is at all severe. On every count, Captain Kennecut met the criteria; he was the living, breathing, sneering definition of the word.

He had kept Longarm waiting in his outer office for fifteen minutes, and when Longarm was at last ushered in, the CO begged forgiveness, citing the stress of a crisis. Longarm saw the captain's young orderly grinning behind his hand.

The office was furnished, decorated, and ornamented with every item allowed a commanding officer of an army post by government regulations. A large photograph of the President occupied the wall behind the captain's high-backed chair. A twelve-by-sixteen carpet covered most of the highly polished floor.

When the door was closed behind them, the unbending officer motioned Longarm to a chair. "I did have a long walk," Longarm conceded.

"You walked from the CP water tower? Why?"

Longarm shrugged and replied, "Thought it might be pleasant. This fort is a garden spot of Nevada."

He found at once that the captain was humorless. The officer nodded in agreement. "I run a spit-and-polish post. I won't have anything less. Why to keep my record looking good is to keep my fort looking good. A clean record is an important thing in the army, Mr. Long. That's the first thing they teach you at the Point. With merits and demerits. Soon you realize that that's the way to run a disciplined world. Reward and punishment. Some of my enlisted men hate me but, by God, they obey me."

He marched across the room to a window overlooking the empty parade ground. He stood for a moment there at parade rest, then strode smartly back to his desk. "West Point molds a way of life, Mr. Long. I feel privileged to have been permitted to attend the Point. Sometimes I actually feel a little sorry for men who haven't learned the beauty of pure discipline."

Longarm smiled. "You actually liked West Point, didn't you?"

"I look on it as the high point of my life, sir."

"You even like it here at Fort Bloody Run, don't you?"

"I understand that I am serving my country." The Captain writhed slightly, fighting to keep his hand away from his crotch.

Longarm grinned tautly. "Heat itch, Captain?"

Captain Kennecut nodded slightly, as if ashamed to confess the human weakness.

"Feel like you'll go nuts if you can't claw your crotch, huh?"

"No, sir. Such conduct is entirely unmilitary. I can refrain. I *shall* refrain." He bit down hard on his underlip. He was about five feet three, blond, going bald. He wore boots that added a precarious three inches to his height, and a full dress uniform that must have been murder in this heat.

"You're among friends," Longarm said. "Go ahead and scratch."

"Sir, if I let minor annoyances unbalance me, I'd not be militarily fit for the bigger campaigns. And I *am* ready. You asked me if I liked it here. That consideration barely enters my thinking. It's a step up on the ladder. I want my next promotion. I shall be moved up after forging a military post, disciplined and battleready. That's what I have here. That is what I like."

"Good for you. I admire a man who accomplishes his goals in life."

"Oh, I've not done the things I want to do. I was prepared and trained and equipped for battle, Mr. Long. I believe in battle, because I believe the rewards go only to the militarily strong and the militarily prepared. A good battle settles everything, Mr. Long. You know where you stand after a battle. On the field, there are only the victors and the vanquished. It's clean and pure."

"It's also bloody."

Kennecut stared at him. "Were you in the big war—the Rebellion?"

"I was young. I saw some action anyhow."

"God, I envy you. My God, I envy you. It ended just before I could get in. I tell you the truth, I broke down and wept. I would have given a leg, an eye, my life, to have been with Sherman when he punished the rebels, burning his way to the sea. There was no doubt after Sherman passed." He shook his head, his eyes anguished.

Longarm spoke in a gently prodding tone. "You've got a battle out here."

"The Great Basin Indians are hardly a worthy foe, Mr. Long."

"Still, somebody is cutting vital Western Union telegraph wires out here. Cutting off government messages."

Captain Kennecut straightened to his full height. His face grew flushed. "I've got a thousand square miles out here, Mr. Long. Most posts have four companies. I've got two companies. I'm not complaining, I'm just stating a fact. My men can't be everywhere."

Longarm grinned. "I know. That's why they sent *me* out here."

Kennecut agreed wholeheartedly. "A good move. A wise decision from Washington. The criminals can move away when they see us coming, but one man might get around and learn the identity of the culprits. Naturally, we'll give you every cooperation we can. You have my word as a West Pointer on that."

"I'm sure we'll all sleep better tonight," Longarm said, aware that the captain would not recognize irony if it clouted him in the head. "And you'll sleep better, Captain, if you'll use a mixture of soda and water. It soothes that itch."

"Thank you, Mr. Long, for your concern."

"Well, I want your help. And you want a promotion."

"Don't worry, sir, nothing will keep me from my majority."

"Good for you. Still, apprehending the Western Union predators might look good on your record too."

"You have my word. You tell us who the culprits are. We'll run them to ground."

"If the wires are cut, I might have trouble getting word to you."

Kennecut flushed. "We're doing the best we can, Mr. Long. We're doing everything regulations require. To the letter. You can be sure of that."

"Reports say most wires are being cut in Indian country around here. What tribes do you have?"

85

Kennecut smiled, his mouth twisted with contempt. "Paiutes."

"Well?"

"Well, I don't think they're cutting wire, Mr. Long."

"Why not?"

"You'd have to know the Paiutes, Marshal. They're the dregs of the Indian race. Subhuman, the best of them. They live like animals. There are whites who kill the Paiutes for sport, because they're less than human. They don't even take their scabrous scalps."

"Could the ones killing the Paiutes be cutting Western Union wire?"

"Why would they?"

Longarm shrugged. "So the cavalry couldn't trail them?"

Kennecut considered this. "That might serve as a motive."

"Can I find these Paiutes?"

"They live—like sand lice—in the open basin. They usually have a central town. They wander around it, coming back to it infrequently. You might find them, but talking to them . . ." He shrugged. "Do you speak a Uto-Aztec dialect?"

"*Ka.*"

Kennecut frowned. "*Ka?* What's that?"

"That's *no* in Uto-Aztec. No, I don't speak it."

"Then you'll never get through to them."

"I was thinking about army cooperation. Don't you people have a Paiute translator?"

Kennecut hesitated. "We've got one enlisted man who can talk with the diggers."

Longarm recognized the word "diggers" as a name given to Indians who eked out a marginal survival by foraging for roots and nuts and trapping small game.

"I'll take him," he said.

Kennecut went rigid again, standing at attention. "No. I'm sorry, sir. I'll have to refuse that request."

"Well, I'm not requesting, I'm telling you. I want that translator ready to travel—with me."

"I've said I'm sorry. It's against regulations."

"What regulations, for Christ's sake?"

86

"The man is a prisoner. He's in the guardhouse, awaiting court-martial. He could be sentenced to up to thirty years. He would like nothing better than to have me send him—unguarded—with you, out looking for diggers."

"What's he in for?"

"Statutory rape, sir."

Vince Thayer had a guest when Longarm was finally able to get to the guardhouse at the rear of the post later that afternoon. Longarm was enthusiastically welcomed on the post. Captain Kennecut himself had ordered his sergeant to arrange for the lawman to use one of the junior officers' apartments during his stay.

Longarm did not request permission to visit the prisoner. Kennecut was obviously iron-handed, a stickler for army regulation, and unbending. Longarm acted as though he had put the young translator out of his mind.

He settled into the apartment assigned to him, and had lunch in the officers' mess. Then he returned to his apartment, saying he was going to take a nap. No one doubted this; he looked as if he'd been dragged from the water tower to the fort. He had spent a sleepless night, but he was unable to sleep.

He showed up at the guardhouse and found a freckle-faced young corporal on duty. "I'd like to see Corporal Vince Thayer," Longarm said.

The guard smiled. "Yessir. Could I just see your pass?"

Longarm slapped his jacket pockets. "Damn. I had it here somewhere."

"I'm sorry, sir. You'll have to have a pass. You know Captain Kennecut, sir. He lives by the rules. The letter of the law. Why, even Vince's *wife* has to have a pass."

"Is Vince married?"

"That's his wife in there with him now."

"Could you let me sort of inspect the guardhouse? In case I want to bring in a civilian prisoner?"

"I guess so."

Longarm exhaled. At that moment the prettiest young Indian girl he'd ever seen came out of the cell block. She had been crying and her black eyes were swollen, her lips puffy and her nose red and wet. She was still lovelier than most females fresh from a beauty salon.

She was slender and fragile, her black hair straight and worn parted in the middle and brushed down over her shoulders. She walked with her shoulders straight and the small of her back held in, as lightly as a ballet dancer.

"Reckon May Cloud would be worth twenty years to me," the corporal on guard whispered.

"Twenty years for what?"

"For marrying her. That's what Vince is in the brig for—marrying her. And he's going to get twenty years of hard labor as sure as Captain Kennecut can read the regulations."

Vince Thayer was a thin, tall boy with dark hair and sun-faded gray eyes. He said he'd been born in the West, to parents who'd come out in a Conestoga wagon drawn by oxen.

"I was a drifter. Then I decided to join the army because pay was regular and a man could have his wife with him. Even at Fort Bloody Run. That's in the regulations, thank God."

"You mind explaining this charge against you?" Longarm said.

Vince spat. "It's statutory rape. I married an Arapaho Indian girl. Pure blood. A beauty . . ."

"I saw her."

"She loves me. I know she does. And I know I love her. It's a lot more than an itch. I don't want nobody but May Cloud. I can't have her, I don't want nobody."

"So you married her. What's the rape charge?"

Vince swore. "That's it. It's a law that nobody pays any attention to. What it is—all Indians by now are wards of the state. That means the U.S. government runs their lives. For any white man to marry an Indian, he must have that woman's Indian agent's permission."

"And you didn't get it?"

"Hell, May Cloud ran away from her reservation. Nobody cared. She and I got married. And now Kennecut has arrested me, and I face twenty years for statutory rape—for marrying May Cloud."

"Who brought the charges?"

"Hell, Mr. Long. You need to ask? Nobody enforces that law. Nobody would even think about enforcing it but an arbitrary army prick."

Longarm cooled his heels for fifteen minutes for the second time outside Captain Kennecut's private office.

"Sorry to delay you like that, Mr. Long," Kennecut said when Longarm was finally ushered into his presence. "I hate to do it to a guest like you. But a man's time is not his own in a job like this. We face a crisis, we have to deal with it, no matter."

"I'm facing a little crisis myself, Captain. First, I want to thank you for how comfortable you've made me. And the food at lunch was better than I could have bought in any Denver restaurant."

Kennecut smiled. "We have good cooks. And they work according to regulations."

"You mean the army tells them exactly how to cook?"

"Down to the size of saucepan to use, Mr. Long. And we obey regulations here, even in the mess halls. Especially in the mess halls. Health is the most important factor in a soldier's regimen, Mr. Long. A healthy soldier is a better soldier."

"How about a *happy* soldier?"

"What are you talking about?"

"Corporal Vince Thayer."

"How did you see the prisoner? You didn't have a pass from this office?" Kennecut was ready to press the battery-operated call button on his desk, thereby summoning the sergeant and seeding a new crisis.

"I didn't even realize the prisoner was anywhere around, Captain. I wanted to look over your jail facilities. I may have to bring in one—or several—civilian prisoners. I was checking your facilities. I did

89

get to talking with Thayer. I found out that nobody enforces that statutory-rape law anymore."

"Because other people close their eyes to murder, Mr. Long, does that make murder right for us?"

"Marrying an Indian girl ain't quite the same as murder."

"I don't have to explain myself to you, Mr. Long."

"You may have to explain yourself to *somebody*. I don't give a damn about Corporal Thayer's married life, but he *is* the only Uto-Aztec translator you've got, and I need him. I'm asking you to drop these ridiculous charges."

Kennecut stood straighter than ever. His sweating irritated his chafing heat itch, however, and he could barely restrain himself from scratching his crotch.

"Ridiculous? Perhaps to you, Mr. Long. But not to a man who has the responsibility for an army post. I am indicting and prosecuting Corporal Thayer as much as a warning to other men in my command as I am because he has broken a federal law and must pay for it. My men will know they will toe the line here or they will suffer the consequences."

"Twenty years for marrying the girl he's in love with?"

"That is entirely beside the point, Mr. Long. And love? I hardly think a white man can love a red woman. Lust? Yes. Unbridled passion. But love? Hardly, Mr. Long. No, I refuse to discuss it."

"I reckon you'd *better* discuss it. I have to write a report on every case I handle. The kind of cooperation I get—or don't get—from other government agencies and departments enters in every report."

"You'll get nowhere trying to blackmail me, mister." Kennecut's face was livid. "I am acting according to regulations. *To the letter*."

"Ordinarily, Captain, I wouldn't give a damn. A soldier in your company gets twenty years hard labor for marrying the girl he *thinks* he loves. You act according to your regulations. Who gives a damn? I don't. But I've got a job to do, and I won't let you stand in my way. We better have that understanding, right now."

"Mr. Long. I am prepared to cooperate with you. To the letter of the law. You'll get every cooperation possible from me. But I won't release a prisoner into your custody. Nor will I *nol-pros* proceedings against a criminal just to make you happy."

Longarm laid the envelope containing his orders on the desk. "There is my assignment, Captain. Top priority. Now, if you're going to win promotions by living according to the letter of regulations, you better start deciding which regulations you're going to follow."

"I'm sorry, Mr. Long. I've made my decision."

"You're a good army man, Captain. But I've got a hunch you're going to be a *captain* for a long time."

Kennecut's face paled, went rigid, but he only stiffened further. He walked to the window and stood there, his hands locked behind him, staring out of the window. Only his shifting legs betrayed the itching agony he suffered.

Longarm picked up his orders from the desktop and walked to the office door. He opened it, then paused and spoke across his shoulder. "Go ahead and scratch your balls, Felder. You're not going to make major anyhow."

Chapter 8

Tension crackled through Fort Bloody Run like those static charges that polarize the atmosphere ahead of savage storms.

Word spread across the fort of the yelling match between the captain and the marshal. The well-kept secret of Longarm's threatening to put "on report" the commandant who *lived* to put men "on report" raged like an infection through the stockade. It was the best joke since the time the captain had promised the men a "girly" show that had turned out to be the women's section from the Salt Lake City Tabernacle choir.

Men and officers whispered together wherever they met, taking sides, making wagers. Able Company formed a pool, winner take all, on which man would win this confrontation. There were those who said that a post commander so far outranked a deputy U.S. marshal that the contest was totally unequal. And besides, who in the memory of man had seen Captain Kennecut bested on any issue?

On the other hand, Longarm's supporters called attention to the marshal's toughness. The marshal wasn't the kind of man to back down from any fight. Odds grew that Corporal Vince Thayer would have all charges against him dropped. Even those who bet against Thayer and the marshal did so for practical reasons. They hoped they were wrong; it was just that they were afraid to bet against Captain Felder Kennecut.

Kennecut called his adjutant into his office and told him to secretly put full-time surveillance on their "guest." This secret, too, soon went around the post like a well-used coin.

Kennecut, outside his office, remained correctly polite and militarily cooperative, but wary toward Longarm. He smiled and gave Longarm a guided tour of the fort. He acted as required by regulations, to the letter. There were going to be a hundred witnesses to this if he ever needed them.

Longarm found that the seemingly heat-struck lethargy of Fort Bloody Run was deceptive. The place was anything but languorous and indolent.

The officers set a brisk pace and the men reacted smartly. The workshops, crafts, skills, and labors of the fort were those necessary in any bustling village of two hundred people who were required to be self-reliant. The smithy employed a sergeant and three men, working full time. The mess hall was fevered with activity, with its assigned men and those working out penalties for minor infractions engaged in kitchen details. Dust plumed like smoke from the corrals and stables where the animal detail worked. Sweat, dust, and noise rose everywhere.

Longarm watched the enlisted men caring for their own mounts. They fed them, checked their shoes, and took them out through a small bar-secured gate beside the smithy to run the animals in the Humboldt riverbed. When they returned, men and horses covered with sweat, the men walked the horses, washed them down, brushed and curried them. By four o'clock they were on the "grinder," in uniform, with their horses saddled for Kennecut's inspection.

When Longarm presented his requisition to the captain for animals and supplies, Kennecut smiled graciously, summoned a sergeant, and ordered him to see to the requisition. Then Kennecut nodded in a pleasant manner toward Longarm. "Why don't you let he help you select a good horse, Mr. Long? You may not respect the way I run my command, but I know horses."

Longarm said, "Don't get me wrong, Captain. I've nothing but respect for the way you run Fort Bloody Run. I accept your offer."

With two junior officers in their wake, Kennecut and Longarm presented a small parade of interest to every eye in the compound. They reached the corral, where Kennecut launched into a lengthy dissertation on the history, qualities, and defects of certain horses.

Kennecut liked a horse that was big and handsome, which was obviously the way he saw himself.

"We've got some lighter animals, Indian ponies," Kennecut said. "Some of the enlisted men like them. But an Indian horse is just an Arabian brought over by the Spanish. They have developed with wild blood in them. An Arab-blooded horse cannot run or last against the English-blood breeds. I tell you, the English always prized the pure blood, and there was never more than a drop of Arabian blood in those animals. Old Henry the Eighth, himself, passed a law that pure-bred English stallions couldn't even run where common horses under fifteen hands were pastured. And he even ordered undersized and inferior horses killed and buried. All to protect the bloodline."

Kennecut waved his arm, signaling a handler, who cut a thick-rumped mare from the corral. "She'll make you a fine animal, Marshal. Carry your weight all day in the heat."

"Captain, I hate to disagree with an expert like you, but sometimes horseflesh comes down to a matter of personal taste. I want to move fast. I'd like one of those quarter horses."

Kennecut gestured sharply in disdain. "No stamina."

Longarm stroked the mare's nose. "On the other hand, Captain, a horse overloaded with fat can be trouble. It may look healthy, but it's likely full of water and fat. And you can never tell until it's too late."

They argued—smilingly and politely—over the horse, down to its hindquarters. But Longarm was pleased to see that in this discussion Captain Kennecut almost relaxed to a state of ordinary humanity. The officer loved horses and knew them well. He dismissed the splay-footed, the pigeon-toed or the cow-hocked—

defects found when one carefully inspected the hind-quarters.

"Check your horse from its hindquarters, Marshal. From behind, your horse should show good square quarters, perfectly shaped *gracilis*—those inside muscles of its hind legs. They ought to be almost egg-shaped and decrease in size to the rump bone. And the bone above the knee—that can't be too large. And the hocks' tendons should be strong and standing up so you can see them. You check a horse's hindquarters and watch when he walks away from you. If he's not turning or straddling, you've got a good horse that won't fail you. All qualities you'll find in this mare."

"I hate to go against expert advice, Captain, but I want a small, lean horse out on that basin. I've walked across a good part of it myself, and I know."

Captain Kennecut shrugged and remained smiling. "Only trying to help, Mr. Long. But it looks as though you and I agree on nothing."

Longarm smiled. "What the hell, Captain. We're not so far apart as you think. We're both fighting—with all our guts—for the same thing."

Longarm's horse was cut out of the corral and put in a stable along with gear.

He was told by the hostler to expect a sore butt after a day in a McClellan saddle. "We call it the 'general's revenge,' " the man explained as he spanked the saddle named for the famous Civil War general. "General McClellan copied these things from the Hungarians. Maybe the Hungarians have more tail padding than we do." The wooden foundation, the side bar ironed to pommel and cantle pieces, was covered only with raw-hide sewed on while wet. The leather shrank in drying, making the saddle indestructible—but iron-hard.

Longarm explained to the hostler that he actually preferred a McClellan because, with its wide slot running down the middle, it was more comfortable on a long haul than most others he'd used, for horse and rider alike. He did admit, however, that "riding with your balls swinging in the breeze takes a mite of getting used to, and there's some gents who find the sensation disagreeable."

He was issued a blue wool saddle blanket, precisely Army regulation, 67 by 75 inches. It had an orange border stripe and the orange letters "U.S." in its center. The supply officer showed Longarm the regulation fold: a rectangle of six thicknesses, folding it first the long way and then twice to make the pad. And since Longarm was a civilian with a government rank equal to a junior officer, he was provided with a saddle cloth.

Longarm walked back toward the front of the compound in the late-afternoon sunlight. All labor had ceased, and officers and enlisted men were bathed and taking it easy before supper. Enlisted men sat on their barracks porch, watching the awkward squad drill under the merciless leadership of a tough sergeant. The men laughed because nobody ever kept cadence or correctly obeyed the rapid-fire orders; it was impossible, and it furnished wild comedy, even to men who might be on report and in those ranks this time tomorrow.

Smoke from supper fires rose from the mess halls and the married men's country. Darkness seemed delayed by remote mountain ranges. The air took on the color of the red dirt of the parade grounds. The bugles sounded, the flags were lowered, the fort was secured.

Longarm bathed, shaved, and put on his only clean shirt. The other he washed out and hung to dry near a window in his room. He met two young officers and walked across to the mess hall with them in the twilight glow. He agreed with them that this seemed a good time of the day. He could see they wanted to discuss Vince Thayer with him, but they did not dare. Officially, no one on the post knew of his confrontation with Captain Kennecut. But there was an undercurrent of tension, of waiting for something to break. They could hear the enlisted men singing, telling the same old jokes, or playing cards after their evening meal.

The supper was steak, red beans, and potatoes. Somebody said he had known that steak would be served; one of the captain's fattest parade horses had died.

The officers invited Longarm to a poker game in the officer's club. He agreed, though he felt as if he'd been drugged after the heavy meal of inch-thick steak, beans, and potatoes. He tried to think back to when he had slept last. He had done little sleeping at the Windsor Hotel with Alicia Payson, and even less on the Central Pacific train out here. The threat of attack had kept him alert and awake all last night. He yawned helplessly.

By the end of the third hand, Longarm's head was sagging. Luckily he wasn't winning. This was one of the most honest, if boring, poker games he'd ever gotten into. The stakes were low, and it was so scrupulously aboveboard that almost everybody won with some frequency.

One of the officers prodded him. "You look beat, Longarm. Why don't you sack out?"

Longarm thanked him and cashed in his chips, dropping the best hand he'd held all evening. He walked out of the officers' club and along the rectangular parade toward his apartment. He thought about this place and the hundreds like it, tossed almost casually across the wild and lonely outlands of the country. The men who served had to be dedicated, or hiding from somebody. It was an isolated life, in voluntary estrangement from the world. Days and nights spent in wilderness desolation. But somebody had to do it.

He grinned crookedly. Probably those officers were pitying him for the solitary life he led, always on the prowl, calling no place home. But somebody had to do it.

He was aware that someone was inside his darkened room even before he unlocked the door. Slapping his jacket away from his cross-draw holster, he drew his Colt, eased the door open, and slithered through.

Across the room, a dark shadow flickered against darker shadows.

"Mr. Longarm?" It was a woman's frightened voice.

"Yes. What are you doing here?"

97

"You can put away your gun, Mr. Longarm. I am not armed. I am not going to harm you."

He exhaled. "You've already scared hell out of me."

Doubting this, the girl laughed softly in the darkness. "A great giant of a man like you? Scared?"

"Anybody who tells you he's never scared is a liar."

"*I* am scared, Mr. Longarm."

"Wait until I light a lamp, and we can discuss it better." As he moved to remove the glass and turn up the wick on the government-issue lamp, the girl drew the shade at the window down to the sill.

The wick flickered and then the fire fluttered into light, cerise and orange. He replaced the glass lampshade and turned. The girl remained at the window, her back turned.

She wore some kind of kimono, brightly woven in Indian reds and browns. It was a lightweight coverlet, and her straight black hair flooded down over it almost to her waist.

"May Cloud," he said, shocked.

"Yes." The Indian girl remained with her back to him.

"You said you were scared, May Cloud." He spoke in a soft tone that he hoped might reassure her. In the middle of speaking, he yawned helplessly.

"I am not afraid for myself, Mr. Longarm. I am brave enough to do what I must do, to face what I must face. But I am deathly frightened for my husband. It will kill him—twenty years in prison. He is a wanderer, Mr. Longarm. He has wandered all his life until he met me, until he joined this damned army."

She continued to talk to the drawn window shade.

He said, "Turn around, May Cloud. I can talk better, or even listen better, looking at you."

"All right."

She turned slowly and leaned against the window seat.

Longarm gasped.

Except for the Indian-bright kimono, a seamless shift that hung shapeless and unpinned, she was naked.

Longarm winced. The drugged sense of apathy spun

98

out of his mind. He wanted to look away from the girl's incredibly lovely body, but he could not. He felt a forbidden arousal deep in his loins.

He shook his head.

May Cloud looked as if she might cry. "You don't like me? I am not pretty? Beside the women you know —I am ugly?"

"My God, May Cloud."

"You do not want to see me."

"I . . . love looking at you . . . Mrs. Thayer."

The Indian girl remained poised there. She was not merely beautiful; she was enchanting. She was the color of tea roses, and her nakedness gleamed heatedly in the warm lamplight. Even her black eyes seemed hot and liquid. Her lips, full and budlike, glistened with reflected fire. Her features had a chiseled perfection unlikely and unusual in Indians of this region. Her throat was a slender column along which his gaze slid to a body that was elegantly structured, as if created with loving care. His aching eyes rested on high, cuplike breasts, topped with small, light brown nipples. Her stomach was flat, her waist narrow, with sculpted muscles seeming to flow into the dark triangle of femininity between her supple thighs. Her long-stemmed legs were perfectly formed with well-turned calves, slim ankles, and high, slender arches. She looked as if she were an aristocrat among her people, a princess born of princesses. He retracted his route, meeting her eyes again.

"If you love looking at me, then what is wrong?"

Longarm tried to smile. "I love looking at you, May Cloud, but I guess the wrong has to do with army regulations, women not allowed in bachelor officers' quarters, and the fact that you are married to a poor jasper who's got enough on his plate as it is, without this."

"There is nothing I wouldn't do for Vince."

"Oh? You're doing this for Vince?"

"Of course. I thought you knew."

"No. I reckon I'm tired. I couldn't figure what in hell you were doing here—dressed so comfortably."

Though she smiled faintly through the sadness shadowing her dark eyes, she did not close the shift. "We need help so bad, Mr. Longarm—Vince and I." She hesitated. "I have heard how you shouted at that evil Captain Kennecut . . ."

"Not evil, just strait-laced. Which makes it worse. He's also puritannical as hell. That'll make it tougher than ever on Vince."

"What could be harder than serving twenty years when you have committed no crime?" She straightened and her eyes flashed. Her taut breasts shivered like gelatin.

"I'm on your side." Longarm shook his head. A poor choice of words at this time. "I agree with you. It is all wrong. But the captain is only accusing your husband. He will be tried before a military tribunal. All the officers won't be like Captain Kennecut. Your husband ain't in prison yet."

"Would you care to have his chances, in a court-martial run by Captain Kennecut?"

"You've got a point there—along with several other assets—but I should warn you, Mrs. Thayer. I am only human. You're a very exciting and desirable-looking young woman. Doesn't that robe have a button?"

She laughed through the sadness eating away like acid at her insides. "You are a good man, Mr. Longarm. I knew that when I first saw you."

"Help me be good, May Cloud. Lock that barn door."

She shook her head. "Look at me, Mr. Longarm. I *want* you to look at me. I want you to want me."

"You got it. Good night. If you'll just lock the door on your way out."

"If you will help us—if you will help poor Vince and me—I will let you . . . do what you wish to me."

"What I wish?"

"*Anything* you wish. You know what I mean, Mr. Longarm. I can look at you and see that you do. You don't need to make me say the words. I would let you . . . go to your bed with me. Wouldn't you like that?"

He exhaled heavily, but did not answer.

100

"The word is about the post, Mr. Longarm. There are those who say you can get Vince free. Others say that the job is too big for you. But one thing all of them say—you are the *only* man who can conquer Captain Kennecut . . . if any man can."

"They are very flattering."

"No, Mr. Longarm. You are much a man. That is clear. One does not meet a man like you every day."

"I don't know what I could do for Vince."

"Get him free, Mr. Longarm. Please, in God's name, I beg you. Don't let them cage him in a prison for twenty years of his life. He is a boy. He will be a broken old man when they are through with him. Is that right? Is that your idea of justice? Do you believe he has committed a crime in marrying me?"

"You've just had bad luck, May Cloud."

"No. I have had good luck. My gods have been kind to me. They have sent me you. You have come, strong and good and kind, to save Vince from hell. For that, it is a small price that I offer my body to you —to use as you wish."

"Why do you think I would help Vince after bedding you down, any more than I would help him just to get my job done among the Paiutes?"

"I believe you might. Sometimes a man who will not do a thing for one reason, will do it . . . when he has a reason like this." She slid her hand slowly down her body, across her breasts, the flat plane of her stomach, to the dark triangle at her thighs.

He winced, feeling the terrible charge of delicious agony surge through him. He kept his voice low, but tense. "Listen, May Cloud. Go on home. Now. I admit you can look at me and see I'd like you. I'd love it. I admit that too. And I admit I've been an ornery varmint in my time, taking what I wanted when and where I could get it—"

"I am here now, you can have me—"

"But I never pulled a trick that low. I never took a young girl because she loved another man enough to sacrifice herself for him."

"Please! Help us! We do need you. Please, take me, do it. I am very good . . . I know many things."

"I'm sure you do. But you get out of here. I don't know many things. Right now, I know only one thing. Looks like it's going to be another long night without sleep."

When May Cloud was gone, Longarm fell across the three-quarter bed and lay sleepless. His eyes burned with weariness, but his belly churned, nerves taut, and his mind wheeled like frightened birds. He wasn't going to be able to sleep, so he gave that idea up.

He listened to the camp sounds falter and sink into deep stillness. The bed smelled good and clean, the mattress was firm, the sheets fresh-smelling from lye soap and drying on lines in the fresh air. Everything was restful. But sleep was out of the question, beyond his reach.

He went on lying there until he heard the midnight duty officer makes his rounds. Silence settled in again.

At last, when he could lie there no longer, he got up and let himself out of the door. The silence was almost deceptive; it was as if unseen eyes watched every move he made; as if he and everybody else on this post were holding their breaths.

He moved softly and silently through the deep darkness. A chilly night wind drove dead leaves across the grinder. A night bird screamed, and a wolf howled at the desolation. A mosquito chewed on him, but he dared not slap it. The sound of a slap would carry in this stillness like a gunshot.

Once past the officers' quarters, he faced the isolated area lighted by the hospital. Even here, action had ground to a standstill; lamps were low, wicks down, and patients bedded. He circled wide around the long sprays of saffron light spilling from the hospital windows. On his right were the married men's shacks and tents, and before him the corral, stables, small storage sheds, livery barns, and the smithy. Everything was silent and dark, deserted in darkness.

He saw a faint lamplight glowing in the foyer of the guardhouse. He knew the layout of the compact building: a foyer, a barred doorway, an aisle with cells on both sides, the cells also barred. In the foyer there were only the essentials required by a duty officer: gun rack, metal desk, sentry's chair—and the soldier on guard.

Longarm ducked into the deep shadows and approached the guardhouse from the rear. He sidled along its shadowed adobe walls, feeling the abrasive material rough against his flesh.

At the corner of the square house, he paused. The door was closed. He didn't believe it would be locked. The duty officer passed every few hours to be sure the sentry didn't lock that door and grab a quick nap. On this post, the guardhouse sentry would be awake—and alert—or he would face the maximum punishment allowable by army regulations for dereliction of duty.

He paused just outside the guardhouse door. He couldn't go on standing there until he was spotted and reported by unseen witnesses. He drew his gun and stealthily opened the door.

The sentry swung around and looked at the Colt .44-40 in Longarm's fist. The youth shook his head and carefully laid his carbine down on the desktop. "You don't have to shoot me."

"All right, son. But I do have to tie you up and gag you."

"I'll go to prison for this."

"At least you won't get twenty years."

"Hell, mister, I don't want thirty *days*."

Longarm jerked his head and the youngster turned his back. Longarm handcuffed him to the bars. Then he stuffed a bandanna into the soldier's mouth and secured it with string.

"You'll be glad you did this," Longarm said.

The young soldier just stared at him, eyes frantic.

Longarm stepped into the cell block. Vince Thayer stood pressed against the bars. He laughed and sobbed in the same breath, "May Cloud said you'd get me out. I didn't believe her."

"Maybe she knows us better than we know ourselves." Longarm unlocked the cell, leaving the big iron key in the lock. "Let's go."

"I'm ahead of you," Vince said. "Which way?"

"Horse and mule back at the stables. Is there a guard down there?"

Thayer shook his head. He went out the front door and ran swiftly across the lighted space toward the stables. Longarm carefully closed the guardhouse front door and then followed.

Thayer was already saddling the horse by the time Longarm reached the stables. "You'll have to ride the mule," Longarm said.

"Mules don't worry me. That mule's sawtooth backbone feels better than that cell cot."

Leading the animals, they walked out to the small, barred gate. Longarm thought how strange it was, and yet totally typical of every army compound he'd ever visited. There was the big front entrance with 'round-the-clock guards in dress uniform, where entrances and exits were accomplished with saluting, official passes, and ceremony. And always, somewhere in the rear, was a gate nobody ever watched, that a night sentry might check casually on his rounds.

Outside the gate, they led the animals into the bed of the Humboldt, then mounted and rode swiftly, following the course of the dry river bed.

Vince kept looking back.

Longarm laughed. "Don't worry, Thayer. Kennecut isn't going to follow us. When he hears about your break, he's going to hate my guts. Maybe he already hates my guts. But in his heart, he knows I'm right."

Chapter 9

Longarm and young Vince Thayer rode, following the torturous course of the dry Humboldt. The arid bed swept in curves and bends, winding through the broken ridges of fault blocks, or writhing like a sidewinder in sage-covered flats. The gray sagebrush, tipped here and there with tiny, yellow, daisylike flowers, smelled spicy—a pungent, green-hued rug thrown across the stark-naked wilderness.

Longarm felt fatigue overwhelming him like some potent drug. His eyes burned and his head swam; he had been too long without sleep. And the fiery blaze of the sun and the intense heat seething in waves from the red, cracked earth, threatened to prostrate him.

He glanced back over his shoulder. There was no sign of pursuit, not even a cloud of dust against the bleached sky. The world lay dead and gray and empty as far as he could see. Thank God. He was too exhausted to run. He had to fight to keep from falling from the saddle.

"How's the mule ride?" he called to Vince.

The youth shrugged. "Don't bother me. I'm out of that cell. I'm shed of that Kennecut. I'm breathing free."

Longarm yawned helplessly. "Have you stopped to think—you'll live AWOL for the rest of your life. What will that do to you?"

"Make me laugh, every time I think of that Kennecut stewing in his own juices."

"You can't ever go back."

"Hell. I don't want to."

"What about a home? Will you be able to settle in one place?"

"I never have lived in one place. Maybe I'll just drift. I'll go where the winds go in the mountains, or the shadows go on the plains."

"But what about May Cloud?"

Vince Thayer's voice took on a savage edge. "What about her? She threw in with me when she married me. She'll take me as I am."

Longarm yawned and stared at the boy, seeing the cold and selfish streak that ruled him. "Sounds like a great life. You running—and her following you."

"We didn't have too much with me facing twenty years at hard labor."

"From the frying pan to the fire."

"What?"

"We ought to stop pretty soon. I'm just about asleep in the saddle."

Vince shrugged, but did not answer.

Sagging in his saddle, Longarm gave the horse its head, letting it plod at its own pace in the river bed. Strange to call a dry gash across a desolate desert a river. And to give it a formal-sounding name like the Humboldt. There remained signs of its violence and its mindless passion, when its tributaries brought flash floods down from remote mountain ranges lost inside ranges in the milk-blue distance. The Humboldt overflowed its banks then, chafing and clawing at the flats, swirling and ripping along in full flood, taking everything in its path. But now the very life was gone from it. Fed by distant rains and unseen snow plains, by uncounted creeks and mesa ponds, it had no life of its own; even its fury belonged to its outreaching tributaries. It lay spent and empty, waiting.

Shaking his head, trying to clear it, Longarm gazed across the eternal vista of this barren basin torn out of far ranges.

"Makes you wonder," Longarm said, hoping the sound of his own voice would keep him awake. "Was this Great Basin once an ocean bed?"

Vince shrugged. "Not me."

106

"Not you what?"

"Don't make me wonder. I don't care. It's just a wide, lonesome gouge in the earth to me, no good for anything but lizards and diggers." When Longarm didn't reply, Vince called out, "You awake?"

"Just about."

Vince surprised him by speaking without even checking their backtrail. "We better stop before you fall. Old man like you. Might hurt yourself."

Longarm yawned with relief, reined in, and swung down from the saddle.

He stretched tall, then ground-tied his mount, wrapping the lines loosely about a clump of cheat grass. "If you're as tired as I am, or as dumb as I hope you are, horse, you'll stay there."

Vince drove a stick into the ground, tied a manila rope around the mule's neck, and let the animal forage in the sparse grass. "One thing, he won't overeat," Vince said.

Vince took gear from the bags on the packmule. Longarm went into the dead center of the river bed and began to dig with a dry piece of driftwood. Soon, water seeped into the hole; he kept scooping it out. When it was about a foot deep, it filled with clear, alkali-tinged water. He tasted it, grimaced, and spoke over his shoulder. "Not bad."

He stared, shocked to see that young Thayer had piled up some prickly greasewood sticks and had a small fire burning.

Longarm stood up. "What the hell are you doing?"

Thayer grinned at him, cool as a gila monster. "Going to make us some coffee." He threw an army-issue coffee pot to Longarm, who caught it. "Fill it up with water. By that time the fire ought to be going good."

Longarm knelt, filled the pot and walked to where Vince was feeding sticks and sage to the fire. "Isn't there an old saying about hiding true love and smoke on a plain?"

Vince shrugged. "You worry too much, old partner.

107

If the army wants us bad enough, they'll find us without reading any smoke signals. And we both need coffee."

Longarm found flour, salt, and a piece of smoked ham. He cut off a few slices, and mixed dough for biscuits. Grinning, Vince took the two flat pans from Longarm and held them over the fire. The coffee smelled good.

Longarm couldn't resist standing up and staring out over their backtrail.

"Relax, old man," Vince said. "You'll feel better with a full belly."

When Longarm didn't answer, Vince glanced up from his cooking. Longarm was gazing at him in such a way that Vince flushed red to the roots of his dark hair. "What's eating at you?"

"You are," Longarm said. "I thought last night I was helping an ordinary young fellow escape a bad deal, doing him and his pretty little wife a favor. You get more complicated by the minute."

"What does that mean?"

"You're a mite more than you let people think you are. You're a wild man, ain't you?"

Vince shrugged. "There have been them that said so. It was the way I was raised, Longarm. My mother sang in the choir of the Baptist church, and my old man came home maybe once or twice a year. When my mother died, I never saw my old man again. Or wanted to. I drifted. Only thing ever stopped me from drifting was May Cloud."

"And now you're going to drag her after you, on the run, all the rest of your life?"

"That's between her and me, mister."

"Thank God. I'll be glad when I'm not responsible for you anymore. You help me talk to the digger Indians, and we're quits. I think I'll be glad to be shed of you."

"Have some coffee, you're just tired."

Longarm hunkered down and drank. "You make good coffee."

"You learn when you're by yourself long enough."

"How'd you learn Uto-Aztec?"

Vince shrugged. "Had to. Like learning to make coffee. Sometimes keeping my scalp on straight depended on what I could say to Indians, or what I knew they were saying. I can talk to any Indians from Socorro north."

"You got a good mind."

"Hell, yes, I'm smart. That's how I've stayed alive. Don't worry about me, Longarm. I'll stay alive."

"You weren't doing so good when I came along."

"What's eating you? You want me to promise you that I'll buy a little cottage somewhere with rosebushes and honeysuckle vines and settle down with May Cloud?"

"No. I don't want you to promise me anything."

"Good."

"What's eating me is that I got you out of that guardhouse. I should have left you there. You could have taken your chances with a court-martial. May Cloud would have been better off. Now I've helped you foul that up. I don't like that on my conscience."

"Just don't try to take me back."

Longarm shook his head. "That's what chafes on me. You haven't learned anything—not by being arrested and threatened with twenty years in prison, not even from being loved by a girl who's willing to do anything for you. You got a good mind; you're almost as smart as you think you are. But you don't learn anything. You'll go on making the same damn fool mistakes until somebody kills you."

"Don't you get any ideas, old partner."

"No. Killing you wouldn't teach you a damn thing."

"Don't get any ideas about taking me back—after you talk to the diggers. We're doing great right now. I owe you. Let's keep it that way."

Longarm held out his cup for a refill of coffee. He shrugged. After a moment, he said, "Did you ever live among the digger Indians?"

"Are you loco? No human beings could live with those vermin. They live like prairie dogs. They don't have guns. They don't ride horses. They eat lizards and rabbits and roots and pine nuts. They are the scum of

109

the Basin. They're like something that lived a thousand years ago. They ain't quite human. And they ain't quite animals."

"Could they cut Western Union telegraph lines?"

Vince shrugged. "You mean are they ornery enough? By a hundred times. Sneaky. Cunning. Treacherous. But why would they want to?"

"They like to wander. The cavalry likes to keep them under surveillance. Cutting telegraph wires is one way they could trick the cavalry."

"That makes them sound one hell of a lot smarter than they were the last time I talked with them. They eat lizards and they're as weak as lizards. They eat rattlesnake, and they're as sneaky as sidewinders. But they also eat rabbit. And they're stupider than any rabbit you ever met."

"You don't sound very impressed with the Paiutes."

Vince grinned coldly. "That's where you're wrong about me again, old partner. I really admire them. I admire them because they can survive under the most hellish conditions on earth. I admire 'em. I just can't stand to smell 'em."

"Eat a lot of stinkweed, do they?"

"And smoke a lot of locoweed. A lot of it."

Longarm ate three biscuits with sliced ham between them and drank another cup of coffee. He stood up, stretching and feeling a lot better.

He saw a faint puff of dust in the distance behind them. Vince was washing up the cups and utensils in the pool of water. He seemed unaware of the dust.

Longarm exhaled and decided not to mention it.

The next time he looked at Vince, the young soldier had spread out a small blanket from the pack and lain down on it, a towel over his face.

Longarm remained unmoving, watching the dust drift closer. He saw the figure emerge in the bed of the river. He was not even very astonished when he recognized May Cloud.

Vince's Indian wife wore a shapeless shift, belted at

110

the waist. Her hair was loose about her face and she wore sandals. She was running at the steady, loping pace he'd seen a wolf employ for hours, relentlessly.

She ran faster when she saw him watching her. Her eyes were sick with fatigue. He knew she had run all the way from Fort Bloody Run without stopping to rest.

He felt slightly better about springing Vince from the guardhouse. Whatever he was, whatever life he offered her, Vince was what May Cloud wanted. That could make up for a lot of hardship, a lot of heartache. They were together, for as long as they could make it, and that seemed to be all that mattered.

She tossed Longarm a tired and grateful smile. Then she cried out, "Vince!"

"I'm over here," he said. He didn't bother to get up. He seemed even less surprised than Longarm had been to see his wife.

She ran to where Vince lay and threw herself upon him, nuzzling his neck, pressing herself upon him. "Hey, take it easy," he said. "You'll wrinkle the shirt."

"Oh, Vince. I'm so glad I found you." She couldn't stop pressing herself close to him, kissing his throat and chest and cheeks.

He shrugged. "What the hell? I knew you would."

Enraged, Longarm wanted to beat the kid's head in. But he didn't move. It was none of his business. Vince was what May Cloud wanted. He had faced twenty years in prison for her. She had run all night and half the day to find him, and he accepted it as casually as he might accept a cigar. There was just no accounting for taste. Women were strange, sort of like butterflies. If a butterfly landed on a rose, it stayed there. If it landed on a horse turd, it stayed there too. . . .

Vince stood up and shook out the blanket. "We better go."

He vaulted up on the mule and let May Cloud walk beside it.

Longarm stared at Vince, sitting on the mule. He

shook his head incredulously, then strode across the sand. He swung May Cloud up in his arms.

"What the hell you think you're doing?" Vince said.

"Try and stop me," Longarm said, gritting his teeth, a muscle clenching in his jaw. "All I want is an excuse to beat your head in." He carried May Cloud and set her in the saddle of his horse. Then he caught the animal by the bridle and started forward.

Vince prodded the mule with his heels and rode alongside of them. He stared at Longarm, eyes wide. "What the hell is the idea of doing that?"

"This girl ran all night and most of today just to be with you. As stupid as you are, you've got to know she's exhausted."

"Hell. We all are. You can't spoil women like her. She knows what to expect from me. It's what she wants."

"Well, the hell with it," Longarm said. "I feel like walking for a while."

Vince shrugged. "All right. But you're just being a damn fool."

May Cloud sagged in the saddle. She waited until Vince fell slightly behind them on the mule before she gave Longarm a shy, frightened little smile of gratitude.

Longarm winked at her. "How'd you know where to find us?"

Her voice sounded sick with fatigue. "I knew you wanted Vince as translator. You mentioned the Paiutes when you were . . . talking to me."

Longarm shook his head. He glanced again along the backtrail. Vince laughed at him. "What's eating you now, old fellow? I swear you're getting to be a real old maid."

"If May Cloud knew where to find us, it's a lead-pipe cinch that Captain Kennecut knows."

May Cloud nodded. "Oh, he knows. He was like a wild man last night. That's how I got away. They arrested me."

"Why?"

"They thought Vince might come back—if I was in jail."

Longarm grimaced. "They don't know good ol' Vince as well as we do, do they?"

She gave him a faint smile. "Vince is good. He is what his life has made him, Mr. Longarm."

"How was Kennecut taking the jailbreak when you left Fort Bloody Run?"

"He was—" May Cloud almost smiled— "he was frothing at the mouth. He was sending messages on the Singing Wire, east and west."

"Messages?"

"Demanding that you be arrested, held, and returned to Fort Bloody Run."

"Me? Not Vince?"

The girl exhaled heavily. "It's you he hates, Longarm."

"And in the excitement, you got away?"

"They forgot me. While they were busy running around, I slipped away."

"Or maybe they let you go. Maybe they figured they can recapture Vince, as long as he has you with him."

She shook her head, deadly serious. "I won't slow Vince down, Mr. Longarm. Before I would do that, I would kill myself."

In the desert heat, Longarm shivered.

When they had gone less than five miles, May Cloud whispered to Longarm, "I better walk now. Vince will be angry."

Longarm started to tell her what she could do to Vince, but figured she would anyway. He swung her down from the saddle. She walked slowly between the mule and the horse, her shoulders back, that slender spine arched, like a ballet dancer barely touching the ground. A butterfly, Longarm thought sardonically. A real butterfly.

The horses plodded slowly in the dry river bed. The hot hours of the afternoon waned. The sun sank and seemed to explode beyond ragged hills so distant that they seemed no more than raw gray shale against the blazing sky. A desert buzzard sailed in long, silent updrafts. Before darkness settled, they climbed out of the deepening river bed. Ahead of them, a clump of stunted cottonwoods promised water. They moved faster; even the animals sensed the cool moisture. They reached a place where a tributary, spilling down from pinyon-dotted ridges, formed a shallow pool in the deep-gouged sump of the Humboldt.

May Cloud cried out in delight. She ran to the edge of the pool, kicking off her sandals. She jerked the leather belt free and pulled the shift over her head. She was as naked and unselfconscious about it as a doe. She ran into the water, falling in it and throwing it up so it fell like raindrops about her. She cried, "Vince. Come on in, Vince. It's cool. Really it is."

Vince was staking out the mule. He stared down at her in the water and shook his head. "Don't need a bath. Had one a couple weeks ago."

She splashed water on her high-standing breasts and laved her hands along the slender lines of her body. "Oh, it feels so good," she called. "If only you knew how good it feels. You, Mr. Longarm. Come on in with me."

Longarm grinned. "My old grandmother had a saying she made me swear to live by. Never take a bath with another man's wife if he's watching. I live by that."

Vince taunted him. "You're a cautious man, Longarm."

Longarm heeled around. "And you're a lucky one, you young fool. You better realize how lucky, before it's too late."

After a supper of ham and biscuits, they clambered up the cool stream onto a rocky ridge. Longarm chose a promontory that looked out across the purpling plain, the soft darkness making the sage look purple. He spread out his blanket and laid down on it.

Vince took May Cloud's hand and led her higher in the rocks. Longarm grinned tautly. He didn't blame Vince. He had been a long time in that guardhouse. May Cloud had been an enchanting picture, splashing in that pool, drying her hair by swinging it madly in a dance that should have brought rain.

He lay in the darkness, listening to their whispering voices. He couldn't hear their words; he didn't want to. It gave him a sense of the rightness of the world that two people could be in love, and making love, even in a wild and desolate desert.

The stars appeared all at once, it seemed, almost as if bursting into the firmament, huge and bright, blazing in the darkness. The wind whispered and frolicked in the rocks and caressed his sun-seared face.

Exhaustion struck him like a club. One moment he was hearing whispers in the wind and voices in the rocks, the baying of a wolf, and suddenly he tumbled toward the stars, flung out into oblivion. All the nights and days and hours without sleep, the tension, everything ganged up on him and battered him senseless.

But even in his sleep he could not escape. In his dreams he fought desperately, unarmed, against an armed man who laughed and waited for him to grow tired before blowing his brains out. A dance-hall girl in a bright yellow dress stood guard over him with a cocked carbine, ordering him to prove he was better loaded than the rifle. He finally got into some blonde's bed five minutes before her husband returned home unexpectedly. Somewhere in the darkness, Alicia was running. She could see in the darkness, and the men pursuing her could not. She called his name, her voice frantic with fear, but when he pleaded with her to tell him where she was, she went into hysterical laughter and the laughter cascaded over him, writhing like sidewinders, cold and slimy to the touch. He was running naked in the snow, and Logan Blackwelder was chasing him with a gun in each hand and a dance-hall girl on each arm. He cried out, shouting, cold, and then May Cloud's gentle hands touched him and soothed him and her lips, light as a butterfly, pressed cool and sweet and good-tasting against his mouth. But when he gave in to his desires and reached out to clutch her to him and to hell with Vince Thayer, she blew away like the dust on a moth's wing. But her kiss had soothed him, and he

115

was no longer cold, and the snow cleared away, and he slept deeply.

The sun, as if intensified through a magnifying glass, burned him and he sweated, aware of the hum of flies, feeling hot and uncomfortable under his hat, which covered his eyes. He didn't remember putting the hat over his face, but he might have, unconsciously, around dawn. He did not know when he had slept better. The sleep of the happy dead. Funny, it had been the brief fragment of the dream of May Cloud's soft mouth, sweet-tasting and cool upon his, that had driven out the tensions and let him sleep. He grinned. Imagine being drugged to sleep like that every night!

He opened his eyes slowly, thirsty and troubled without knowing why. The sun, bright orange- and crimson-splashed, hung well above the eastern horizon.

He sat up, taut. The morning was half gone. He yelled, "Vince! You up?"

There was no answer from the rocks. His voice clattered and reverberated and died on the wind.

He levered himself to his feet, automatically checking for his derringer and his Colt. Both guns were in place. He stared down at the campsite where they'd cooked supper last night, and the pool where May Cloud had cavorted naked.

There was a dark, burned sore in the red earth where last night's fire had grown cold. There was no sign of fire this morning. And something else was wrong. He stood, legs braced apart, and stared down at where his horse was hobbled.

The mule was gone. Sweat broke out on his face and chest. The terrible thought of Vince's betraying him flashed through him, flaring in his mind as if his brain were some hot material that refused to absorb anything.

He felt wild rage, he felt unnerved. The ungrateful young bastard! He had risked his life and his job getting that treacherous renegade out of jail. At least Thayer could have waited until after they'd parleyed with the Paiutes before betraying him. Was that too much to ask of the selfish, no-good young tramp?

116

Obviously it was. Longarm shaded his eyes and searched the open prairie. There was no sign of movement in any direction. They'd been gone since sometime last night. About the time he had dreamed of May Cloud's cool lips on his, she had kissed him softly, and gently placed his hat over his face. Her last kindness, her only way to say thanks, and then she was gone. He shivered. Gone! Where the mountain winds go, where the shadows on the plains go.

He felt overwhelmed with a terrible sense of sadness. He could hate Vince, but he could never hate May Cloud. That would be like hating flowers for growing, breezes for caressing you, water for tasting sweet and cool.

Why hadn't they trusted him? But that was the answer. They hadn't trusted him. They could never trust anyone anymore; they could only run.

The hell of it was, he could even understand why they mistrusted him. He reckoned that when a man like Captain Felder Kennecot represented authority in your life, you would find it hard to have much faith in anybody.

Chapter 10

Longarm plodded through waist-high gray sage. The distant hills receded in heat waves as he stalked them. He was hungry. Vince and May Cloud hadn't bothered to leave him even a can of coffee. He understood Vince's reasoning. Vince's need was greater. In Vince's mind, Vince's needs always rated top priority. The bastard. Longarm reckoned he was lucky they'd left him the horse. He supposed if Vince hadn't believed a blanket wife's place was running behind her husband's horse, he'd have been left afoot. He swore silently, counting his blessings. Maybe, if he ever came upon an Indian settlement, he could make them understand his hunger. He wished he knew the Uto-Aztec word for coffee.

Ahead loomed a buttress of tan fault rock, a wild and jagged upheaval of boulders and shale running north and south across the basin. The promontory topping it promised him a wide-ranging look at the country around him, maybe to help him locate the Paiute camp. He ground-tied his horse and started upslope at a run. But the climb was rougher than he'd anticipated. The rise seemed easy, but was abruptly broken and steep. He paused, common sense telling him to turn back before he fell and broke a leg and died out here among the ants, snakes, and horned lizards. Shadows turned into crevices, and rents in the rocks yawned like bottomless abysses. Sweat poured from him, gluing his shirt to his skin, stinging his eyes. He clambered up, pulling himself over ragged ledges until he sprawled out atop the flat outcropping.

At last, gasping for breath, he stood up. Shading his

eyes with his arm, he turned slowly, like a tired weather-vane in a dead calm. He breathed through his parted lips. He found nothing out there except the same sand and sage and alkali that he'd been tramping across all morning. A far bird, perhaps a heron, fled from its shadow across the bleached sky.

He sagged to a flat rock and rested until the intensity of the sun drove him off the exposed rock. He let himself down the fault rock slowly, but by the time he reached the ground he was panting, exhausted.

Staggering, he turned toward his ground-tied horse—and then stopped as if he were about to step on a coiled and rattling snake.

At first he thought he was in a waking nightmare, overcome by the sun. The basin did waver strangely in the heat waves. He shook his head, recoiling in shock at the two creatures who squatted near his horse among the clumps of sage.

He could not believe human beings could be so filthy, so dehydrated, and so nearly starved. These men wore filth-matted hair, shaggy about their necks, under primitive conical sun hats woven of grasses and haphazardly secured in front with a hooklike bone.

Their wrinkled faces were withered and shriveled by sun and deprivation. There was no way to judge their ages. They may have been young, but there was about them a look of Biblical antiquity. Their necks were like turkey necks, with Adam's apples and tendons outthrust against loose skin. Their shoulder bones were knotted prominently, as if about to burst through sun-dried papyrus flesh. Their chests showed each rib, and their bellies sagged, ballooned from malnutrition. They wore only breechcloths, sodden and grimy and fetid. Their thin, sticklike legs were caked with muck. Their feet were wrapped from ankles down in strips of hide or dry-rotted canvas; there was no way to tell anymore what that fabric once may have been.

They were as astonished to see Longarm as he was stunned at the sight of them. They stared up at him, unmoving. Each of them carried a hardwood digging stick called a wand. The ends of the shafts were sharp-

119

ened and fire-hardened. With these implements they killed rabbits, birds, and rats, dug lizards and ground squirrels from the ground, and, in extreme moments of rage, slew each other. They carried no other weapons or personal gear. One of them wore a five-strand necklace of colored stones.

They shook their heads, speechless. They looked as if they would scream, but they were afraid to scream. They looked as if they might cry, but they had no tears. They felt helpless terror as they looked at the tall giant throwing his shadow across them, but they were too sickly and debilitated to fight or run.

Making weird and meaningless grimaces, they stood up slowly, watching him as they might a hawk or a lizard. They were barely five feet tall, wretched little creatures. They said something. It sounded like "Ho."

He supposed they were explaining themselves, their presence, their ascendency in this land. They were Ho —the People, the Real People.

He said, "Saltu." This seemed to please them. They nodded, retreating in the patches of grama grass and sage. Suddenly they turned and ran.

Longarm yelled at them. The sound of his voice speeded them up. They ran, low to the ground, loping like terrified animals. He could see how they could lose themselves in the growths of plains sage.

He ran to his horse and leaped into the saddle. He didn't want to lose them. Plodding, checking, asking questions, going where the trouble was: that was his lonely job. Right now he was belly-sick of it, but he had no intention of letting those little subhuman creatures escape him.

He raced after them, letting them stay far enough ahead that they did not panic. He was sending them the signal that he was not an enemy. Though he was not one of the Real People, as they were, he wanted to be friendly.

They ran longer than he believed they could endure. And then, suddenly, before his eyes, they disappeared. Maybe he'd blinked against the burn of sweat, maybe

120

they'd lost themselves in a thick heat wave, but they were abruptly gone.

He pulled up on the reins and sat staring at the empty ground ahead of him. His eyes widened. At first it seemed a trick of the sun. There seemed to be ten or fifteen strange mounds in an irregular circle of a scabrous area where no grass or weeds could grow anymore.

They were not mounds, but flimsy brush wickiups in a rancid and random grouping. The offensive fetor of decay rose on the heat waves.

He prodded his horse slowly forward. The wretched huts were built by driving a forked limb into the ground, lacing cleared limbs to it, and then covering this shell with anything they could find to form a roofing: matted grass, sticks, pieces of old blankets, canvas, boards. It was almost as if the diggers, like birds, formed their structure from any available waste they could tote home. The huts were open across the front; the ground inside was covered with mats woven of grass or made of stolen blankets. They appeared to have no worldly goods of any kind, no food stored anywhere. He saw the two diggers peering at him from one of the wickiups, and he could see other terrified faces framed in other darkened holes.

He turned and rode away. Less than a mile from the Indian settlement he found an outcropping of rocks. He staked out his horse, removed its saddle, and let it graze. He found a shallow run of water in the bed of the Humboldt. Across it he saw the poles and wires of the Western Union telegraph.

As he stood there, a stunted pronghorn crept down to the river to drink. Pulling his rifle slowly from its saddle scabbard, Longarm steadied himself on one knee and shot the animal behind its front leg.

At the sound of the gun, the diggers came running. They lined up along the ridge in the stunted sage and scabrous buffalo grass, staring at Longarm and the slain deer.

Longarm ignored them. He found limbs long enough to form a tripod, then hung the animal on it, head

121

down, and skinned it. He placed the skin on the ground and began to carve open the belly and remove the viscera. The diggers inched closer.

Longarm continued to work without glancing toward them. He piled rocks, making a hearth. Inside it he built a fire. Soon the Indians were gathering greasewood sticks and running close enough to toss them near the fire. He still did not acknowledge them.

He thrust the longest limb through the decapitated animal and placed it across the rocks as a spit. Blood and fat dripped into the fire, making it flare up. The smell of cooking meat rose. The Indians crept closer, squatting and staring at Longarm and the cooking deer.

It took a long time to cook the animal, as undersized as it was. The Indians remained squatting, unmoving, watching. Some of them salivated, wiping their palms across their mouths. Others continued stoically to balance themselves on their wands, which they had driven into the ground between their knees.

None of them spoke, not even to each other.

At last Longarm was able to tear the meat from the animal. He turned then, and motioned with his arm for the Paiutes to join him.

No one moved for a moment, and then a thin and wizened man got up and came downslope from the group. He wore a breechcloth made of a San Francisco hotel towel, and a bright necklace.

His prune-wrinkled mouth watered, but he remained proud and straight, if not very tall.

"Novoko," he said. *"Ho. Novoko. Ho."*

To Longarm, "Novoko" sounded as much like a name as it did like "howdy," or "how much is that?" or "we're going to kill your grandmother." Pointing to his chest, he said, "Longarm."

"Longarm," Novoko said. *"Saltu Longarm. Novoko. Ho."*

"Sounds good to me," Longarm said. "Why don't you have something to eat?"

He nodded his head toward the cooking meat. Novoko nodded back, turned, and ripped off a hunk of meat. Grinning wildly, he backed away, eating it although it burned his mouth so badly that his sunken eyes watered.

The other Paiutes ran down the slope and surrounded the fire. When they had finished stripping the meat away, only the bones remained.

When they had eaten, Novoko bowed toward Longarm again. He pointed to three of the men. Again, Longarm had no inkling of their ages.

The men got up and began to dance. Each did his own interpretation. Longarm sat on a rock and watched politely. When Novoko saw that his guest was less than impressed, he called Longarm's attention to himself and, by pretending to sleep, with his eyes closed and head placed on his folded arm, then moving in a circle, suggested that these men were dancing their dreams for him.

Longarm nodded and smiled.

Once he smiled, it looked as if he were to be entertained forever. Everyone had a dream he wanted to dance for him.

When at last they had spent their energies, they squatted again and stared at Longarm. Longarm chose a stick much like one of their wands. He motioned Novoko to come near. The man approached warily.

With the stick, Longarm drew three or four telegraph poles and wavy lines between them. Then he pointed to the telegraph equipment in the desert across the shallow Humboldt.

Novoko smiled and waited politely.

Longarm drew a stick figure at the base of one of the poles. Then he drew another figure at the top of the pole. Then he erased the wavy line and drew it sagging to the ground beside the first figure.

Novoko nodded and smiled politely.

He slept that night beside the river. When he awoke in the first pale light of false dawn, he saw Novoko and ten or twelve other Paiutes squatting on the ridge, gazing silently down at him.

He was able to shoot a couple of rabbits, and the Paiutes joined him for breakfast.

Afterwards, Novoko motioned him to follow. They went up into the rocks. Novoko motioned him to silence. Longarm sat in the sun and waited. Two of the men made grass lassoes with slipknot nooses. They prodded in the rocks until a lizard appeared. Quickly they dropped the noose over the lizard's head and yanked upward. Catching the animal and breaking its neck was accomplished in a single motion.

The patient, short-legged, dark-skinned desert Indians captured half a dozen lizards up among the rocks. They ate them, biting off their heads first and then consuming the entire animal. They offered Longarm a lizard, but when he refused, they laughed and nodded. He saw that they felt far superior to the Saltu.

When they came down from the rocks, Longarm stood, feeling queasy, and watched toothless old men eating grasshoppers. By this time the women had returned with their intricately woven baskets filled with seeds, roots, and pine cones.

Three men tried to head off and kill a stunted deer with their wands. They were not fast enough. Longarm took up his rifle and glanced at Novoko for permission. When Novoko nodded, he shot the deer.

The Paiutes ran to it, but Longarm had decided on a plan that would not absolve the Indians from wire-cutting, but would determine whether they *could* be guilty or not. He had learned early in his job to take one indisputable fact and match other facts to it. Those that fit, like pieces in the puzzle, you kept, building your case that way; the others, no matter how intriguing or promising, you discarded.

He strode out to the dead animal and stood over it. He pointed first to Novoko, then to the three hunters, then to the deer, then to the telegraph poles.

Puzzled, the Paiutes followed him up the slight incline to the ridge where the Western Union lines were strung.

By the time they reached the poles, the rest of the settlement had silently joined them. They sat down and stared at Longarm.

On the hard ground before Novoko, Longarm drew

124

first the deer. Novoko nodded; the representation was close enough.

Next, Longarm scratched out the poles and the wires again. Novoko merely stared at him. Longarm drew a stick figure climbing the pole. Then he pointed to the picture of the deer. Novoko smiled and nodded.

When none of them moved to accept the challenge, Longarm decided to clarify the matter by acting it out. He removed his jacket and gunbelt and laid them at the foot of the pole. Then he climbed it. He did it the only way he could, sinking his boot heels into any breaks in the poles and moving his hands upward over and over again.

He made it. Below him, the entire settlement stood up, nodding their heads toward him. He came down as quickly as possible, and waited again. None of them moved. He pointed to the men, the deer, and then the pole.

At last it was clear. Self-consciously, the Indians went to the pole. Watching them, Longarm replaced his gunbelt and slung his jacket over his shoulder.

The little men tried, straining desperately. They were wiry enough; they were strong and agile enough; what they didn't have was the stamina. They were too nearly starved, too debilitated and weak. They fell from the poles and lay gasping on the ground.

Longarm felt a certain satisfaction. As far as he was concerned, he would have to look elsewhere for the culprits who were destroying Western Union property and thus interfering with government business. One fact was that somebody climbed the poles in this wilderness and cut the wires. These miserable little creatures, existing in brush huts and living on lizards and seeds, simply didn't match the first fact. They didn't climb those poles.

Whoever had listed the Paiutes as possible suspects may have had proper motives. The hungry people were forced to wander in wide circles around their settlements, seeking nuts and roots and seeds; they hated the cavalry's coming out and herding them in. Cutting the wires so they couldn't be traced easily might have

125

satisfied the Paiutes, but Longarm was ready to absolve them of any involvement in this crime.

He dragged the deer to the firepit and motioned the hunters to take it over. Working with their wands, they slashed off the hide and gutted it.

Longarm bowed to Novoko and gestured toward the west. Novoko nodded, and Longarm took a last look at the noxious and scruffy little people. He walked down to the banks of the shallow creek and along it to the place where he had staked out his horse.

He was aware that Novoko was following him, ten or twelve paces behind.

He came around the boulders and stopped. His horse was gone. His saddle was where he had thrown it; the stake and the rope were still there.

His stomach churning, he stared at the remains of his horse. The Paiutes had slain it and chopped off the meat from its carcass.

He spun to face Novoko, who had stopped, holding his wand like a scepter. He stared at Longarm, expressionless.

"Why did you do that?" Longarm yelled at him.

Novoko merely stood there.

Longarm peered at the wizened, sun-cured little man. Novoko said, *"Ho."*

"Sure, you dried-out son of a bitch. You're the Real People, all right. So nice. So polite. And all the time your people were butchering my horse."

Novoko remained unmoving. He said, *"Saltu."* It was as if this explained everything, as if this were the only possible explanation.

Longarm stared at him, inwardly raging. "Hope you can eat the saddle too. Hell, if I'd known you were going to eat my horse, I'd have taken Kennecut's advice and brought you a fat one."

Novoko went on standing, unmoving, wizened, like something graven on that ridge. Longarm gave him a little farewell salute. "See you in my nightmares, old son."

Picking up his saddle and saddlebags, he turned and strode down toward the river. He heard something whistle, almost like the whir of a rattlesnake, and tried to turn. The wand—fire-hardened, sharpened—struck him in the side above his hip.

Fire erupted through him. He dropped his saddle and saddlebags. His hand slapped the butt of his Colt. By the time he was completely turned, the gun was fixed on Novoko, who stood unmoving on the ridge behind him.

When Novoko saw the gun, he cried out with the sound of a choking hawk. He fell to the ground on his knees. He bent his head and covered his eyes. His entire body quivered as he waited to die.

Longarm stared at him. What had Vince said of these strange little desert people? Treacherous as sidewinders.

He slammed the gun back into its holster. "The hell with you," he said. "Killing you won't teach you a damn thing."

Holding his breath and biting down on his lip as hard as he could, he jerked the wand from his flesh, feeling blood oozing hotly from the hole. He held the wand a moment, staring at its blood-covered point.

Still shaking visibly, Novoko removed his hands from his eyes and lifted his head.

Longarm broke the wand over his knee and threw the pieces up the slope toward the kneeling man. Then he backed away, staggering slightly.

That gash in his side scared him. If that wand were as filthy as its owner, it could be deadlier than a tarantula. He wanted to wash it out, cauterize it, do something, but he knew better than to stop.

He looked back over his shoulder. He did not see any of the Paiutes, but that didn't mean they weren't stalking him, hiding, waiting for him to falter or fall. He could see them running to stand over him and hurl their wands into his body. They knew how to cut a Saltu down to size.

He kept walking. Pain flooded up through him, and he became dizzy. He figured the best chance he had of being found was to follow the Western Union poles. They had repair people out on patrol in this deadly country.

He staggered up the slope. The sun seemed more intense than ever, and its rays, reflected off the pastel earth, blinded him. He fell against one of the poles and leaned there until he caught his breath and his head cleared slightly.

He thought he heard something in the sagebrush, and panic flared through him. He leaned against the pole and widened his eyes, trying to see through the dazzling sunlight and the occluding haze that closed in upon his mind. Fall here, he kept warning himself, and you'll be as dead as your horse.

The blood seeped down his hip. The rip in his flesh burned as if it were poisoned. A creeping horror was slowly paralyzing him.

He turned and located the next telegraph pole. Filling his lungs with a deep breath and holding it, he strode along the broken ground, wavering slightly as if drunk, always keeping that pole directly ahead of him. It danced, shimmering in the heat, and he felt a wrench of terror, afraid he'd lost it, afraid he would black out before he reached it.

He stumbled against the pole and hugged it, laughing in exultant triumph.

"I'll keep going," he said aloud. "They can't trail me. They're too weak and too scared . . . sons of bitches . . . they eat lizards . . . they eat raw lizards . . ."

After a moment of reasoning, he laughed again. Holding onto the pole, he located the next one in the progression and then ran toward it. He fell once before he made it. He got up and turned all the way around, disoriented, unsure which pole he was trying to reach.

He laughed savagely. God in heaven, all he needed was to spend his last energy running back and forth between the same two damned poles. Well, he would not do it. That was a hell of a stupid way to die. It was like eating lizards with their heads on, or chewing on grasshoppers, with the brown liquid running from the corners of your mouth.

He stumbled against a pole and clung to it, breathing raggedly. It was really simple. He only had to keep the sun on his left and slightly ahead of him, and he was all right. He rushed on to the next pole. The one ahead lay across a slight defile. He went swiftly, heading downslope.

The descent was sharper than it seemed, a long slant of rocky ground, strangely golden and ribbed with red cactus, reflecting the sun, dazzling him, blinding him.

He stumbled on a rock and plunged forward, falling to his knees in the dry bed of the Humboldt.

Pulling off his coat, he unbuttoned his shirt and loosened his trousers, touching the fiery skin around the gash in his side. All he could think of was blood poisoning, mortification, corruption.

Working feverishly, he dug the sand away, frantically scooping up the earth and feeling the water seep slowly around his fingers. He kept digging. He could think only of survival. There was no memory of the past or contemplation of the present, or even any hope for the future. There was just the thought of staying alive, the obsessive idea that to stay alive he had to clean the carrion filth from that wound.

His groping hand found a piece of flint so hot it seared his skin. He took it up and shoved it into the ragged tear in his side and nearly blacked out. The searing heat of the rock stung his flesh. He threw it aside and lay down beside the slowly filling hole. He scooped the water up into the wound, washing, scrubbing.

His mind spun, but he knew that if he passed out and lay without his shirt, he would be burned beyond hope. Forcing himself to take his time, he replaced his shirt with great care, buttoning it securely at his throat and arranging his string tie. Then he forced himself to shove his arms into his jacket. Uniform. He had to be neatly attired. If they found him dead out here, he wanted old Billy Vail to be proud of him.

Dressed again at last, he scooped handfuls of water up to his face. Then he drank from his cupped hands. The taste of the water nauseated him.

He straightened, fighting the dizziness that swirled around him. It was time to go, time to find that next telegraph pole and stagger the impossible distance up-slope to it. Keep the sun in the west and God in his heaven and the poles in reach.

He tried to stand up. He couldn't do it. The sickness boiled up through him and he toppled as if he'd been struck by a giant fist. He fell on his side. He rolled over on his back. He tried to find the telegraph pole and couldn't do it. It was lost in the blinding core of the sun. He closed his eyes and turned away. When he opened them again, he stared up into a whiskered ancient god's face.

Chapter 11

Somewhere within that hot, deep darkness into which he had plunged, a faint stirring of consciousness flared. It was an awareness of pain—fiery, naked, raw pain. Longarm fought against it. He was satisfied, content in the oblivion of blackness and its total forgetfulness. Some instinct, fighting up through the overwhelming messages of burning pain, warned him that if he wakened, it would be to a dread reality uglier than anything he had ever faced before.

He tried to burrow back into the warm sand of the riverbed, into that safe pool of nothingness, but the more he tried, the more wakeful and agonized he became—the more aware of a chilled, strange reality around him, a blaze of fire in his side, an ache of savage cold at his ankles and wrists.

He opened his eyes unwillingly, discovering one thing at a time above him and around him. He lay sprawled on his back. He seemed to remember from some distant past that this was the position into which he'd fallen as he'd blacked out. A year ago? Two? An eternity? Some other lifetime?

For a long time he lay passively between painful sleep and the agony of waking. Suddenly he remembered the treacherous little Paiutes trailing him. He yelled in fevered terror. He felt a desperate sense of urgency. He had to get to his feet; he had to get away from the diseased little diggers. But when he moved, pain shot through him like a hundred poisoned darts. His breath quickened, thick and forced. How long ago had he passed out? How long had he lain helpless like this?

He tried to move, but could not.

Panic seized him. He tried to spring up and found that he could not move. Gradually he became aware of the restraining thongs about his wrists and ankles.

He tried to pull free and could not. He lay still for one moment longer, eyes shut against the painful lances of light. This was just part of the nightmare brought on by the gash of that putrid wand in his side.

He heard movement around him and opened his eyes wide, expecting to see Novoko and his filthy little side-winders surrounding him.

He stared up at a face it seemed he'd seen some-where before, perhaps in some other nightmare. It was the set, stern face of a man in his late forties or early fifties, but aged and gray beyond his years. He was a big man, bald across the pate, but with long silky hair growing white down to his shoulders. His eyebrows were white caterpillars, shading a fanatic's blue eyes. His mustache was thicker than his hair and drooped on both sides of his mouth, growing into his white, care-fully trimmed, Van Dyke–type beard.

The man wore wire-rimmed spectacles, a white, ruffled shirt buttoned at the throat, a broadcloth suit, and dark boots. His voice was mellifluous—the trained, round tones of the actor or the evangelist. He said, "Decided to join the living, have you?"

"Who are you?" Longarm said. "Where am I?"

The golden-voiced man spoke to the two women on each side of him. They were many years younger than he, but they were plain and severe, and looked as if they had never really been young inside. Their mouths were pursed, vinegary. "Listen to him. Comes awake yelling his head off. Now he's full of fight and questions."

"He's a Gentile," one of the women said, as if this were the only necessary answer.

"Now, let us not judge harshly," the man said, and then added, "not yet."

"Who are you?" Longarm persisted.

"Well, at least we know who *you* are, don't we?" said those pear-shaped tones.

"Why am I tied down like this?"

The whiskered face bent closer. "You were wild, my son. Feverish. Suffering from sunstroke. A virulent knife wound in your side. You yelled about Indians and fire sticks. You swore that ants were stinging you. Your whole body—your mind, even—was poisoned by your wound. We had to cleanse it. We had to bleed you so you would calm down. We tied you down for your own safety, my son. We would not want you to slip away from us, into death."

One of the women laughed, a bitter sound, not laughter to be shared.

Longarm stared up at her, his mouth twisting. "You're a barrel of fun."

The bald man spoke, his voice riding over Longarm's. "We have done our best by thee. You are a stranger and we brought you into our midst. You are a nonbeliever, an outsider, and yet we prayed for thee and we did for thee and for thy immortal soul."

"You're . . . Mormons," Longarm whispered.

"Disciples of the Church of Jesus Christ of Latter-Day Saints. We who have been persecuted and tormented and slain by you Gentiles have returned good for evil unto thee." His face twisted slightly with disdain. "As I told thee, we know who you are. We know thee and thy works. We went through your papers. We wanted to know thy name."

"But we learned much more," one of the women said.

"You came to betray us," the other said.

"That's enough, Prudence, Charity. His time will come to answer our charges against him. For the moment, until he can face the Council, he is our guest. I ask thee, Prudence, and thee, Charity, to remember this."

"What kind of charges?" Longarm said.

"In the right season and at the right moment and the right place, all things will be known."

"Until that joyous day," Longarm said sarcastically, "must I be tied down this way?"

The glorious voice flowed over him like healing oil. "I am afraid it is God's will."

The two women tittered in appreciation of the elder's

heavenly humor, but the bewhiskered man frowned at them and they fell silent.

Longarm slept. When he woke, it was to the faint, pleasant scent of a young woman, or some pale memory of cologne haunting him from his past. He opened his eyes. Night shrouded the windows of the bedroom. A young girl—she was no more than twenty, if out of her teens—stood over him. Her hair was a red-gold color, and her ceramic-smooth cheeks glowed with ruddy health. Her lips were rose-red, entirely free of lip rouge or any paint. Painted faces were an abomination in this place, disavowed by the faithfuls' adherence to the Thirteen Articles of Faith. They put away worldly cosmetics and abstained from tea, coffee, tobacco, and spiritous liquors. People like these had to create their own entertainment; having females like this must have made it easier.

He said, "What is your name?"

"Purity Garrison," the girl said.

"I take it you're the daughter of the old man here. That his name? Garrison?"

"I am his wife. His latest wife."

"Oh? I thought the faithful had given up plural marriages."

She just gazed at him with a crooked smile. "I haven't always been one of the faithful."

He grinned. "I'll bet you haven't. It can't be easy being married to a man old enough to be your father."

"Life was not meant to be easy," she quoted. "Life is our training for eternity with our Father."

She spoke these words in deadly seriousness, almost in the stentorian tones of her aging husband, then abruptly she giggled impishly.

He stared at her. "What kind of vixen are you?"

She stopped smiling and met his eyes evenly. "If you were less ill, and I could lock the door, I would show thee the imp of Satan I can be—with the right man."

"How do you know I'd be the right man?"

Boldly she rubbed her hand between his legs and

stroked him lingeringly. "I know," she whispered. "I have bathed thee."

A lance of fiery desire pierced through him from deep in his loins and he felt his heart pound. He struggled helplessly against the thongs, feeling himself growing rigid under her hand. "Can't you lock the door?"

She sighed and withdrew her hand. "Not in this house. Keys make possible dark secrets, and dark secrets are—"

"An abomination before God."

She smiled and sighed heavily. "I have not been here long. Less than a year. It seems most of my life. I have learned how many things are abominations before God."

"Why'd you come if you don't like it?" Longarm asked with a frown, remembering the case of Emilie Boggs, a young girl whom he'd had to rescue from a group of dissident Mormons who'd called themselves the Avenging Angels. In that affair, the leader of the splintered-off sect had kidnapped the girl after seeing her in a vision as his Celestial Bride. The Avenging Angels had been quite a bunch, all right; they'd left him to die in the Great Salt Desert, a wilderness about as dismal as the Humboldt Basin. Somehow he'd come through it without winding up as salty and dry and dead as a side of bacon, but he didn't crave a repetition of the experience. "They, uh, didn't force you here against your will, did they?" he asked hesitantly.

"No," she replied, and Longarm breathed a small sigh of relief. "I wish they had," she went on. "Then I could fight them. I could hate them instead of hating myself—and my father."

"Your father arranged your marriage to old Garrison?"

She nodded. "My father was my only family. We lived in Denver. My father gambled. On everything. On cards, on horses, on silver. He was desperately in debt when he met Nolan Garrison and brought him home with him. I hardly looked at him—a bald old man who was a friend of my father's. But then, a few nights later, he returned to our house. There was a strange

135

look of excitement in his face. He said he had experienced a divine revelation. In a vision, one of the original disciples of Christ himself had told him he could fulfill his obligations and responsibilities to the Church and his flock of faithful only if I were his Celestial Bride. We would be joined in a Celestial Wedding."

She spread her hands, her lovely young face bleak. "I did the best I could to keep from laughing. I giggled once, in spite of myself. My father said I was just nervous. For the first time I realized my father wasn't laughing. He was serious. Garrison knew the precise amount of father's gambling debts, the urgency of his paying them before he was liquidated by vengeful gamblers. Father said my marriage to Nolan Garrison in a Celestial Wedding sounded like a sacred idea to him."

She sat a moment, remembering in pain. "After that, I really didn't have a chance. It was something that was inevitable. Father wasn't cruel or insistent, but he was persistent. He told me how rich Nolan Garrison was, what a wonderful life I would have as the wife of a leader of the Mormon Church, one of the Council of the Twelve Apostles, a member of the First Council of Seventy. He told me everything except that Nolan already had five other wives."

"I'd heard that polygamy was outlawed by the Church."

She gave him that odd smile again. "Even Nolan Garrison says that will come—that the Salt Lake City Church will actually disavow plural marriages within ten years or so. But among the faithful out here? Never, he says, because polygamy is a vital part of the true teachings of Brigham Young and Joseph Smith."

She gestured with her hand toward the books lined up between two bookends representing Christ's nail-pierced hands. "These are the books we read—the *only* books we read—and it's all in here." She read off the titles: *The Book of Mormon, Doctrines and Covenants,* and *The Pearl of Great Price.* "From *The Book of Mormon* came the visions and the revelations. It tells of the revelation of Joseph Smith's establishing the

Church in the wilderness in purity and with responsible authority. Nolan named me Purity after we were married. I guess I should be thankful. He could have named me Responsibility or Authority."

He grinned at her. "At least you can laugh about it."

"Oh, I can cry too. Would you like to see me cry? I've just found out, crying is no good. And laughing is like living well—it's the best revenge."

"What was your name—before Nolan Garrison bought you?"

She shook her head, her eyes swirling with hurt. "No. Elder Garrison didn't *buy* me. My father *sold* me. I have to keep remembering that, or I couldn't stand it at all. My name was Peggy O'Moore. And my stalwart, honorable father was Sean O'Moore—of the gambling O'Moores. I grew up longing to be a singer. I wanted to appear in beautiful musical shows like the ones that Trixie Mondale brings to Denver. I know I could succeed as a singer."

He smiled. "The way you look, you could succeed as a singer if you had to carry your tunes in a bucket."

She nodded, touching his chest. "Oh, how I wish for a key for that door! I've sat here night after night, looking at you, wishing. I've got a long, empty life ahead of me here. A key might not help much . . . but it would be a memory." She tilted her head, shaking the thought away. "When I knew that Father actually was going to sell me for his gambling debts, I thought about running away and trying to get in those shows as a singer, and maybe I should have. But I didn't have the nerve. I didn't know then what I know now . . ."

"What do you know now, Purity?" he inquired in a gentle tone.

She sighed. "I was kept in a detention dormitory with other unmarried girls—being purified—until I agreed to marry Nolan."

"Then you *were* forced into it?"

"I told you, no. I came of my own free will. I came in my innocence—which is just another way, Mr. Long, of saying my stupidity. But I am here, and I am on a road that lasts all my life, on which I can never turn back."

Longarm heard Purity gasp. She lunged away from the bed and turned, facing Nolan Garrison. Her husband wore his nightgown stuffed into his tweed trousers, and he was barefooted. His hair and beard and mustache stood up wildly, and his white-caterpillar eyebrows were mussed. His eyes blazed with rage.

He drew his arm far across his body and backhanded Purity across the face. The young woman staggered and fell against the wall. She stayed there, the livid imprint of her husband's hand across her cheek.

"Let me up from here, you old bastard," Longarm said, "and I'll kill you."

Garrison turned his wrath on Longarm. "Let me advise thee well, Gentile. Never interfere between a man and his wife. She knows she has erred and done wrong and sinned." He glanced at Purity, still slumped on the floor against the wall. "What did I tell thee before prayers tonight, Purity?"

Purity swallowed hard. "That the patient did not require my presence tonight, that I was to sleep, that I was no longer to nurse the patient."

"You heard my instructions precisely, thou Jezebel, but attended them not."

"I am sorry. I thought . . . he might be ill."

Garrison looked as if he would strike her again. His eyes blazed with his rage. "You thought only that I slept, thou harlot. Thou shalt pay for this. I tell thee now. Go to my room, prepare thyself, and wait for me there."

Purity nodded, pale and contrite. She got up and, head lowered and averted, went out of the room.

Nolan Garrison stood like a statue of a Biblical prophet until she was gone, then he said, "I am sorry, but she is not permitted to converse with Gentiles. Her purity must not be contaminated by such as thee."

The Mormon elder blew out the lamp and left the room. The house and the desert settlement grew quiet, but Longarm could not sleep. The long hours dragged out. A cock crowed, and others answered across the compound. First lights showed in other windows, and the first breakfast fires rose against the pastel sky.

He waited for Purity to return. Once, perhaps when the bald elder was out of the house, he heard Purity singing. He knew it was she; her song was a hymn, but her voice was Irish and warm and full of secret laughter.

He strained helplessly against the thongs, secured to the walls by heavy pegs.

Purity did not come back to the bedroom where he lay as their prisoner. He felt gratitude for their having lugged him in from the bed of the Humboldt, but his indebtedness, along with his patience, soon died in rage.

The other two women, Prudence and Charity, sat with him during the hot, silent days. They changed his bedclothes—everything was spotlessly clean and fresh—and allowed him to attend to his bodily functions. They fed him, but they did not speak to him. He tried to force them to talk. He told them ribald jokes, and offered to let Charity—or was it Prudence?—fondle his tally-whacker. Finally he asked if either one of them had ever seen a man's privates before: "I mean a real man, Prudence, not an impotent old billy goat."

It did not matter what he said to them, he could not provoke them to reply. They merely stared at him in cold and implacable hatred.

At night he was left alone and, as far as he knew, untended or unguarded. When his strength returned fully, he found it impossible to go on lying helpless there. In boredom more than anticipation, he started to yank on the thong securing his right arm.

He shoved his arm out as far as he could, getting slack in the leather thong. Then he yanked it toward him with all his strength—and bit his lip to keep from yelling in agony. The thongs closed on his wrist, cutting the flesh and stopping all circulation.

This delayed him, but did not stop him. He pushed his arm far enough toward the wall that a small loop appeared in the thong. He gripped it in his fist, relieving the pressure on his wrists somewhat.

Gripping the thong in his fist, he yanked on it repeatedly. He felt his heart quicken. The large peg in the baseboard loosened; he could move it back and forth like a loose tooth. He overlooked the fact that his wrists were cut deeply and bleeding.

He tried to ignore the pain. How pleased Billy Vail would be if he could see what his deputy endured for the government's hundred a month and found.

He yanked again . . . and again. The peg was loosened, but it was well seated, driven into sun-cured wood with great force and unyielding strength.

When dawn broke over the Saints' settlement, the peg was still in place, but Longarm's sheet was spattered with his blood.

Charity came in with his breakfast. She hesitated, holding the tray. She stared at the blood-splotched sheet, at his torn wrist. Coldly, without showing any expression, she placed the tray on a table and walked out.

She returned in a moment with Nolan Garrison. He looked sad, but not enraged. With a heavy-headed hammer, he reset the peg in the wall.

He stood then, looking down at Longarm. "You must learn patience. You are recovering swiftly. Soon enough you will be free of these fetters."

Charity stood gazing at him in chilly triumph. They did not bother to tend or bandage his torn wrists.

"You are a bitch, Charity," he said. "Did you know that? A real eighteen-carat bitch."

"I am Prudence," she said.

"Maybe you are, but all the rest of it applies."

She stared at him, her pale eyes swirling with hatred, but did not reply.

He felt as if his wrist were staked in an ant bed. Each time the thong rubbed against his raw flesh, pain flushed through him and exploded behind his eyes.

He lay sweated, wondering if the elder would post a guard in his room that night. He hoped it might be Purity, but told himself ironically that his pain was softening his mind; old Garrison would never let that lush quail near him again.

Longarm grinned. Garrison is doing unto me, he told

himself, as I would do unto him. Only he's doing it first.

Night closed in over the desert village. The room grew dark. No one came near him. The valley grew quiet in the darkness. By nine o'clock, all lights were extinguished in the compound. Through his window he watched the fire of a blazing desert star; the air was so clear that the distant light seemed to shine just beyond his window.

Absently he began to jerk on the thong with his left hand. Smarter now, still learning from his mistakes, he caught the thong in his fist before he yanked on it.

He worked without hope, but he worked relentlessly. Now both his wrists bled, but he did not care. The peg loosened with the first three or four yanks he gave it.

In less than three hours the peg broke free and he fished it in across the floor. The loops around his wrists were formed by running the thong through braided eyelets. He loosened the bindings on his right wrist and then sat up and slipped the thongs over his feet.

Blood ran down both his hands, coagulating between his fingers. He ignored the blood and the pain. During the preceding days he had watched Charity—or was it Prudence?—putting his freshly washed and carefully ironed clothing on a shelf in a standing chiffonier.

Holding his breath, he got off the bed and padded across the room. He put on his underpants and slipped his trousers over them. His shirt smelled of soap and fresh desert sunlight. "Thanks, Prudence," he said under his breath. "Or Charity."

Dressed, he patted his hands around in the darkened dresser. He found his boots, his wallet, his holster, and even his watch. Both his guns were gone. He was not surprised; he would have been astonished to find them. Then he realized that his cheroots were also gone, and this made him angrier than the loss of his guns.

He ripped towels and bandaged his wrists. Walking in his stocking feet and carrying his boots, he tiptoed across the room and eased the door open. The hinges whimpered faintly and he sucked in his breath and waited, counting to fifty before he moved again.

He pulled the door ajar only far enough to sidle through. Aware of human presence in the darkness, he stopped. They loomed in the darkened hall, barring his way.

As his eyes grew accustomed to the stygian darkness of the narrow corridor, he recognized Nolan Garrison. The bald elder was damned near as tall as he was, and towering in his wrath. On either side of him stood his favorite harpies, Prudence and Charity. They wore nightgowns, their hair in braids. Nolan carried a long rifle, and both women had handguns.

He winced. He wasn't convinced that Garrison would shoot him in cold blood, but he had not the least doubt that Prudence and Charity waited only for him to make any move at all.

He made none. He sank against the wall. Garrison gazed at him, looking along his nose like some furious deity. But the two women were worse. Their chilled laughter struck him like spittle in the face.

Garrison's mellow voice anointed him. "We did for thee what we could, heathen. Now we know who you are, what you want, why you were on your way here. Whatever pity, concern, or compassion once we held for thee is quite dead. Do you want to return quietly, or do you want us to shoot you? It is all one with us. It is your move, Mr. Long."

Chapter 12

Longarm was led in shackles across the Saints' Golconda Valley compound to the meeting hall. It was nine in the morning but the sun was blisteringly hot, an angry fireball blazing in the crystal-clear atmosphere.

He took his first look at the Mormon settlement and found it a strangely laid-out town—not really a city at all, but a loose gathering of widely separated structures. There was no village center except the meeting hall, set down among a dozen newly planted pinyons. All other buildings were distantly spaced along wide streets where a few hardy cottonwoods and twisted Judas trees struggled for life. The homes were often a quarter of a mile from the nearest neighbors. These people held the entire valley and utilized every square yard. And they were getting results from their careful husbandry. Far along the road across the compound from Elder Nolan Garrison's farmhouse, stacks of hay had been rounded like great tan breasts on the bosom of this arid land.

The Council members were already seated and silent —grim, cold, and unforgiving men—when Longarm was brought into the room and seated in a chair in front and apart from them, his wrists and ankles shackled.

Elder Nolan Garrison wasted no time in getting the proceedings under way. He asked God's guidance in bringing just judgments and in protecting the bounteous life in this glorious valley into which God had led them. Longarm could not say why, but this prayer hardly reassured him. He had learned in his dealings with these people that they often interpreted God's will to their own ultimate benefit.

"We will describe first the events which bring us

143

here," the elder said in that resonant voice. Longarm had thought Garrison would describe how he had come upon the Gentile unconscious in the bed of the Humboldt, but instead, Garrison chose to go back a little farther than that—back, in fact, to the early years of the century.

"We of Golconda Valley are fundamental adherents of the *original* Church of Jesus Christ of Latter-Day Saints, as organized through revelations from God Himself by Joseph Smith at Fayette, New York, in 1830. This means we are faithful followers of Joseph Smith in every sense and essence of the word."

Longarm stared at the huge, balding elder. Either Nolan Garrison liked to hear the mellifluous sound of his own voice, or this opening sermon was for Longarm's benefit. The faithful knew all this. In fact, Longarm himself could have advised the bald elder to save his breath, because he was quite well received and trusted by the Mormons of Salt Lake Valley. He had saved one of their women from an abductor when the Church was helpless in its own land, and he had received vows of eternal gratitude. But he sat silently while that deep voice flowed like pudding over the silent room.

"The Council of Jesus Christ of Latter-Day Saints accepted the Church Council of the Council of Twelve Apostles headed by Brigham Young, and began in 1846 and 1847 that terrible trek overland to Salt Lake Valley. This means we are truly faithful adherents to the teachings of Brigham Young. We live according to those teachings of *The Book of Mormon, Doctrines and Covenants*, and *The Pearl of Great Price*. This means we live totally and strictly according to the teachings of our holy Church. We believe then that from revelations of the original three of Christ's own disciples, Joseph Smith was endowed by God with the priestly power for Gospel dispensation.

"This has brought us our beautiful Thirteen Articles of Faith by which we are guided. One of those Articles of Faith is our privilege to worship Almighty God according to the dictates of our own conscience.

"Worship according to the dictates of our own conscience; for this we have removed ourselves to this valley—an arid place to which we have brought water and flowers and food. All we ask is that we be permitted to worship God Almighty according to the dictates of our own conscience. This means without the interference of local, state, or national governments.

"And so this is the basis of all our complaints and charges and accusations and indictments against the infidel spy from the United States government who was on his way here to probe and inquire and investigate and report to his government on our *privilege* to worship God Almighty according to the dictates of our own conscience! This is unendurable! It is indefensible! It is a violation of privacy and our privileges! These are our charges against this man, and it is your judgment we ask upon him."

Longarm said, "Aren't you interested in why I was on my way here?"

Garrison's caterpillar-like brows writhed, and his fanatical blue eyes glittered. "You have impeached yourself, Mr. Long. You have convicted yourself before us—"

"I ain't said anything."

"Your papers. Orders from your government . . ."

"It's your government too, Elder."

"Without the right to invade our privacy, to interfere with our religious ceremonies or the God-given privilege to worship Him in our own way. That is our government. But it seems to have little kinship with the probing, prying, harassing bureaucrats you represent. Your orders from that government are most explicit. You are to come among us and report on our activities—"

"*Not* your religious activities."

"Our lives *are* our religion, Mr. Long. And you have convicted yourself of betraying and attempting to abridge our rights and privileges and privacy. I read your orders, Mr. Long. I felt pity for you. I felt sorrow for you. I wanted to find out who you were and how we might notify your family. It was as if I did not put my hand in a man's wallet, but into a nest of sidewinders.

145

Your orders, your badge, and your gun—they had testified for thee. They have spoken for thee. They have condemned thee. They have indicted thee. We do not need to hear your lies from your mouth. This Council has voted not to hear the testimony of your voice. We have seen the evidence. We have seen the truth. And you stand convicted."

Longarm stood up and almost fell. He was deadly serious because he saw that Elder Nolan Garrison was deadly serious. This was his life they were about to "abridge."

"I've got no interest in your privileges or your privacy," he said. "I am interested only in who's cutting the Western Union lines and disrupting government communications. That is all I'm here for."

Nolan Garrison gazed at him sadly. He shook his head, the long, silky hair bobbling against his shoulder. "You do yourself no favors to invoke the wires of Satan. The very existence of those lines is an abomination before God, a threat to our own safety and security. Those lines carry your lies about our way of life. Those lines reach out like tendrils from the vineyard of the Devil. Their roots go down to Hell."

"Won't you listen to anything I have to say?"

"This is not the time, and not the place, Mr. Long. We are here to learn the verdict of this Council of Elders. What is your judgment, Elders? I call for a voice vote regarding this man charged with crimes against our Church."

"Kill him," an elder said.

"Kill him."

The verdict was unanimous. Their voices were cold and low and almost sad, but without hesitation or reluctance.

Nolan Garrison nodded, bowing to the will of the Council. "It is the judgment of this Council, Custis Long, that you be taken to a place of detention and held there until such time as you shall be taken before a firing squad and executed. May God have mercy on your soul."

● ● ●

The settlement prison was a single, stone-walled, dirt-floored cell behind the blacksmith's furnace. The iron door was closed behind Longarm and locked. At first he was bat-blind in the dull darkness that was relieved only by light through a window eight feet in the wall and barred.

"So you're the U.S. marshal," a voice said.

Longarm closed his eyes tightly and then opened them. He saw a man wearing trousers and an undershirt, but no shoes. He lay on a metal cot without mattress. "Make yourself at home, Marshal." He gestured toward another cot across the cell. "You won't be here long. Neither one of us will."

"You mean we can get out of here?"

The man grinned like a coyote. "I mean that Mormon justice is swift. Especially in Golconda Volley. They have quick trials and even quicker executions. That way, no matter who comes out here to protest an execution, they'll be too late to stop it. The elders will weep and gnash their teeth and wail in their regret, but the fact will be accomplished. You'll be dead. And I'll be dead."

"You sound resigned to dying."

"I'm not resigned, Marshal. But I am trying not to deceive myself, or build up any false hopes. I've been here three days. There were two other fellows here when I was arrested—a rustler and a man who tried to run away with one of the women. One was executed yesterday. The other went this morning. I figure I'm due tomorrow."

"They execute one person a day?"

"When they got 'em to execute. I've found they have no trouble—and no prisoners—for months and even years at a time. Looks like you and me just got here in the busy season."

"What did you do? Spit on a sidewalk?"

"I killed the son of one of the elders. He caught me stealing. I admit that. I was hungry. Empty-bellied hungry. Maybe you've never been that way. This young fellow came on me. He wouldn't listen. He didn't believe a man got hungry enough that he had to steal to

147

eat. I tried to talk to him. He began to shove me around. I killed him."

"What were you doing out here in Mormon country?"

"I came out prospecting for silver. Since the strike over beyond Claim Jump, there's been a lot of prospectors spreading out, because a couple of the mines near Claim Jump have already petered out. I had some trouble. My horse was bit by a snake. Lost my way . . . ended up here." He shrugged.

"I'm only looking for somebody who might be destroying government property."

"You mean cutting Western Union lines?"

"Western Union has a federal government franchise west of the Missouri—"

The other prisoner laughed without mirth. "Mister, you picked something to investigate that's the hate closest to these elders' hearts. They call the Western Union lines the Devil's toy of the Gentiles. I don't know if they cut lines, but they've got a lot of reasons for wanting them down."

"Have they?"

"Well, look at it this way. In Salt Lake Valley, the Church has said it doesn't approve of plural marriages, but it'll be at least ten or twelve years until the Church *rules* against polygamy, which is something else. These people practice it in this valley. The Western Union lines carry news fast—news about their marriage habits, among other things that they wouldn't want spread around."

"What other things?"

The man laughed coldly. "Well, I'd say you were dead the minute old Nolan Garrison found out you were a U.S. marshal. Tell you how good I think your chances are. They're going to execute me in the morning, come sunup. I got no chance at all, and I don't think your chances are as good as mine."

"Is Garrison wanted by the federal government?"

The prisoner shrugged. "Let's just say I believe old Garrison will want you safely executed before those

148

wires can get word to your offices that you're a prisoner here—even if that means cutting those wires."

"Do you believe they cut wires to stop messages going east or west?"

"You mean do I have proof you could present to a court of law if you get out of here? Which you won't." The prisoner shrugged. "No. I got no proof. It just makes sense to me that if someone came along who might send out word of Nolan Garrison's crimes, old Garrison might cut wires or anything else until he could . . . liquidate the troublemaker. And that's you. Right now, he's probably got the runs. He's afraid you know something about him and Mountain Meadow."

"You mean he was there?" Longarm said, openly surprised.

"Yes. I got it from one of the prisoners, the one who tried to run away with one of the wives. He says he knows that Nolan Garrison was at the Mountain Meadow Massacre, because he was there and saw him. He says Garrison was even more of a fanatic then than he is now. If anyone opposed the Church, Garrison couldn't sleep until that person was removed. Garrison was one of the leaders of the Mountain Meadow Massacre. These people—Gentiles—were surrounded by Indians, cut off from help, and these people came as their deliverers. They promised safe passage out. But they went among them and shot them dead—men, women, and children. You can believe me, Nolan Garrison has plenty of reason to hate federal marshals who come around—and those Western Union wires that might carry out the truth about him."

The hours dragged by slowly. When nightfall came, Longarm got up and prowled the cell. He finally lay down; he did not believe he could sleep. Late at night he heard the man on the other cot, crying softly in the darkness. Longarm lay unmoving.

His cellmate had not exaggerated. At the first hint of dawn light, the heavy, iron-barred door was unlocked and swung open.

Longarm lay immobile. The three black-suited men

who entered the cell wore black hoods over their heads and were armed with rifles. One carried a lantern, another held handcuffs and a chain at his side. They caught the arms of the prisoner, twisted them against the small of his back, and snapped on the cuffs. He did not speak or resist.

They pulled him to his feet and marched him out of the cell between them. The iron-barred door clanged shut. Darkness swallowed the prison room again, barely touched by the faint flush of daylight.

Longarm heard men marching on the stony ground outside the wall of the prison. Pulling his bed under the high window, he stood on it and peered through the inset opening.

He flinched. A morbid scene greeted him in the false dawn. A line of six black-suited, hooded men, carrying carbines, stood about fifteen paces from the stone wall. They stood at one-yard intervals from each other, cold and silent. Lanterns were placed on the ground at each end of the line of executioners. They cast eerie shadows across the yellow ground.

The prisoner, blindfolded now, was brought out and stood against the wall. Dawn spread faintly pink, adding a ghastly glow to the scene.

Nolan Garrison appeared around the corner of the jail. He walked with his head bowed and both hands clasping a large black book in front of him. He was the only man present who was not wearing a hood. He stood between the condemned man and the firing squad.

Garrison's resonant voice droned in prayers for the redemption—in heaven—of the condemned felon being dispatched this morning.

At last Garrison stopped praying. He turned and stalked away without glancing toward the doomed man.

Longarm sprawled facedown on the cot. No one came near him after a man brought his breakfast. The sound of that gunfire seemed to echo and reverberate inside his head all day.

He had stood at the window with feelings of fascination, dread, and horror washing through him. When the

150

prisoner fell, riddled with bullets, he was pronounced dead. A squad of men with sharp-bladed shovels dug a narrow slit about four feet deep near a cottonwood tree.

The prisoner was dragged across the rough ground and dropped into the narrow gash in the earth. The men with shovels threw the dirt back into the hole and then beat it as flat as they could with their shovels. Then they went away, and for another two hours the whole settlement was silent and empty.

Longarm remained as if paralyzed at the window. Finally, when the first workers appeared from the houses and rode their mules toward the fields, he retreated from the window and fell across the bunk.

His mind began to plan ahead; the prisoner had accepted his death as if he believed his string had run out. Longarm didn't buy such negative reasoning. He wasn't ready to die in this godforsaken valley. And to be shot and thrown in the ground, without a marker or even a pine box, seemed a hellishly callous and unattractive way to die. One thing he knew; three armed men or six, they wouldn't drag him off to his death without a struggle they'd be telling their grandchildren about. He was not going to be fertilizer for some cottonwood tree. Not without a fight.

The people of the settlement did not come near him. He heard men talking in subdued voices as the smithy worked in the building beyond the iron door.

At nightfall two men arrived, bringing his last meal on two tin plates. They set the meal on the floor of the cell, then they stood beyond the bars, watching him with looks on their faces that raised the hackles along Longarm's neck.

He gazed appraisingly at the food. It looked ordinary and innocent enough. But when he recalled how quietly that other prisoner had gone to his death, and considered the smirks on the ugly faces of the men beyond that door, suspicions flared. One way to execute an unprotesting prisoner was to drug him the night before.

"Eat," one of the men said.

"Your last supper," the other added, grinning vacantly.

Longarm shook his head. "I'm not hungry. I'll eat it later."

The two men glanced at each other and shrugged. They walked away, and Longarm stared at the plate of steaming food without moving. Maybe he was making a mistake, but it was a chance he wasn't going to take. He wouldn't be the first man to go to hell on an empty stomach.

After a long time he got up, took the pans of food, and scraped them out of the high window. Then he threw the pans between the bars of the door into the narrow corridor.

For a long time he prowled the cell. He studied the cots to see if they could be dismantled into metal clubs. He exhaled, frustrated, looking around. He climbed up on the bed again. The window bars were sunk solidly into the rock and adobe wall.

Standing there, he thought at first that he was getting a preview of the fires of hell. Then he realized that the flames licking upward against the night were real. The haystacks far down the compound were burning; smoke and fire were exploding upward on updrafts of desert night wind.

Lights appeared in every house. Somewhere, someone began hammering frantically on an iron hoop. Then he saw half-dressed men riding horses and mules, carrying pitchforks and shovels. Then the women ran along the roads, carrying oaken buckets, watching the fire illuminate the whole desert world.

Behind him somebody said, "Well, you going to stand there all night?"

He leaped down from the bed and ran across the cell to the iron-barred door. He gripped the bars, staring wide-eyed in the thick darkness. "Purity," he whispered, stunned.

The blonde girl was sawing at the lock tongue with the blade of a heavy hacksaw. "Don't ever call me that again," Purity said. "My name is Peggy."

He took the hacksaw from her and worked it be-

152

tween the lock and the doorjamb. "What are you doing here?"

"Well, after I set the haystacks afire, there wasn't any sense staying down there."

"Tarnation, girl, you did that? They'll shoot you."

"They will if they catch me."

"What are you going to do?"

"I'm going to be a singer in musical comedies. I made up my mind since you got here. Can't you hurry? We don't have all night. Hay burns fast, and some of those old men think faster than fire."

"I'm hurrying. I'll never be able to repay you for setting me free."

"Oh, yes, you will. When you get me to Claim Jump —or when *I* get *you* to Claim Jump—our debts are cleared."

"I can't take you. I'd only get you killed."

"Work faster. Of course you can take me, you ought to know that. If you don't take me, you won't even go."

"Honey, once I get out of here, nobody can stop me."

She laughed and showed him his own Colt. "I can and I will. I didn't risk my life to be left behind here."

"I'm thinking about what's best for you," he said.

"No. You're not thinking at all. I've got your gun, I've got two horses saddled, I've got everybody in the settlement fighting a fire three miles from here. It's real simple, Mr. Long. We both go—or neither one of us goes."

"If you shot me, you'd never get away."

"If I don't get away, I'd want them to execute me. I won't go on living here. And there's one more thing. I know the way to the nearest town. Do you?"

The lock bent and then snapped. He threw the door open, caught Purity to him, and kissed her soft mouth fiercely. "Later," she laughed. "There'll be plenty of time for that."

She handed him his Colt and his cross-draw rig. They moved out of the building as he belted the gun at his hips.

In the shadow of the cottonwood that shaded the

smithy by day he saw the two saddled horses, ground-tied. "Let's get out of here," he said.

"Just a minute."

He turned and stared at her in the darkness. She reached in under her dress and took something from between her thighs. He shook his head, disbelieving, laughing. It was his derringer. She held it out and he took it. He grinned in the darkness. "Hot," he told her.

Purity laughed. "You better believe it," she said.

Chapter 13

The fires were already dying out as Longarm and Purity rode southwest across the settlement. In the distance they saw people running back and forth, dwarfed shadows against the failing conflagration.

The sky was somber, the ordinarily blazing stars wan and ineffectual, the moon a thin, faint sliver in the black canopy. As they sped their stolen horses into the darkness beyond the last of the Mormon farmhouses, someone yelled. Dogs barked. A rifle cracked, reverberating across the valley. Before they were a mile from the cultivated fields, following a narrow roadway, they heard the clanging of the alarm, the furiously beaten iron ring summoning the faithful to the chase.

Longarm rode blindly in the night. At the moment he didn't look very far ahead; he planned only to put as much distance as possible between himself and the firing squad led by the vindictive-god figure, Nolan Garrison. Strategy could come later. Galloping his horse, he bent forward, urging his mount to race faster in headlong flight.

Purity stayed close behind him. They rode silently. The echoing thud of hooves on the hoof-packed earth was the loudest sound they made, an unbroken and steady rhythm, at this moment the loveliest sound Longarm could remember.

The first pale glow of dawn showed Longarm the fatal error of his and Purity's planning. They had followed the riverbed to keep from getting lost in the night. This had been like leaving a clearly marked map for their hunters. Knowing the country, the pursuers

155

had ridden in a beeline across the plains and now waited ahead to intercept them.

Longarm slowed and whispered to Purity, "They've cut us off."

He pointed toward the rise where several horsemen were silhouetted against the sky.

Purity swore and turned her horse, prodding it up the steep bank to the head-high gray sagebrush. Moving into the thick growth, she pointed toward a high hogback ridge rising in a rocky fault and cutting across the plains, studded with pinyon and juniper.

"You got any idea how far away that is?" Longarm protested. "You know how close your husband is up that riverbed?"

"You got any better ideas?"

He laughed ruefully. "Let's go, sweetheart. We're doing it your way."

"I hope so," she said over her shoulder.

Suddenly brightening daylight showed them the posse had spotted them and had split into three squads, covering the plains west of them and closing in. Longarm and Purity were forced to veer north again.

"We don't want to go north," Purity wailed in protest.

"I know that. You know that. Our horses know that. But all that really matters is that old Garrison knows that, just as he knows we'll keep trying to turn back west. And when we do, he's got us."

They rode under a section of telegraph lines. Those poles and gleaming wires seemed to beckon them toward the west. The lines would be their only hope for a trail out of this wilderness, now that Garrison's riders had denied them the Humboldt riverbed.

The dust clouds raised by their now unseen pursuers forced them to continue north and west.

"Maybe we can veer west just enough to keep those poles in sight," Longarm suggested, more to reassure Purity than as a practical suggestion. He knew better. Garrison's men were closing that whole area to them.

"Claim Jump is that way." Purity's voice was hoarse with frustration and desperation in the abruptly blazing heat. She swung her arm hopelessly toward the south-west.

"Your husband's out that way too," Longarm told her.

She nodded and rode silently for a long time. The sun cooked the sweat from them, simmering them in the incredible heat, scorching their necks and shoulders, broiling the tops of their heads. The fiery orb was reflected from the flat, pastel-red earth, from bald rocks and bare plateaus in blinding brilliance.

"I'm thirsty, Longarm," Purity said. For the first time, despair quavered in her voice.

"Soon," he said.

"I was too frantic trying to think of everything last night," she confessed. "I forgot water. I'm sorry."

"We'll find water soon."

She stared at him but didn't say anything. She knew he was lying to her.

When the horses faltered, they slowed the pace. Letting the tired animals plod across the rock-hard earth, Longarm squinted against the blinding glare, looking for the dust clouds that would pinpoint the three squads of searching riders. He found two plumes of dust against the sky, well to the south, but he was troubled by the absence of a third cloud.

Bringing his gaze back around again, south to north, he realized suddenly why he could not locate the third set of riders. That high, flaring butte toward which Purity had pointed them when they relinquished the riverbed now blocked their view. It loomed above them, dark with huge boulders and broken ground, and topped with pinyon. Distances were deceptive in this basin, but if the Mormons had circled west of the butte, it had to be within an hour's ride.

"Your ridge," he called to Purity. "Head for it."

She responded, but only listlessly. Nothing but determination kept her in the saddle.

They rode suddenly upslope into an outcropping of rock. Above them reared boulders bigger than a Mormon barn. Feeling his first glimmering of hope since he and Purity had ridden out of the valley settlement

157

last night, Longarm swung down from the saddle. Clutching the lines, he ran upward, leading his faltering horse into the outcrop.

He located a small clearing, walled in by high boulders. He removed the saddles from the perspiring horses and ground-tied them in the sparse grass. If the animals were hungry enough, they would eat the cheat grass and bitter-tasting sage. Sage was a last-resort food for horses, and Longarm didn't know how to tell them, but that's where they were—at a last resort.

"Come on," he said to Purity. He caught her hand in his, and staggering with weariness and the unsettling strangeness of walking after unbroken hours in the saddle, Purity followed him up a concealed goat path between the rocks.

"We'll find water, Purity," he whispered.

The exhausted girl tried to smile, but failed.

For what seemed an interminable climb, they scrambled up through the rock outcroppings. Then, his heart pounding, Longarm spotted further up the high wall a dense outgrowth of mesquite and sage. The moldy color of the brush promised water. Water! He dragged Purity after him now, climbing and clambering to a deep-set ledge where a sandy sump smelled cool and wet, with the pungency of damp pine. Trembling, he pushed through the hedgelike sage and stared, laughing, at a bubbling spring of crystal-clear water. A stunted pinyon, sedge, and green mesquite hedge insulated the oasis from the blazing desert, cooling, concealing, and isolating it.

"Oh, Longarm," Purity cried, exultant, "we've found water. They haven't beaten us yet, have they?"

"Anyway, we won't die thirsty."

Purity dropped to the grass surrounding the tiny spring. She pressed her face into the pool and drank frantically.

She managed to turn her head for a moment, smiling, revived. "Oh, God, Longarm, would you believe water could ever taste so good?"

Longarm watched her, grinning down at her beautiful reflection in the pool. Even fatigued after hours in the saddle, her blonde hair wild, she was a lovely young vision. No wonder old Nolan Garrison had gone home after he'd seen her the first time and had a revelation about her—a wet revelation, no doubt.

Sinking to his knees beside her, he drank, taking the water up in his cupped hands, gulping it down, and letting the cool drops run along his fevered chin and throat.

As he drank he was aware that Purity had slaked her thirst and now rolled over on her back. She lay prostrate, staring up at him, smiling tremulously. "Oh, Longarm," she whispered, "I've waited so long."

He bent down and kissed her, lightly at first. They had no time to waste; they had to stay alert and watchful. But her mouth was soft and cool and he felt a sharp, hot twinge flare up from the depths of his loins. He said, "God knows I want to, Purity. But there's two things I've got to do first."

"Oh, Longarm."

"Our lives might depend on my doing them."

"My life . . . depends on your doing it . . . to me . . . now."

"You just say that because it's true," he told her. "But there are always things that have to be done first in this life. It's hell, but it's true."

"What?" Her head rolled back and forth on the grass, her breath hot and forced. "What could be more important?"

"Water for those horses. If they can't run fast in this heat, we can't run."

"All right." She nodded, contrite. "But hurry. Please hurry, Longarm. I was that old man's wife for almost a year."

He kissed her again and grinned. "And the other thing—we've got to know where that third set of riders is." He tried to laugh. "They could catch us in the act, if we don't know where they are."

"Can you think of a better way to die?" she whispered, licking her tongue across her lips.

"I'd rather think about doing it and not dying at all," he said. "If we're smart enough."

Purity drew her hand along his face, stroking it longingly. "All right," she said. "Be smart. But for God's sake, be smart fast."

When he returned, Purity lay beside the pool as naked as the day she was born and as unselfconscious as a doe. She reclined on her outspread dress, waiting, her bent knees waving back and forth in a restrained but tormented rhythm of their own.

"Did you find them?" she whispered, watching him through heavy-lidded eyes.

Gazing at her nude beauty, Longarm nodded abstractedly. He could feel himself rising rigidly to the occasion. "And watered the horses and left undone all those things I ought not to have done."

She gazed up at the bulge in the front of his skin-tight trousers. "Are the riders . . . very far away?"

He did not take his eyes from the soft, full rise of her breasts. "Far enough."

"Thank God." She smiled like a sleepy but sensual and voluptuous baby, and held out her arms to him. Just enough sunlight penetrated the cool bower to highlight the ruby and gold color of her breasts, drawn taut when she raised her arms.

He knelt beside her on the grass. She moved close to him and began talking in a low, overheated whisper about what she wanted him to do to her, what she had dreamed of his doing to her, what she had wanted all those nights at the settlement when she had stared at his wonderful maleness and could do nothing about it. He wanted to warn her once more that they might be throwing away their only chance to get out of this alive. He felt it was only honest to warn her that wasting time and precious energy like this could be fatal. But she needed loving, and besides, she'd already said it: God had yet to invent a better way to die.

She pulled away his clothing and drew him down to her. "I'm wild for you," she whispered. "I'm boiling hot. Touch me there . . . touch me . . . you'll see."

He touched her, breathing raggedly, and tried to smile. "Does part of the excitement come from the dan-

160

ger of making love when you know damned well we ought to be running?"

"We'll run," she whispered, her eyes fluttering closed. "Only I can't stand it anymore. Do it. Oh, please, do it to me."

She held him close in her arms. All the foreplay she needed had been accomplished in her lonely bed during all those thwarted, repressed nights at the settlement. She removed his gunbelt, tossing it behind him. She unbuttoned his shirt and then ripped open the buttons of his fly—and finally got what she so desperately wanted.

As Purity slaked her long-inhibited, wildly aroused, and seemingly insatiable hunger, Longarm forgot the armed men riding steadily across the sage toward them. Purity was right—this was a hell of a lot better than chopping cotton, though the way she did it, it was much more strenuous. She reached her first climax almost immediately, but wouldn't even slow her rhythmic thrusting or release him for a second. She clung to him and kissed his face, his jawline, his throat and shoulder, her mouth parted, her breath hot and fast. She seemed to drink in the salty sweat of his body thirstily.

Her lips and hands suckled and caressed and seduced him, her lips flailed under him, slowly at first and then more violently. She breathed loudly, gasping and whimpering and saying his name over and over as if its very sound were an aphrodisiac. She sank her teeth into the soft flesh between his shoulder and chest, and seemed not to breathe at all.

Fiery, blinding flames of desire raged upward from the deepest well of his groin. He felt her ankles lock tighter and tighter at the small of his back. He couldn't move now even if Elder Nolan Garrison himself stood over them and pumped hot lead and the wrath of God into them.

Longarm felt as if the sun had seared away a circle of leaves and concentrated all its fire on his spine. As wantonly as Purity bucked and boiled and writhed beneath him, he was not dislodged. He was part of her

161

in that instant. They flailed and battered each other in delicious madness.

She sank her teeth with silent ferocity deeper into his shoulder. He clutched her surging hips in both his hands, digging his fingers into her buttocks and forcing her up to him with all his strength. She twisted and pressed upward, trying to extract from him his last full measure of devotion!

He erupted, feeling himself ejaculate in smoldering, simmering, seething release. Purity's whole body quivered, shuddering and trembling in her own sweetly agonized satisfaction. Once more, before she would release him, she reached a fiery, helpless climax and then sagged beneath him, exhausted but still clinging to him, her arms and legs and teeth locked tighter than ever.

At last she lay back, pallid and sweating and smiling, her blonde hair spilling across the grass.

"It was what I dreamed, Longarm," she breathed. "It was everything I dreamed."

Panting with fatigue, he tried to smile down into her pale, happy face. "You willing to let them kill you now?"

"The hell with that," Purity whispered. "I want to live now, more than ever."

Even though Purity tried to delay him by kissing and nuzzling him in erotic abandon, Longarm pulled away from her and rebuttoned his clothing.

On his knees, he crawled to the rim of the shaded pine bowered oasis. He parted the limbs of the stunted pinyon and surveyed the flat, hot country east of them.

He signaled to Purity to join him. She crawled to him and pressed against him, her bare breast flattened on his arm. He pointed toward a boll of dust on the plain. Three somber horsemen rode slowly, warily away from them toward the east.

"They passed us," he whispered, awed.

"Of course they did." She clutched his arm, smiling. "While we were doing God's work."

Longarm exhaled heavily. "Dress. We've got just one chance to head west on them. Let's take it now."

She nodded and grabbed up her clothing. She dressed as they crept swiftly but silently down through the rocks. "I'm with you all the way," Purity said. "All the way to the nearest hotel bed."

The low snuffling of their horses, slightly rested and grazing on meager clumps of cheat grass among the rocks, reassured Longarm. Those men had undoubtedly searched down here, but they had missed the small entrance into the walled clearing.

He saddled the horses and lifted Purity in his arms. For one long moment, instead of sitting her on her horse, he held her. His hand covered her breast, feeling the pounding of her heart through its fullness. No matter what happened now, they had shared an idyll in that copse above them that few people ever experienced. They would never find another moment quite like this again. In that isolated oasis, they had loved each other with the fury of the doomed, the avidity of the starved, the ecstasy of the passionately attracted. One perfect moment in life. Millions of people lived and died and never had that.

He kissed her gently and set her in her saddle. Leading his own horse, he went quietly through the twisted path out of the huge corral of boulders.

They came out on the lower slope and Longarm hesitated, searching the open country. In the distance he saw telegraph poles like tiny sticks in the sagebrush, their lines glittering. The basin land between looked empty and open to them.

"Let's go," he whispered.

He swung into the saddle, trying not to hurry but nevertheless unable to shake a sense of unexplained wrong. A tense stillness hung over the rocky upland. He listened, but heard only the soft clopping of the hooves of their own horses.

He sidled cautiously out of the barricade of rocks, pushing aside a bush, and stepped out into sunstruck brilliance. He hesitated, holding back the prickly underbrush and motioning Purity to ride slowly and warily past him. She nodded, restraining her horse and turning the animal west toward the open basin land.

A whisper of sound ten feet behind and above him galvanized Longarm. He jerked his gun from its holster and spun around, crouching. The sun glittered on a gun barrel in the brush above him. The gunfire cracked sharply from the rocks, echoing clearly across the plains.

Devilish cunning guided that gunman's attack. He not only sent the alarm to the other riders, turning them back from the plains, but he killed Purity's horse.

Shot in the head, the animal buckled to its knees. Purity leaped free of the saddle just in time, before the horse fell sideways and trapped her. The animal struggled for a moment, head rearing in a terrible instinct to persist, then it toppled, dead.

Longarm saw all this in the flash of time that it took him to swing up his gun and fire directly into the red center of that puff of gunsmoke. He heard a man gasp from the rocky plateau.

"Keep down," Longarm said to Purity. "Stay low, behind your horse."

Flinging his horse's reins behind him to the ground, Longarm ran back into the rocks and scrambled over them, his rage giving him the agility of a maddened mountain goat.

He leaped through the rocks as he heard someone running and stumbling downslope. The man heard him, a broad-shouldered, black-suited fellow in a squared hat. He stopped dead in his tracks and spun around, levering the rifle in his hand, firing from the hip as if he held a pistol.

Before the man could squeeze the trigger, Longarm shot him. The sound rattled and echoed outward from the rocks. He saw the bulky man half-drop, half-throw his rifle from him, and plunge down the incline in a shower of stones. Longarm waited to see no more. He threw himself along the broken path through the rocks, searching for the man's horse.

He could not find the animal. The men on that plain were riding fast toward the ridge. Damn clever, these faithful.

He paused, seeing three clouds of dust smoking upward in the breathless stillness of the basin. The hard-riding Mormons were converging on him.

He waited to see no more. He abandoned the hope of taking the hidden horse, and ran through the narrow path and grabbed the lines of his own mount. Moving out of the copse, he swung up into the saddle. Purity stood up. He reached down, caught her about the waist, and hefted her up behind him.

The horse was already trotting, ears pricked high, heading west across the open basin.

Chapter 14

The desert sprawled out before them, a blazing crucible from crimson horizon to blue-hazed infinity. Barren, gray, dead—and deadly—wastes. Longarm felt the strange and terrifying pressure of awesome silence, relentless and unbroken stillness, the fearful quiet of isolation and cosmic solitude, of the terrible loneliness of remote and hostile wild lands, and no place to hide.

Behind them the dust clouds blossomed, big-bellied, threatening, mushrooming on three sides, closing in with a steady and implacable deadliness.

The tired horse faltered, stumbling, and Longarm swung down from the saddle and caught the checkrein. "Stay in the saddle as long as he can carry you," he told Purity.

But she swung her leg over the saddle horn and slipped to the ground in the riverbed. She strode along beside Longarm.

"No use fooling ourselves," she said. "That horse has done all he can for us."

"I thought I was fooling you," he said.

Purity shook her head. "My father bred horses before he gambled them all away." She laughed in remembered pain. "As he raised a pretty daughter with a nice Irish singing voice, until he gambled *her* away."

"Men do hellish things."

She sighed. "But you'd think a father . . ." her voice trailed off. She exhaled heavily and swung her arm helplessly toward the growing dust clouds. "I guess we've got enough milk about to go sour so we don't have to worry about milk already spilt."

He grinned. "Very well put, like a good Irish lass."

Suddenly the exhausted horse jerked back on the reins and tried to rear, but the animal was almost overwhelmed by fatigue. It could only set its forelegs and stand unmoving, quivering.

Longarm heard the blood-chilling whir and jerked his head around.

Three or four feet ahead of him, coiled in the dead center of the sandy riverbed, a rattlesnake sunbathed in that most dangerous state of lethargy, sluggish but testy, and far from comatose in the blaze of the sun. The reptile was like some prehistoric serpent that had slithered from the earliest vales of time, in size and ugliness. It measured seven inches in diameter across its sleek body. Its head was large and poised, weaving from side to side. Its thirteen or more rattles—no time for an accurate count!—whirred in the silence like frenzied castanets.

Longarm glanced over his shoulder toward those ominous, approaching dust clouds, then looked again at the monster snake, the monarch of this area, its kingdom this riverbed and the unmarked acreage in every direction around it.

The horse stood, legs quivering but head erect, nostrils dilated. Longarm found a long greasewood stick, as hard as steel. He couldn't shoot the varmint; that would bring those riders straight in upon them. Garrison's men were gaining fast enough as it was.

He threw river rocks, trying to chase the creature out of the channel bed. The rattles whirred faster, frantic and angry, like the warning buzz of a thousand hornets.

Purity said, "That thing's not even afraid of God. You'll have to kill it." She handed him a varnished, knobby pole that was as out of place in this wilderness as a diamond tiara would have been. It was heavy hardwood that had been shaved, stripped, and stained —and for some reason discarded in the middle of nowhere. "Kill it with this," Purity told him.

Longarm took the rod from her. He hefted it in his hand. It made a hell of a club. He wanted to run the serpent out of here if he could, but time was running out.

Longarm removed his coat and secured it on the thorny greasewood stick. He extended it to within a foot of the rattlesnake. The huge reptile drew its head back and, with a bullet's speed, struck it, its fangs glistening wet with venom, sinking into the fabric. Longarm clubbed at that wedge-shaped head, catching it cleanly. The snake folded to the ground, writhing but not lifting its head.

Throwing his coat behind him, Longarm used both poles to heft the ten-foot-long creature up and out of the riverbed, onto the rocky bank.

He tossed the sticks aside. "Let's go. I don't know how bad that critter's headache is, and I don't want to find out."

He caught the fallen lines. The horse tried to move forward, but it could not, and gave up. It trembled, stumbled, and almost fell, its head sagging.

Longarm removed the saddle and bridle from the lathered animal. He hurled the gear into the waist-high sage clumps and slapped the horse on the rump. "Get out of here," he shouted. "Find water."

He hoped his raised voice would shock the animal into one last burst of energy. The freed horse lurched, hesitated, and, when Longarm shouted again, suddenly jerked its head up and trotted away, faltering, along the riverbed, as if following a scent too faint for human senses.

"Ho!" A shout came from beyond a knoll that rose abruptly from the river, with a telegraph pole sprouting from it.

Purity and Longarm halted, taut, stunned.

Longarm stared toward the crest of the knoll. Beyond it he could see the parade-dress column of telegraph poles and lines.

He gazed at Purity a moment, then drew his gun and called, "Anybody up there?"

"Nobody but us chickens!" came the answer, followed by a belly-laugh.

Holding his gun at his side, with Purity at his heels,

Longarm ran up the steep incline. At the crest he hesitated, crouched to his knee, removed his hat, eased up behind a rock outcropping, and peered over it.

His mouth sagged open. A highly polished but now dusty runabout carriage, with narrow-rimmed tires for speed, and a canopy top and upholstered boot and backrest, was pulled up on a dim trail under the telegraph wires, perhaps the memory of some forgotten wagon trace west.

The glistening single-seated carriage bore a sign on its side: *"Read the Claim Jump LEGALIZER and Go to Bed at Night With Nothing on Your Mind."*

But neither the vehicle nor its sign surprised Longarm as much as the appearance of the man gripping the reins and grinning up at him against the sun.

The first thing that Longarm noticed was that the man was big—probably six feet tall, standing—but at two hundred and forty pounds he was bulky, thick-shouldered, keg-chested, beer-bellied, thighs and upper legs like rough-cut chunks of marble encased in Levi's. His square-jawed head was large, and his nose was broad and hooked. One leg was wrapped in a heavy cast from toes to hip; it extended out the side of the carriage and was braced against an iron hand-rest. The man wore a battered Stetson pushed back on his yellow hair that faded rapidly to gray along the temples and sideboards. He wore rimless glasses over tired, astigmatic blue eyes. Somewhere in his early forties, his face was creased with baked-in laugh lines, and he brayed a loud laugh toward them.

"You folks plannin' on stayin' up there, hidin' from me?"

Longarm stood up. He replaced his gun in its holster and walked with Purity in the searing sunlight down to the carriage.

"Where you folks headed?" the man said. He laughed. "Or are you setting up houseless housekeeping in them rocks up there?"

"Our horse just gave out on us," Longarm said.

"Ain't that the way with a horse? They always pick the worst possible times to fall down on you. I mean, you ride a horse double for three or four days in this heat, and that worthless critter is liable to get the mollywobbles for no good reason." He laughed, enjoying his own humor vastly.

"Didn't seem all that amusing to us at the time," Longarm said, glancing over his shoulder.

"Forgive me, friend, forgive me . . . I'm noted for saying the wrong thing. Once asked the mother of a condemned man if she was hanging around after the tie party. Called a bald man a long-faced liar, and just yesterday told the fattest woman in town that somebody said she was taller layin' down than she was standing up. Always saying the wrong thing. Crazy about one-line jokes. Crazy. Groaners, I call 'em. That propensity has cost me some rewarding employment. By the way, sir, I am Eastlake Hollinsworth, editor of the Claim Jump *Legalizer*. And that's my real monicker. Eastlake Hollinsworth. What a name for a tramp journalist like me. Probably the biggest joke of all. Tell you, though, the most popular column in my paper each week is one I call WARTS—that's 'Worst Awful Rotten Tall Stories.' Folks send 'em in or tell 'em to me. I collect groaners. I always say a good groaner is better than a broken leg most any day in the week."

"Been out here collecting groaners?" Longarm gave the approaching dust clouds another nervous glance.

Hollinsworth shook his head and laughed immoderately. "Well, kind of. Came out to the Shaftsville Mine. Heard there was a robbery-killing. Sounded like the headline story I needed. But I reckon I won't be able to use it. Our sheriff, Wyatt Peale—you acquainted with Sheriff Peale? No? Well, it turns out Sheriff Peale did the killing. Man was robbing the mine guard. Sheriff Peale shot the guard instead of the robber. Killed him dead as my story, because I also found out accidentally that Sheriff Peale made the mistake on purpose. So I got no story. Got this broken leg writing things the town fathers objected to . . . don't write stories like that anymore. Save 'em up. Write jokes, groaners . . . I don't learn fast, as the fellow said when he shot his mule after being kicked in the head for the third time, but I learn good. Where you folks headed?"

"Claim Jump," Purity said, with some anxiety in her tone.

"Well, why didn't you say so? Get in. It's a right smart ride, but this buggy moves fast. Man don't own a fast buggy ought not to fool around with other men's wives, eh, friend?"

"Sounds reasonable to me," Longarm said.

"Then I can't use it in my column. No good if it makes sense. Don't want to make sense. Want to make you groan."

They got into the carriage. Eastlake Hollinsworth slapped the reins and the horse moved forward smartly. "If he don't move fast enough to suit me," Hollinsworth said, "I yell my groaners at him. He's a right speedy critter."

Longarm glanced back over his shoulder. The dust glowed larger, clearer in the plains behind them. He wondered how long the canny Mormons would follow the tracks laid down by Longarm's horse in the riverbed. Every moment was urgent. He'd feel better when he got to the Western Union office at Claim Jump and sent his report to Vail. The fact that he would report Garrison's condemning him to death to the federal government would not stop the righteous elder, but it would point a finger of guilt at him in case the unforgiving man refused to give up this chase, and Longarm knew that nothing and nobody was going to stop the vengeful lord of Golconda Valley.

He wished he had the telegraph key he always carried in his saddlebags, but he had lost most of his possibles, along with his army horse, to the Paiutes. One of the diggers would likely make a piece of jewelry out of the hunk of gleaming brass.

Longarm had to bite hard on his lip to keep from suggesting that Eastlake Hollinsworth step up the pace of his horse. The big man knew the capabilities of his animal, the distance to Claim Jump, the danger of pushing a horse in this heat.

Longarm could not resist checking over his shoulder.

He knew that the observant Hollinsworth was aware of the way he watched the backtrail, but almost pointedly the editor ignored it. Maybe he'd learned to stay aloof from the troubles of strangers, especially strangers found prowling in the open desert country.

Hollinsworth studied Purity with some interest. He said, "Ain't you a Mormon, young lady?"

"I was," Purity said. "I resigned. I'm going to become a singer with Trixie Mondale's musical comedy company."

"Oh, do you know Trixie Mondale?" Hollinsworth said.

"Not yet. But I look pretty good when I'm dressed up. And I can sing."

"Sing me a little something."

Longarm listened to them, deciding that either he was suffering from sunstroke or they were. Not even the belly-laughing Hollinsworth could be unaware of the growing clouds of dust converging into one in the plains behind them, and following them like a hungry cat.

Purity glanced over her shoulder, drew a deep breath, and sang a few bars of "Kathleen Mavourneen" for Hollinsworth. Her lovely voice ate through the acid of anxiety consuming Longarm, and when Purity stopped singing, he applauded.

"You're really good, young lady," Hollinsworth said. "But a musical comedy company—that ain't no easy life."

"It doesn't matter. It will be better than my life back there."

Hollinsworth whistled. "You're running away from a Mormon settlement?"

Purity nodded. Hollinsworth glanced across her at Longarm. "And you're putting your neck in the noose by helping her?"

"It's a long story," Longarm said. "And leaving was a kind of mutual deal."

"And you figure those dust clouds are being made by the Mormons?"

"Very likely," Longarm said.

"We'd appreciate it very much if you could get us to Claim Jump alive and ahead of those men," Purity said.

"You think you'd be safe in Claim Jump from them men?"

"I don't know," Purity said. "But we won't know if we don't try, and we won't make it if we don't move a little faster. I know it's your horse, and I hate to ask you."

Eastlake Hollinsworth laughed deep in his rotund belly and laid the whip across his horse. The light buggy bounced, speeding ahead. The hot breeze slashed like fiery knives at their faces. "Don't mind," Hollinsworth shouted. "What the hell? Got to hurry anyway. Got a hell of a story to write—about two people escaping from the Mormons."

The horse kept a steady pace along the road, which gradually took form and became more than a dim cart path through the wilderness.

"I had a girlfriend once that wanted to be an actress," Hollinsworth said. "I told her she'd never make it. But she thought she would because she had everything a man wants—a hairy chest and big muscles." His laughter boomed above the rattle of the carriage, the clopping of hooves, and the pounding of blood in Longarm's temples. The big, booming voice rose. "And that fat woman I mentioned? I told her I could get her a job with the circus, but that she'd have to work for peanuts. Get it? Big? Fat? Have to work for peanuts?"

"I got it," Purity said in a flat tone.

"Well, you didn't groan," Hollinsworth said.

"I groaned inside," Purity told him. "Do they have any shows in Claim Jump, Mr. Hollinsworth?"

"They got some, but they're all in saloons. No place for a pretty little miss like you, straight off a Mormon farm. Seems to me you ought to go to Denver to get started."

"I need a job. I won't be taken back by those people," Purity said. "I don't care where I sing."

"I would agree, anywhere but in Claim Jump, missy. We got the dregs of the world out here. A slab-sided, lean-to-and-tent-town with a population about equal to

Denver's. Why, the best man in our town in Sheriff Wyatt Peale, and if he was an outhouse, they'd condemn him, that's how low he is. I tell you, Claim Jump is a great town for animals. A wolf comes through town, and a few months later, here comes the stork. I tell you true, I could not believe it when Plitt Shawlene wanted to start a newspaper out here in Claim Jump. You know, ol' Plitt owns a string of cow-town newspapers. But most are in county seats or in state capitals, like Carson City. I told him, I said—"

Longarm leaned forward. "You know Plitt Shawlene?"

"Like that." Hollinsworth twisted one finger over another. "That's Plitt on the bottom, of course. Hell, I was in Denver not long ago. Visited ole Plitt. Just a few weeks ago, as a matter of fact."

"That's the answer," Longarm said.

"Sure it is," Hollinsworth agreed. "Now all we need is a question to go with it."

"Who is Trixie Mondale's best friend in Denver?" Longarm said, grinning. He forgot to glance over his shoulder for the moment.

Hollinsworth shrugged. "Beats me. Who?"

Longarm frowned, staring at him. "Why, Plitt Shawlene. If we both sent wires to Shawlene, and sent Purity on to Denver as quick as possible—"

"There's a Central Pacific train east at four o'clock. Stops at Claim Jump, too."

"Can we make Claim Jump by four o'clock?" Longarm asked.

Hollinsworth pulled out his watch and consulted it. "We can just make it. If the creek don't rise, horse doesn't stumble in a hole, and we can outrun your friends, we can just make it."

Purity grabbed Longarm's arm, gripping it fiercely. "Oh, Longarm," she whispered. "Must I go? So soon?"

"Aha," Hollinsworth laughed. "I see it wasn't all shooting and running out there in the boondocks."

"It wasn't all fun and games, either," Longarm said. He nodded toward Purity. "It's the only way you'll be safe. On a train that doesn't stop between here and Salt

Lake City. A train they won't even know you're on. When you get to Denver, you go straight to a man named Chief Marshal Billy Vail. Tell him I sent you. Tell him to get you to Plitt Shawlene. And tell Plitt Shawlene that he owes me, and that this will wipe out all past debts when he takes you for a tryout with Trixie Mondale. I've got an idea Trixie is going to love you."

"Sounds practical and sensible. Sounds like it will work," Hollinsworth agreed. "And I'll send a hymn of praise by wire to Plitt about you. Don't see how you can lose. There is one thing, though . . ."

"What's that?" Purity said.

"You catch that four o'clock limited, missy. But that name, Purity. You leave it behind you in Claim Jump. That name will get you nowhere in musical comedy."

Claim Jump was all that Eastlake Hollinsworth had said it would be—and less.

Longarm stared, shocked at a town such as even he had never seen before. Sun-stunned, slab-sided, jerry-built structures sprawled carelessly over the broken ground, as randomly as tossed dice. The most carefully constructed abode within the town limits looked as if it had been thrown together overnight, between beers. One long, wide avenue cut arrow-straight from one end of town to the other. Like dirty, grasping fingers, sin-ister alleyways crept off from the main street, strong-armed between the close-packed hovels. Every habitation had been wrought of the handiest materials available, and in the desert country this could be down-right makeshift. There were adobe walls roofed with domed or gabled canvas. Tenting draped from flat, tarpapered roofing. There were tents of every size, shape, color, and design. Clothes were hung on grass ropes to dry in every alleyway and open space. There were even a few respectably constructed wooden and adobe-brick structures boasting shingled roofing—the railroad depot, the office and printing plant of the Claim Jump *Legalizer*, the county building, a couple of the dozen or so saloons, a general store, a feed-and-grain warehouse, a hotel, and the local offices of the silver-producing companies.

Eastlake Hollinsworth drove his horse imperiously through the teeming streets. The pedestrians did not look at moving vehicles, in the belief that if you didn't look at them, the drivers wouldn't run you down—a proven fallacy. Hollinsworth ignored the people he met as he drove, letting them fend for themselves, lunging frantically for safety at the last minute.

"Almost made the headlines," he would yell at the pedestrians as he skimmed past them. "Another tragic traffic fatality."

Hollinsworth had not exaggerated. The population of Claim Jump equaled or exceeded that of Denver—crushed into one-tenth the land area. The streets looked like a huge cauldron into which the dregs of western humanity had settled—temporarily.

Hollinsworth drove them to the adobe-fronted hotel. He checked his watch and told them they had thirty minutes before the Central Pacific eastbound was due, and it had never been on time yet. He smiled and wished Purity great good fortune and success in her new career. "Just get on that train, missy. Just get on that train and get out of here."

"She'll make it," Longarm told him.

Hollinsworth nodded. He said, "And you, Longarm, you'll find me the most knowledgable person in Claim Jump on the lowlife and vermin that infest our environs. And since we have at the present *only* lowlife vermin, I'm a veritable fund of information. If you need my help in apprehending your culprits, call on me, my man. I'm like the golden-hearted fancy lady—I want to help."

While Purity bathed and refreshed herself in the hotel room, Longarm bought her ticket to Denver. From the general store he bought a picture hat—which the clerk said was all the rage in San Francisco—a dark veil, and an extremely modest dress. The gown he chose was of fashionable fabric, but sedately cut. He chose it purposely. He hoped to conceal Purity's identity as much as possible under picture hat, veil, and shapeless frock—all the way to the safety of Chief Billy Vail's staid protection in Denver.

"Don't you talk to strangers," he warned Purity as she dressed. "Not even nice little old ladies. And no traveling salesmen."

"I wish I thought you were jealous," she said.

"I *am* jealous," he said, to please her. "And not half as jealous as I am afraid for you. There are a lot of miles of Mormon country between here and Denver."

It was four o'clock long before Purity was ready to part with Longarm. She kept remembering those heated moments in that hidden oasis. It wouldn't have been so bad, but she insisted on remembering out loud. He felt the stormy stirring of excitement inside him, but it couldn't eat through the fear he felt for her. She had to be on that train before Nolan Garrison and his riders got into town.

Purity's lovely eyes brimmed with tears. She tossed the veil back from her face, gazed at Longarm, and sighed. "When you get back to Denver," she said, on the verge of unhappy tears, "save a weekend for me. Please. Just one weekend in a nice soft bed somewhere. That's not too much to ask for saving your life, is it?"

He laughed, caught her in his arms, and kissed her. She pressed her body to his, and he felt her sensuous form writhing against him. Her heart thundered through the fulsome insulation of her breasts.

He backed away, grinning. "Oh, no," he said. "You'd miss your train."

"Wouldn't it be worth it?" she whispered, eyes glazed.

"No. You've got a fantastic career in singing ahead of you—if you get out of here fast enough. I'll see you in Denver."

"You promise?"

"You can sue me."

They left the hotel and walked through the streets to the depot. Longarm insisted that Purity keep her veil draped over her face. He kept watching the wide, busy street and the open country beyond. There was no sign yet of Garrison's riders. But there was no sign of the train, either.

They stood together on the platform. Purity clung fiercely to his hand. When the train paused long enough to pick up mail and passengers, Longarm kissed her through her veil and put her in the coach. She sat at the window, crying softly and throwing him kisses.

Longarm stood on the platform, smiling up at her with a bravado more feigned than real. He still could not discern dust clouds from the east, but the train seemed reluctant to depart. He wished it would get on its way.

As the train coughed and shook and chattered forward on the rails, Longarm felt a surge of hope for Purity, and at the same time a sense of loss and, over it all, a chilling fear that things hadn't even started to go wrong yet.

He stood there until the train was gone, then shouldered his way through the crowds on the main street and went into the Western Union office.

The telegrapher, sitting at a silent key, began to shake his head. Longarm spread out the messages he wanted to send on the desktop—two concerning Purity, one from him and one from Eastlake Hollinsworth to Plitt Shawlene—and a report on his investigation to date for Billy Vail.

"I'm sorry, can't take in any messages," the clerk said.

"This is government business." Longarm showed his marshal's badge. "Urgent."

"We don't get messages in this place unless they *are* urgent, Marshal," the operator said. "I'm sorry, but the lines are down east of here again." He shook his head, frustrated. "We got crews out looking for the breaks, but meanwhile, no messages go east of Claim Jump."

178

Chapter 15

"Those blasted wires," Eastlake Hollinsworth roared. "Cut again. This is intolerable, Longarm. Intolerable."

"The government isn't exactly thrilled about it either," Longarm said in a mild tone.

The bulky man struggled out of his squealing swivel chair. Bracing himself on an odd hardwood single crutch with a deeply padded head, which snuggled under Hollinsworth's armpit as if it were an appendage of his body, the editor paced back and forth in the crowded, cluttered front office. In the rear of the print shop a lone woman worked under a single lamp that was suspended from the ceiling on wires with pulleys, so it could be shifted as she worked in various areas. At the moment she was at the old square print cases, with a metal stick in her hand and a pair of tweezers. She was setting type. She did not turn around or look up from her task.

"Did they say where them wires were cut this time?" the editor wanted to know.

"They don't know yet. Only that it's east of Claim Jump."

"I know what you're thinking," Hollinsworth said, prowling awkwardly up and down between stacks of boxes, old newspapers, and flat printing forms. "You're thinking that this points directly at them Mormon farmers as the culprits. Am I right?"

Longarm nodded. "It could be them."

"Yes." Using his crutch as a weapon, Hollinsworth swung at a spider on the rafters. "Hate them things. Bit by one of 'em once. Swelled up four times normal. After that, I put one on my privates, but the damned unobliging creature wouldn't bite it. Have hated 'em ever since." He laughed and secured the knobby crutch under his armpit again. "One thing about them—them Mormons, I mean. If they did cut these wires this time—let's say they did, 'cause they wanted to come up on you and Miss Purity before you got word back to your people in Denver."

Longarm nodded. "They could have done that. But if they did, they only muddied up the waters."

"My sentiments precisely. I don't see them Mormons cutting telegraph wires as a steady practice. They know —as much as they hate them wires—that cutting them would bring investigating teams in. And that's the last thing they want."

"That's the way I feel about it. They got a motive— for this one time. They want to stop me and Purity from getting away. But I got a feeling that it's something bigger than anything those Mormons are mixed up in. They want, above everything else, to be let alone."

"There's a lot of that going around, that wanting to be let alone." Hollinsworth hobbled in his office from desk to stack of litter and back, like a wounded, caged buffalo.

"That's what I wanted to talk to you about," Longarm said. "You know all the people around here—and I imagine you know a lot of their secrets. Who has the most to gain when those wires are down, time after time?"

Hollinsworth plopped down at his rolltop desk. He shouted, "Hey, Mother, get me my medicine, will you?"

The woman in the rear of the shop laid down the stick of type on which she was working. She padded up the dark aisle beside the old flatbed press.

Longarm caught his breath. "Mother" was an Indian girl, a beauty somewhere in her twenties. Her beauty reminded Longarm of Vince Thayer's Indian wife, May Cloud. But this young woman was mature, serene, and coolly lovely, where May Cloud was immature, unfinished. This girl was breathtakingly lovely, where May Cloud was an extraordinarily pretty young girl.

The Indian woman went to a chest near Hollins-worth's desk and took out a bottle of bourbon and two glasses. She set the glasses on the desk between Long-arm and Hollinsworth. "Help yourself," Hollinsworth said. "I have Setao lock the booze away from me, because I'd rather drink than work any day. In fact, if Setao didn't set type and lay out the pages, this damn paper would never make it to the streets every Thurs-day. Setao's a smart Indian girl. Not too much educa-tion. Way she sets type is by letters and divided words —whether she recognizes the words or not. You give Setao perfect copy, she gives you back perfect sticks of type—letter for letter, word for word. Any mistake you make for her, she's going to make for you. By the way, Setao is my wife. Legal as hell."

Longarm hid his astonishment behind the glass from which he took a long pull of raw whiskey.

"Got her a long time ago. Had a paper farther back east. In Oklahoma. Marrying Setao was a lot cheaper than hirin' a printer's devil. And besides, she slept in." He waved his arm, dismissing the beautiful young woman. "You can get back to work now, Mother. I know you got a lot to do."

Setao gave Longarm a warm, devastating smile, then turned and padded back along the dark aisle to her work.

"To get back to your problem, Longarm. The bad part of it is, there ain't no simple answer to who would benefit when the wires are down. As you have already seen today, we've got some of the *scum de scum* of the lawless here in this boomtown. Men who don't want their whereabouts known to the federal government. To me, that's one possibility. Another is the very make-up of this town's government. The men behind it are in here to rake off everything they can. Let me give you an example. Remember I told you about Sheriff Wyatt Peale? Well, Wyatt never was rightfully elected sheriff. The fellow that ran against him, Palmer Troy, was elected. Palmer was killed that same night—and the word came down from somebody here in town that

Wyatt was to be sworn in as sheriff as if he had won the election.

"And that's the cleanest side of politics. It's getting so people won't even vote for these rascals; they say votin' for them just encourages them. No, sir, I hate to say it, but this town is run for the profit of a few. There's somebody here that runs everything. I don't know who he is, though of course I have my strong suspicions. Anyhow, they all got reasons to cut wires. And then there's always greed and graft and duplicity at work wherever there's big money at stake, like in the silver mines that have opened up here. Take an example. Today you got a mine running full force and bringing out silver worth millions. Suddenly you got a mine that's petered out. Just like that. Now if you knew that, and also knew that money men back East had been pestering you to buy you out, wouldn't it be nice if the wires went down suddenly until you could unload your worthless silver mine on some unsuspecting Eastern swindler?"

"That suggests a hell of a motive," Longarm agreed. "But mines don't fail fast enough to explain this rash of vandalism."

"No. Just throwing out lines for you to fish with, Longarm. Hell, there are all kinds of profits to be made, losses to be avoided, if you could just control the passage of information for a day or two. Even the ranchers might be cutting the lines. Seems to me they got less motive, but still a motive that would prompt them to act. They own their own land, but most of them graze federal grassland. They hate it when the government sells off some of that prime grazing land for homesteading. They hate homesteaders, bobwire, and probably the telegraph. You got a big country here, old son, and a big job. A hell of a big job. I don't envy you one damn bit."

The sun was setting when Longarm came out of the office of the Claim Jump *Legalizer*. He paused for a moment on the front steps of the building. People had quieted down some now, preparing or eating supper, or bunched into saloons. The streets were still crowded with people who seemed to straggle up and down because they had no direction, nothing to do with themselves when the mines were closed.

"You, there! You!"

Longarm stiffened, recognizing that stentorian voice. He stared as Nolan Garrison, looking like some feudal lord hewn from stone, rode toward him, backed by a dozen tired and dusty riders.

Garrison rode his horse up close to Longarm. His hat, tied with a string under his craggy jaw, was pushed back from his sun-baked face. His eyes seemed exaggeratedly pale, his beard, mustache, and eyebrows whiter than ever. The twilight wind from the plains swept along the street, striking against Garrison's flint-hard face.

"Where is she, Longarm?" Garrison's voice battered the sounds of the boomtown to silence. And, Longarm saw, it did one more thing not to Garrison's advantage. It attracted a curious and hostile crowd of boom-towners. They recognized the Mormons, and they didn't like them.

Longarm was even aware that, behind him, Eastlake Hollinsworth had hobbled on his crutch to the door and now stood there with a gun in the crook of his arm.

Around them on the wide, wind-rustled street, other cold-eyed, hostile men gathered, watching the Mormons with hatred and mistrust.

Longarm saw that Garrison was aware of all these negative factors. The crowd of hostile men, many of whom despised the Mormons simply because they didn't know them beyond rumor and lie, tempered any action Garrison may have laid out in advance.

But he had come to get his wife, and he was not to be denied. Perhaps the death penalty and the charges against Longarm could be adjudicated some other day, under more favorable circumstances, but he wanted his lovely wife. "Where is my woman, Long?"

"She left, Garrison. When we first got to town. She

said she had been thinking about it for a long time and she was going back."

Garrison sat motionless in his saddle, gazing at Longarm as if he were not outnumbered and surrounded by unfriendly Gentiles in an alien area. His pale eyes impaled the lawman. "I hope you understand, Custis Long. This is my notice to you: If you ever enter our lands again, as long as I live, your life is forfeit. To my people and my people's God, Custis Long, you are a condemned fugitive."

Longarm said, "I better warn *you*, Garrison. My reason for coming into your area has not been settled. It has not changed. I'll come back, Garrison, if I find that any of you are cutting government telegraph wires."

Garrison seemed pleased about this. He nodded, gazing down from his horse like an angel of vengeance. "Do that, Mr. Long. Come back. For any reason. We look forward to that day."

Longarm was exhausted by the time he reached the hotel where he had rented a room. He yawned helplessly as he crossed the open porch to the double doors of the lobby. Like everyone else on the streets, he had remained unmoving until Garrison and his armed men had turned their horses and ridden east out of Claim Jump, unhurried and unyielding.

He entered the crowded lobby and walked across it toward the stairwell. It was suppertime, but he was too tired to eat. Maybe after he rested awhile. In a nightmare town like this, there would always be a cafe or saloon open where he could get something to eat— when he had energy enough to chew.

"Mr. Long. Mr. Long." The desk clerk was waving his arm and snapping his fingers to gain Longarm's attention.

Yawning, Longarm went to the registration desk. The clerk reached into a mail slot and brought out two slips of paper. On both of them were written: *"See me. Urgent. W. P."*

"Who is W. P.?" Longarm asked.

The clerk looked astonished. "Why that's Mr. Wyatt Peale, Mr. Long. Sheriff Wyatt Peale. He's been in here twice, very anxious to talk to you."

Longarm yawned helplessly. "If Mr. Peale comes in again, send him up to my room, will you?"

His shoulders sagging, his legs leaden with exhaustion, Longarm crossed the lobby and climbed the dark stairwell.

Sounds of gunfire awakened him. He awoke with a start, sitting up on his bed in his darkened hotel room. For a moment he didn't know where he was. The rumbling echoes sounded like a desert storm. Thunderous volleys rattled pictures on the wall.

He got up from the bed and went to the window, where he stood staring down at the main street.

No street lamps glowed down there, but the lamp and lantern light from stores, saloons, and other buildings radiated brightly across it. The center of the street was an open arena. People had cleared it and crowded against storefronts. After a moment he located the combatants. They faced each other like embattled gamecocks at fifty paces, angled across the avenue. One duellist stood in front of an adobe-walled, canvas-roofed saloon. His opponent was poised before a well-lit wooden structure, a competitive saloon.

That the two foes *stood* to face each other was not strictly accurate. They wavered drunkenly like reeds in a hurricane. They had fired three times at each other, and not even a bystander had been winged so far.

Longarm shook his head. Another ordinary evening in Claim Jump. He lost interest, but stood another few moments until the gunfighters steadied themselves to fire another salvo. Then he turned away and lit the lamp on his night table.

He checked his watch. He had been sleeping almost three hours. He felt refreshed, even hungry. He washed up, dressed, and left the room.

When he entered the lobby, the desk clerk called out to him, "Mr. Long, the Western Union office sent word.

The cut lines have been repaired. They're accepting messages again."

Longarm went directly along the street to the Western Union office, pushing his way through the crowds. The gunfighters had abandoned the feud, at least temporarily. One of the combatants had fallen and everybody had run out to him, thinking he had been hit, but he had not. He had passed out. The crowds spilled off the walks and life resumed its usual hectic boomtown pace.

He sent the messages regarding Purity and her flight to Denver. He decided against a lengthy report, after all, and sent three lines to Billy Vail, saying only that the investigation continued. He didn't want to implicate the digger Indians or the Mormons, which meant that so far he had little to recount.

When he was through, he stood at the desk and listed the names of the town fathers whom Eastlake Hollinsworth had mentioned earlier. He added Hollinsworth's name to the query and sent it off, asking Vail for as complete a report on each as the government could supply, as quickly as possible.

"Where was the cut in the lines?" Longarm asked the telegraph operator after he'd turned in his last message.

"Near Golconda Valley," the operator said. "They didn't pin it down any closer than that."

Longarm spread out the sheet of paper on which Billy Vail had indicated where each of the previous cuts had been made in the telegraph lines. He found Golconda Valley and made a dot on his map. Maybe he was wrong about the Mormons, but he couldn't believe it. They had more to lose than to gain by cutting those "devil's toy" wires.

He gazed at the map, finding no pattern except that most of the cuts—all but one, made near Elko, across the state—were within a day's ride of Claim Jump. The more he stared at that map, the more he was convinced that he had finally reached the seat of the trouble. People in this area had big investments in the game; they could make and lose fortunes just by tampering with the only communication lines.

He refolded the map, shoved it in his jacket pocket, and walked along the street to the sheriff's office.

A deputy glanced up from behind his desk, where he was studying the rotogravure pictures of a *Police Gazette*. He grinned. "This stuff gives you a hard-on," he said. "Shows their legs up above their knees, for God's sake." He slapped the garish newspaper in enthusiastic approval. "What can I do for you, sir?"

Longarm showed the deputy his marshal's badge. "Name's Long," he said. "Out of Denver."

"You the fellow they call Longarm?"

"Yeah. Where'd you ever hear of me?"

"Sheriff Peale. He said he heard you were in town. He's been looking for you. Acts like it's something urgent—to him, anyway. Sure wants to get in touch with you, all right."

"Has he packed it in for the night?"

The deputy shook his head. "Oh, no. He's prowling around town somewhere. Nights are our busy time, you know. All of us—even the sheriff hisself—we get most of our sleep from four till noon. That's our quiet time. If he drops by, I'll tell him you were looking for him, Marshal. Where can he find you?"

Longarm shrugged. "I'm going to get a bite to eat, then I'll be at the hotel."

"Where you going to eat?"

"I don't know, anyplace I can find open."

"Try Ptomaine Sal, across the street yonder. Food's no good, but Sal—hell, man, she's built like a Jersey milch cow."

Longarm finished off his steak and potatoes at Sal's, marveled one last time at the proprietress's truly enormous bust, and then went back out onto the main street, which was busier now than it had been at noon.

He checked in at the sheriff's office, but Peale had not been in again. He decided to check with Eastlake Hollinsworth, who might have some idea where Sheriff Peale hung out late in the evenings.

187

At first he thought the newspaper office was closed. Then he saw light breaking around the edges of drawn shades. He went close to the door, drew back his fist to knock, but then hesitated. Through the slit between the curtains, he got a slantwise view of the plant. Setao was setting type far along the aisle, and Hollinsworth was entertaining a visitor.

Longarm might have knocked on the door anyway, but there was something unusual in Hollinsworth's manner. His guest sat in an old wicker chair with his back to the door—not that Longarm would have recognized him anyway. He found nothing memorable about the guest; the only distinguishing mark about him, as seen from the door, was a monklike, round bald spot in the man's crown. Otherwise the man's hair was dark and he seemed heavyset and well fed, though possibly trim compared with Hollinsworth's bulk.

Hollinsworth wasn't laughing. This was what made Longarm pause and decide not to knock at all. When he had been with the *Legalizer* editor he had found him laughing, even when the subject was serious. There was tension in the way Hollinsworth leaned forward toward his guest and rested his weight on that single crutch. Something seemed to be troubling Hollinsworth deeply, and Longarm shrugged. He turned away, deciding not to intrude at this time of the night. Hollinsworth seemed to have his own woes.

Maybe the fellow didn't laugh at his one-liners.

He spent the next two hours nursing single beers in several saloons, talking to strangers, listening, asking questions. The talk was silver; that was the only topic of true interest. Even in those places where there were hostesses, the women were of secondary interest. A woman could let you down, break your heart, put you in the hoosegow or the madhouse, but a man who had enough silver could own the world.

It must have been after one o'clock in the morning before Longarm left the saloon. He had learned a couple of facts that interested him in line with his investigation. Silver ore mined out here had a value on the

Denver and New York silver exchanges in relation to how much was being mined, what quality, and how rich the veins were.

It seemed to him that anybody who could control the flow of information going out from Claim Jump and the silver mines to Denver and New York, for even as long as one day, might profit hugely and illegally. If they could buy silver much cheaper than the metal was selling in the eastern exchanges and suppress that news for a day or so, they could make a killing in a market that was buying on outdated information.

It presented a much more reasonable motive for periodically chopping down Western Union lines than the ranchers or the Indians or the Mormon settlers would ever have.

He walked out of the saloon and headed down the half-lighted street toward the Western Union office. If he could learn the names of individuals or corporations making huge deposits soon after the wire-cutting, he would have an interesting list of suspects.

He found the Western Union office closed. He swore and stood a moment in the darkness, listening to a rinkytink piano in one of the saloons.

He stepped off the sidewalk to cross an alley. From the black depths of the narrow passageway, a gun cracked. A bullet ripped past his face and he lunged backward, flattening himself against the wall of the Western Union office.

Far down the alley he saw a figure, crouched low, running. There was no doubt about it. Whoever had fired that shot had put Longarm's name on it.

He whipped out his gun, aware that men were spilling out of saloons and other buildings on both sides of the alleyway.

He saw only that his assailant had raced to the left around a building at the end of the dark alley, running like a pronghorn with the hots.

He ran along the alley, gun drawn. He half expected the gunman to sidle back to the corner of the alley and take another shot at him.

He kept his gaze fixed on that building at the end of the alley. He didn't bother to look down. He didn't even think about looking down.

When his feet struck the body of the man in the alley, Longarm went sprawling. He would have struck the ground, but he managed to throw himself against a wall and steady himself. He did land on his knees, but managed to hold onto his gun.

Then he turned and stared down at the unmoving body. Men with lanterns came running from both directions. They held the lights high.

The first man that reached the place where Longarm stood, shook his head and bawled, "Good name of God! It's Sheriff Peale. This son of a bitch has shot the sheriff."

Chapter 16

His gaze riveted to the dead man crumpled in the mud of the alley, Longarm straightened up. The lanterns and torches danced in the narrow passage, seeming to wheel and skid around his head like bats in a cave.

"Somebody killed him," Longarm said.

"You killed him, you son of a bitch," a man said.

Another nodded. "Couldn't have been nobody else. Couldn't of been no other way. Heard one shot. Ran out here quick as I could. Here he stands over pore ol' Sheriff Peale."

"I never much admired ole Wyatt," a man said. "But hell, he tried to do his job. He deserved better than this."

A man knelt beside the slain sheriff. He caught the corpse by the shoulder and turned him facedown. A bullet hole an inch in diameter blossomed redly in the sheriff's back. "Shot in the back. The pore son of a bitch. Shot in the back in an alley."

"String him up," somebody yelled.

Longarm remained standing over the slain official. He forgot the gun in his hand, the bullet hole in the sheriff's back, the mob howling for quick vengeance with a hanging rope.

He stared at the crown of the corpse's head. It was that round monk's-cap of baldness. This was the man he had seen earlier tonight in Eastlake Hollinsworth's office. He couldn't help thinking that maybe if he'd followed his instincts and knocked, gone inside, met Sheriff Peale, heard what was troubling the harried lawman, Peale might still be alive. God knew the man had tried hard enough all day to get in touch with him.

It was no wonder that even the jocular editor of the *Legalizer* had looked so intense and worried. Peale had had a problem all right, and it had been fatal.

"Wait a minute," Longarm said. He raised his voice to be heard over the animal growling of the mob.

"We heard the shot."

"Damn right we did, and we found you standing over the sheriff's body."

"What kind of proof do we need, mister?"

"You haven't any proof at all," Longarm told them. "There was a shot. One shot. Somebody shot at *me*. One shot. It grazed my face—"

"Ain't that always the way?" Somebody laughed. "When a man needs an alibi, the shot was at him, and it always just grazed him—didn't hit anything so he can prove where the bullet went. Look, mister, we all heard that one shot. It went in Wyatt Peale's back. And we found you standing over him. You look guilty as hell to me."

"But that's it," Longarm said. "The sheriff wasn't shot in this alley. He was killed somewhere else and dumped here. I was running after the jasper that shot at me. I tripped over his body."

"That kind of talk won't wash, stranger," a man said. "You got a hundred witnesses against you."

A roar went up from the mob that crowded the alley; newcomers were still pressing in.

"String him up. Hang him."

"Let's hang him. That'll stop his lying."

Longarm put his back against the wall. "I didn't do this," he said. "You people have got to listen to me."

"We heard all the lies there is, stranger, a hundred times, and that ain't stopped us from a hangin' yet."

"Get him out there," somebody said. "String him up."

The men closest to Longarm pressed in close. He tried to bring the gun up. As he turned, somebody struck him across the back of the neck. He stumbled forward and they had him. Men caught him and wrestled him to the wall. Somebody brought rope. In a moment they had snubbed him down like a rodeo calf.

He could barely walk with his ankles roped. But he didn't have to walk. The mob, growing louder and more bloodthirsty by the second, pressed him along the alley toward Main Street.

They spilled out of the alley, half carrying, half dragging Longarm. The lanterns spun and flew about him, the voices struck him like stones.

Outside the Bear Paw Saloon, the mob halted. Longarm stared up at a wooden frame fifteen feet above the ground, extending over the street from the building's front. Even in the lamp light, Longarm could see that the scaffolding had seen plenty of use. Hanging was the leading sporting event in Claim Jump.

In the lantern light the drunken faces were hideous, grinning, panting masks from a nightmare. He searched the shadowed faces of the mob, looking for one sign of sanity, one man to appeal to. He found none.

"Listen to me," Longarm said to the men around him. "This is murder. I'm innocent."

Laughter assaulted him. "Hell, mister, we must have had fifty hangings on this scaffold. We ain't never hung a *guilty* man yet."

"You've got to give me a trial."

"That's where you're wrong, killer. We don't have to give you nothing."

Somebody laughed. "Killer wants a trial. All right, wo'll give him a trial. I say the bastard is guilty. Anybody say he's innocent?"

"Guilty."

"Hang him."

"Okay, mister. You've had your trial. You satisfied now?"

"Well," Longarm said, "as long as everything is legal."

The hanging rope was thrown over the high scaffold and tied off on a peg driven into a building wall stud. The noose dangled seven or eight feet in the air.

"Bring a horse. Somebody bring a horse."

The crowd parted and two drunken men staggered through the mob, leading a saddle horse. "This here is

Sheriff Peale's own hoss," one of them said. The mob roared, finding poetic justice in this.

"Hang the bastard from the sheriff's own hoss!" a man yelled, and the mob took up the chant.

"Hang him. Hang him."

One man held the reins of the horse. The others tried to force Longarm to mount. When he refused, four men hefted him up and threw him in the saddle.

Somebody from the crowd yelled, "Aw, shit, that ain't the sheriff's horse."

"What the hell difference does it make? It's a horse, ain't it?"

"Hang him!"

A rifle shot broke across the shouts of the mob. Silence settled for an instant, and in that time, three deputies, armed with guns, pushed through the crowd. Leading the group, Longarm recognized the young deputy who'd been so enthralled earlier with the *Police Gazette*. Maybe they'd have made it sooner, but the deputy probably had to check the magazine one more time—a woman showing her legs above the knees, for hell's sake!

"Hold it!" the young deputy's voice blared, trumpet-like. To Longarm, it was a beautiful sound. "I'm Deputy Sheriff Duncan Murphy—"

"Git on back over to the whorehouse, Dunc, and let us alone," somebody yelled.

"I'm acting sheriff here," Duncan Murphy went on. "Me and my deputies are prepared to shoot the first man that tries to carry out this hanging."

"You know who this bastard shot and kilt, Dunc?"

"I don't give a damn. How many times have we told you people you got to stop these hangings? You're going to get the state militia over here from Carson City. Look at this man you're about to hang right now —a United States deputy marshal. You bastards don't show good sense. Now go on, get out of here."

"He kilt Sheriff Peale."

"Shot Wyatt Peale in the back."

"Hid in the alley and shot him in the back."

Duncan nodded. "We don't always enjoy protecting

194

the people we have to protect. But we got our job. Our job is to lock this man up until we can straighten this out. He's got a right to a trial, no matter who he killed." He jerked his head at his two deputies. "Get him off that friggin' horse and let's go."

The deputies helped Longarm down from the disputed horse. The animal was led away, with some man complaining loudly, "I tole you bastards all along, it wasn't the sheriff's horse."

The deputies surrounded Longarm and walked him through the mob to the jail. They held their guns at the ready. The mob yelled insults and threats, but its fight was gone.

Inside the sheriff's office, Duncan Murphy locked the front door. "We better keep you here in a cell until things quiet down, Marshal. Call it protective custody."

"Thanks for saving my life."

"Nothing we *wanted* to do," another deputy said. "Peale wasn't a charmer, and he was a crook, but he was the best goddamn sheriff this town ever had. You had no right killing him."

"I didn't kill him," Longarm said patiently.

"Don't lie, mister. That makes it worse. We know Wyatt was looking for you all day. You knew him, huh? Had a hate on, huh?"

"I didn't kill him."

"Hell, don't lie. We got to protect you. It's our job."

"That's enough, Lou," Duncan said. "Though I can tell you, Marshal—U.S. lawman or not—Lou kind of speaks for the rest of us."

Longarm opened his mouth to protest again, even though he knew it would be fruitless. Then he spied his own Colt .44-40 lying on the sheriff's desk. "That's my gun, Duncan," he said. "Check it. See if it's been fired."

Duncan Murphy picked up the gun, smelled it, and spun the cartridge chamber. He winced. "Jesus Christ," he whispered under his breath. He looked up, embarrassed. "We owe you a hell of an apology, Longarm. We almost waited around until *after* they hung you to break it up."

* * *

From his cell, where he was held in "protective custody," Longarm could hear the activity, celebration, and official business going on in the outer office. He heard a judge swearing in Duncan Murphy as sheriff of Bear Paw County. Then he heard champagne corks pop and a woman squeal delightedly, "Oh, Sheriff, that feels *good*."

"And that *looks* good," the new sheriff's delighted voice wafted through the cells. "Come on, hon, let me see that pretty leg—all the way—come on up *over* your knees, hon."

"Why, Sheriff," came the giggling voice, "you little devil, you."

There was a moment of taut silence, and then the new sheriff entered the cell block. His tie was loose, his face smeared with bright red lip rouge, a woman's yellow garter on his shirt sleeve. He said, his voice resentful, "You got company, Longarm."

"Why, thank you, sheriff, you little devil, you."

Duncan Murphy grinned sheepishly. "Take it easy there, Marshal. You're still my prisoner."

He held open the iron-barred door and Eastlake Hollinsworth's Indian wife entered the cell block. Duncan pushed a kitchen chair close to the corridor bars outside Longarm's cell. "I reckon you can stay awhile, ma'am," he said. He locked the corridor door. "You call me when you're ready to leave."

Longarm crossed the cell and gripped the bars in his fists, staring at Setao. She was even lovelier by daylight than in the feeble lamp glow of the print shop. She was built like unalloyed silver—malleable and ductile, a better heat conductor than copper, more lustrous than gold. Her breasts stood full and erect against the fabric of her cheap and shapeless shift. No fabric could ever totally conceal her radiant beauty. He saw a deep sadness in her black eyes that he had never seen before, a serene acceptance of pain as old as her misused people.

Puzzled, Longarm stared first at the classically lovely

young woman, then searched the corridor behind her. "Where's Hollinsworth?" he said.

"My husband wishes me to say a thousand apologies to you, Mr. Longarm. He wanted to come. He wants me to say that anything he can do to help you, you need only ask. But I regret to say he hurt his leg last night."

"Again?"

She hesitated, frowned slightly, and then smiled. "Oh, yes. Again. He hurt his leg again."

"Well, I'm sorry to hear that."

"Yes. He must learn to be more careful."

"I'm pleased that he sent you, Setao, since he couldn't come himself."

She smiled and nodded. Her head was perfect, as if delicately modelled, her hair severely and precisely parted down the center and braided along each side of her face, her ears like dark tan, flawless shells.

"It's funny," he said. "The way Hollinsworth calls you 'Mother.' You're one of the most beautiful women I ever saw."

She shrugged. "It is his little joke."

"I don't mean to be insulting—well, maybe I do— but not long ago I met an Indian girl. She had married a selfish white man who treated her like a blanket squaw. What is it with you Indian women—marrying men who overwork you? You like to be mistreated?"

She sighed and gazed at him sadly. "I am not mistreated, Mr. Longarm."

"Maybe it just looks that way. You do all the work—"

"I want to. You see, Mr. Longarm, there is so much you do not understand. I feel a great debt to my husband. A debt I can never repay. As long as he lives I must repay it. I do not mind. I want to. Whatever he asks me to do, this I will do. You see, Mr. Longarm, my husband rescued me from an Indian reservation some years ago . . ."

"You must have been a child."

She shrugged. "The reservation was on dead and barren land. We lived like animals. We never had enough to eat. We were robbed and cheated by the Indian agent. My husband took me away. For this I am eternally grateful. My obligations to him will not be satisfied except in death. His death or mine. Only death will free me from my deep, deep debt to him."

"I see. Forgive me for poking my nose in."

She smiled. "You are forgiven."

He sighed, unable to take his gaze from her serenely lovely face, the soft lips, the perfectly hewn nose, the wide-set black eyes under arched brows, the porcelain-like forehead. He said, "Do you know what your husband and the sheriff were discussing in the newspaper office last night?"

Her head jerked up, her eyes frantic for a moment. Then the old serenity flowed back through her and she smiled gently.

"No," she said, shaking her head. "I do not know. I was in the back—"

"Setting type," he said, grinning.

She smiled. "I know only that they talked for a long time. Very seriously. But I do not know what they said."

"All right. Thanks for coming, Setao. You made this day for me, no matter what happens next."

She smiled again, lowering her dark eyes under his gaze. "You are most kind."

"Just truthful, Setao. Truthful as hell."

"A woman does not hear so many pretty words in her life that they are not as welcome as flowers, Mr. Long-arm. Truthful or not."

"You can believe what I say about you, Mother."

She smiled. "My husband asks that I tell you he hopes all goes well, and that you will come to visit him as soon as you have been freed from—" she gestured with her arm— "this place."

"And you, Setao? How would you feel if I came to visit?"

She nodded, not meeting his eyes. "I would be pleased," she said.

● ● ●

Longarm was well fed with food from Ptomaine Sally's cafe, across from the jail. The food was delivered personally by the astoundingly endowed proprietress herself. She sat on the cot and chatted with Longarm while he ate.

The afternoon was quiet in the jail. The front door was locked, the deputies were out; this was the quiet time of the day while Claim Jump gathered its energies for another raucous night.

Longarm spent the time productively. He was actually thankful he had been arrested. He was forced to lie in the cell silently and use his brain. He thought back over all that had happened on this assignment, spending most of his concentration on the time since he and Purity had been rescued by Eastlake Hollinsworth in the desert.

He shook out the map, with its dots showing the cuts in the Western Union lines. The newest cut was in the same area as one of the earliest breaks, out in the Golconda Valley area. But this was not only the Mormon settlement region; it was silver mine country. What had Hollinsworth said? He had been out to visit the Shaftsville Mine.

He went over it all: clubbing that snake; meeting the editor of the *Legalizer*; the sheriff's futile attempt to contact him; the sheriff's murder; the attempt on his own life. It was like a jigsaw puzzle; it almost formed a picture, only there were vital pieces missing, if only he could find them.

He was still going over it in his mind. Who could have wanted to kill him? Who could be profiting from the silver trade when those lines were down? What did Setao look like under that shapeless shift she wore?

He hardly realized it was dark in the jail cell until Duncan Murphy entered the corridor, carrying a lantern. The new sheriff set the lantern on a chair. "That visitor of yours—Hollinsworth's wife. She's some beautiful piece of cake."

Longarm grinned. "I'll bet her legs go up clear past her knees."

"Wouldn't you love to find out, though?" Duncan

sighed. "You know, I heard something about that Indian girl today. It's bothered me all day. She's always so quiet. Works so hard. Acts like she's Hollinsworth's slave instead of his wife. Rich as he is, he works her like a dog."

"Oh? Is Hollinsworth rich?"

Duncan shrugged. "I don't know. Ol' Wyatt Peale always said he was."

"What did you hear about Setao?"

"Oh, hell, I don't believe it. I hope it don't get back to Hollinsworth and make trouble for her. Fellow told me this morning that he saw Setao walking down a dark alley last night late, with a man leaning on her, his arm around her shoulder."

"No," Longarm said. "I don't believe it."

Duncan grinned. "I know how you feel. I don't want to believe it either. But she is young—half old Hollinsworth's age—and she *is* an Indian . . . . Well, what the hell, there are always rumors going around."

He unlocked the cell door. "I reckon it's safe for you to leave here now, Marshal. If somebody did try to kill you last night, you better be on your guard tonight."

"I'm always on guard, Sheriff. But there's no way to stop a fellow if he wants to kill you bad enough."

"Reckon that's true." Duncan followed Longarm into his office, and gave him back his derringer and Colt. "I like that little double-barreled trickster. Could come in handy."

"It's good, if you're close enough."

"Like a woman. Just like a woman, Marshal." Duncan laughed and took up a sheaf of papers from his desk. "Look at this. If you wasn't a U.S. marshal, I swear I'd have to hold you. You've made some powerful enemies on your way out here. I hear the Mormons want to execute you. And these are telegraphed requests from Captain Felder Kennecut up at Fort Bloody Run to hold you for his arrival."

Longarm thought for a moment, and then nodded. "Why don't you send a wire to Captain Kennecut, Sheriff? Tell him I'm here in Claim Jump, and if he wants me, he can come and get me."

200

Duncan laughed disbelievingly and shook his head. "You really going to turn yourself in to that stiff-backed prick?"

"No. But he's a good soldier. And he'll likely bring at least a platoon of his soldiers with him. I don't know why, but I got a feeling that having him around will be very damned convenient."

Longarm walked along the crowded main street of Claim Jump. Chills crawled along the nape of his neck. He could not say why, but he felt he was being watched, as if somebody were waiting to pounce on him, or maybe take another shot from a black alley. He found himself studying faces, trying to find among these thousands of strangers the one stranger who wanted him dead.

He fought the strong urge to glance over his shoulder. He didn't deceive himself. Silver was big business; it generated big profits; he could be in somebody's way— somebody who was willing to pay to get him out of the way permanently.

He exhaled heavily when he entered the hotel lobby, and went directly to the registration desk. "Any messages for me?" he asked the clerk.

The clerk handed him a stack of yellow Western Union flimsies. Longarm decided not even to go up to his room to read them. He went to a butt-sprung club chair near a large potted palm.

The message on top concerned Purity—or Peggy O'Moore, as she was now billed. She had been hired by Trixie Mondale and would become a member of that lady's touring musical shows.

There were reports on most of the men he'd inquired about. One showed that Wyatt Peale had served a prison term in Oklahoma Territory. Longarm wadded this up and threw it in a wastebasket.

He stared for a long time at the report on Eastlake Hollinsworth. Born in the midwest. Began working on newspapers as a copy boy. Had worked his way down from daily newspapers in New York City. Had worked in Oklahoma, Texas, and Central America, where he

201

was jailed for a year on some kind of gold fraud. Deadly shot with a gun. Was known to have killed at least five men, all in self-defense or in duels arising from his news stories. Had large bank accounts in several Denver banks.

He sat holding all this information, unable to make it all jell. Maybe if he talked to Eastlake Hollinsworth. He folded the telegrams and shoved them in his inner jacket pocket. He bought a pack of nickel cheroots on the way out of the hotel.

Pausing on the top step of the hotel veranda and cupping his hands over his face, he lit a cheroot, sucked in the smoke greedily, exhaled it, and walked down the steps to the crowded street.

A panhandler staggered up to him before he'd gone half a block. He said, "Par'm me, mister. I'm a silver prospector. Down on muh luck. Can happen to all of us, you know. Wonder if you could let a fellow have a silver dollar for a cup of coffee."

"Coffee costs a dollar?"

The panhandler shuddered visibly. "Oh, mister, I *hate* coffee. I can't lace it with Irish whiskey, man, I can't drink it."

Longarm grinned and shoved his hand into his pocket. Behind him a voice said, "Now."

As Longarm tried to turn around, something cracked him across the skull. He was aware that the panhandler had wheeled about and was running through a blaze of desert stars. His cheroot flared into a million fiery bats, wheeling and flitting around his head. His knees buckled and he pitched forward, but he never felt it when he struck the ground. He was warm and lost and comfortable, if only they'd quit shooting off Roman candles just behind his eyes.

Chapter 17

Longarm never knew how long he was unconscious, only that it was more than a few minutes and less than a vacation with pay. He became aware first of movement—swiftly rolling wheels and racing horses' hooves on flint-hard, rocky land.

He opened his eyes slowly. The movement of his eyelids sent shafts of pain shooting to the top of his skull. He closed his eyes and lay still for a long time, surrendering to the dictates of his pain.

He heard muted voices as if from a great distance and muffled by the pounding of hooves and the rattling of the vehicle. He believed two men were talking, their voices low and tense. He was unsure whether he had heard either of those voices before. Anyway, he could not distinguish what they were saying.

He was confined in a space much too small for his large frame. He tried to straighten out, but could not. He succeeded only in bumping his head against an iron support. Lights flickered weirdly yellow and green and pink behind his eyes.

He lay still, cramped and in pain. He found that his ankles were bound tightly, as were his wrists. He must have been trussed up for a long time because his hands and feet felt swollen and numb from a lack of circulation.

He opened his eyes and managed to hold them open. What he thought to be eruptions of light from the pain fulgurating through his body were really the brilliantly blazing desert stars.

He winced. His first thought was that the vengeful Nolan Garrison had sent men to kidnap and return him to Golconda Valley. But when he glanced around the small bed of the carriage, he found it too fancy for the tastes of the stolid Mormon farmers. This single-seat carriage was even richer than the runabout owned by Eastlake Hollinsworth. The narrow wheels and light-weight construction stamped this buggy for speed, pleasure, and show.

He turned his head, trying to see the two men sitting on the carriage seat above him, but he could see only unidentifiable portions of their anatomy. He gave up, surrendering to the pain that charged through him on crossed wires from his nerve centers. For instance, he felt as if he'd been kicked in his belly, but the pain throbbed in his eyetooth.

There were no landmarks in the night. The sage-brush-covered plains lay flat around them. They seemed to be following a well-traveled, hard-packed road; this was his only clue.

Suddenly the driver yanked hard left on the lines and the two horses wheeled off the road onto another path, with hardly any loss of speed. Two things were evident: driver and horses knew this terrain well, the driver at least was reckless of self, buggy, and passengers.

The man on the front seat with the driver complained, "Take it easy, kid. I got no craving to break my neck on no buggy ride with you."

The driver laughed, a fluting sound that was somehow familiar to Longarm, yet one he could not quite pin down. "Hell, Mr. Hagadorn, I didn't know you was scared of nothing."

"Well, now you know, kid," Hagadorn said. "I'm scared of riding with you."

They covered at least five miles from the turnoff, with no breathing spell or let-up on the horses. They raced in through a fence and sped toward a pond of light in the endless prairie darkness.

The buggy was driven directly to the front steps of a house the likes of which Longarm had never expected to encounter in this wilderness. Built of adobe brick, with Spanish tile roofing, it was a mansion, with brilliant lamplight spilling from every one of its numerous windows.

Longarm lay in the narrow bed of the carriage and gazed up at the wide front veranda with its slanting roof, the row of windows across the second floor, and the smaller set on the third.

The driver leaped down from the carriage. By this time two or three animal handlers had run across the ranch yard to tend the horses. The driver said, "These animals are beat, Ramon. I want them washed in warm water and rubbed down good and toweled off till they shine. You hear me, you lazy bastard?"

That voice was familiar. It rang in Longarm's mind, and he had just realized it belonged to Logan Black-welder when the youth bent over him, grinning down into his face.

Logan's smile was savage, nothing to be shared. "Well, you're awake, huh, Longarm? Welcome to Snake Head Ranch." His laugh rang in the late-night stillness. "I hope you'll think of this place as your home away from home. Because that's sure as hell what it's going to be for a long time."

Longarm stared up into those dead-hawk eyes under the brim of the ten-gallon Stetson pushed back, devil-may-care, on wheat-colored hair. Funny how you could take a cold dislike to a man on sight, and then grow to hate him in time.

"You just can't learn when to let well enough alone, can you, kid?" Longarm said.

Logan laughed at him. "Oh, you ain't my guest, Longarm. Hell, I wouldn't of brought you this far to bury you. Bringing you to Snake Head Ranch was the old man's idea." He turned and spoke to the man easing himself leisurely down from the carriage boot. "Mr. Hagadorn, you want to help me get this critter out of the cart?"

Hagadorn didn't speak, but came around the carriage to stand beside Logan. Longarm caught his breath. The respectful way that Logan addressed this fellow had prepared Longarm for an aging and distinguished man.

Hagadorn was Logan Blackwelder's idol, that was

obvious. The spoiled rich boy gazed at him with something approaching reverence; Hagadorn was obviously what Logan wanted to be if he ever grew up.

Hagadorn's face was the kind that gave ordinary men bad dreams. Not that it was misshapen or ugly in any way; it was not. It was the kind of face one sees on wanted fliers.

A dead and savage intensity glittered in his killer's eyes. His features were sharply cut; there was something almost feminine and too-perfect about them. His flat-brimmed hat, thrown back off his head, was secured about his throat on a stout silk cord, and rested against his shoulders. His hair, looking freshly shampooed and brushed, shone like cold milk. He wore a string tie, a ruffled shirt, and a cutaway coat especially tailored for him. The lapels reached almost to his belt line, but then the fabric flared back clear of the guns holstered at his hips, and ended in tails. His whipcord trousers were carefully tailored and stuffed into hand-tooled boots. He was not a man one quickly forgot, no matter how devoutly one might wish to.

"So you're Longarm?" Hagadorn's voice, a Texas-accented tenor, showed his contempt for the lawman. "I been hoping we'd meet, Longarm, for a long time."

"This is the way to meet me, Hagadorn," Longarm said. "Sneak up behind me, tie me up, and take my gun. You feel safe, Hagadorn?"

The pale face flushed red to the roots of his cotton-blond hair. "Wasn't my idea, Longarm."

"Hell, Mr. Hagadorn, don't let this law-dog get your goat," Logan said. "You could take him any day in the week. We both know that."

"I want *him* to know it," Hagadorn said in a taut whisper.

"Hell, Mr. Hagadorn, you'll get your chance. I'll see that you get your chance." Logan smiled and nodded, trying to reassure and appease the hired gun. "No matter what Pa says, I'll see you get your chance."

They grabbed Longarm by the shoulders as if he were a sack of grain—which neither of them had likely *ever* handled—and dragged him from the rear of the carriage. He struck the ground hard, knocking his breath out.

Logan glanced at Hagadorn and laughed. Then the two men lifted Longarm and dragged him up the steps and across the fifteen-foot-wide veranda. By the time they reached the front door, it was being held open for them.

A woman stood bracing the door. As Hagadorn and Logan dragged Longarm past, he stared up into Emma Frye's face. No sign of recognition flickered there. She gazed at him impassively.

Logan said, "Is the old man sleeping, Emma?"

"He went to bed hours ago, Mr. Logan. He said I was to tell you to put your guest in the strong room."

Logan laughed. "Right. You feel like dragging this carcass up three flights, Mr. Hagadorn?"

"Hell, no. Cut those ankle ropes. Make him walk."

Logan nodded eagerly and bent over Longarm to loosen the ropes binding his ankles. Longarm said, "Untie my wrists, Hagadorn, and you and I can have that little talk you've been looking forward to for so long."

He heard Hagadorn's sharp intake of breath, a sound like the whir of a rattlesnake's rattles. The hired gun helped Logan yank Longarm to his feet. "Don't be in a sweat, Longarm. You'll get your chance."

Logan and Hagadorn marched Longarm up the wide staircase to the second floor. They walked down a cavernous second-floor corridor to a less imposing set of stairs leading up to the third floor. On this level, revealed by the lamp carried by Emma Frye, there were three doors, two facing each other and another at the end of the corridor. No light showed in the slit under the rear door, but there was a line of yellow spilling under the door directly to the left, across the hall.

As Logan pushed the key into the lock of the door on the right, a woman screamed in the room across the hall. Hagadorn stiffened, as nervous as a cat, but Logan only shrugged. "Crazy woman," he said, and laughed. "What the hell, Mr. Hagadorn, every family has one, huh?"

"If you say so, kid." Hagadorn did not smile.

The woman screamed again. Logan yelled, "Shut up, you crazy bitch! You want me to beat your face in again?" Then Logan smiled toward Hagadorn. "You got to know how to handle women, huh, Mr. Hagadorn?"

"If you say so, kid."

Logan smiled and nodded. That Hagadorn deigned to speak to him at all was obviously the high point of Logan's spoiled young life.

Longarm shook his head, watching the enraptured youth. Young Blackwelder wasn't the first youngster to choose a wasted life as his goal. How many gunfighters had Longarm seen end up in unmarked graves? Hell, how few had he ever seen end up anywhere else? But this wasn't something you could tell a headstrong hellion like Logan Blackwelder.

Logan shoved Longarm into the room. Emma followed with the lamp, which she set carefully on an old mahogany dresser. The room was spartanly furnished with a bed, a washstand with earthenware pitcher and basin, and a framed painting of a desert range. Two windows opened on the front yard. The windows were barred.

Logan removed the ropes from Longarm's wrists. Longarm stood for a moment, massaging blood into his paralyzed hands. Then he reached into his vest and took out a cheroot. Both Logan and Hagadorn slapped at their guns, Hagadorn a full breath ahead of the young rancher.

Longarm grinned at them. "What's the matter, boys? Nervous? Relax. Nervous men don't live half as long." He slapped the empty holster. "Besides, you took my gun."

Logan grinned coldly at him. "My father will see you tomorrow sometime. Meantime, if you want to occupy yourself, try to get out of here. I'd like to see that."

Across the hall, the woman screamed again. Hagadorn winced, and Logan cursed and said to Emma, 'Can't you keep her quiet?"

"I do the best I can, Mr. Blackwelder," Emma Frye said. She still had not given Longarm more than the

208

faintest glance. She looked taut-drawn, as if she feared he might speak to her. He watched her. She was wound tight enough to fly apart. The girl screamed again, and Emma held her breath until the sound died away.

"Must be upsetting, hearing that all the time," Longarm said.

Logan shrugged. "Can't hear it, except on this floor."

Hagadorn backed to the door. Longarm grinned coldly. This was the way a top gun departed any room. He had stayed alive perhaps twenty or twenty-one years by trusting nobody. He had slain enough men to get a rep and a price on his head, but he was six feet of raw nerves, jumping at whispers. Logan Blackwelder's idol.

Logan followed Hagadorn to the door. "Come on, Emma," he said.

Emma nodded. "Yes, Mr. Blackwelder." She stared up into Longarm's face as if she had never seen him before. "You will find towels in this drawer, sir." She tapped the top of the washstand. "Someone will bring your breakfast in the morning." Her hand remained for a moment on the top of the washstand. Then she looked through him and walked past him. When Logan closed the heavy door and locked it, the woman across the hallway screamed again. Then the key turned in the lock and they were gone.

Longarm stood for a long time in the middle of the room. Then he walked to the window and stared down into the lighted yard. The animal tenders had removed the carriage to the sheds off to the right in the darkness. He could see a single lantern glowing outside a long, barracks-like bunkhouse. The woman across the hall cried out and he turned away, chewing on his cigar.

He wondered what time it was. When he checked his watch, he caught his breath and pulled on the chain looped across his vest, then pulled out his two-shot derringer and stared at it. His captors had removed his Colt, but it had never even occurred to them to check for another gun. Logan was a rich boy and Hagadorn was a rich gun for hire. Neither had been interested in stealing his watch.

Grinning coldly, he unsnapped the derringer from his

209

watch chain, made sure it was loaded, and placed it behind an iron bar at the window. Across the hall, the girl cried out again.

He crossed the room to the washstand and took up the pitcher to pour water in the basin. Something glittered on the top of the old dresser. It was a key.

Longarm grabbed it, remembering the way Emma Frye had tapped this dresser and kept her hand atop it for a moment. She had left that key for him!

Elated, Longarm ran across the room. He shoved the key into the lock, but it did not even fit. Whatever lock this key fit, it was no use in getting out of this room. He stared at it and shook his head. He stood, puzzled, listening to the girl's sobbing across the hall. Then he shoved the key in his pocket and prowled the room in the oppressive silence.

The door was unlocked at about eight the next morning. Job Blackwelder entered, followed by Hagadorn. In this small, third-floor room, Job looked bigger than ever, but there was little resemblance to the laughing, expansive, and outgoing man Longarm had met on the siding outside of Clump, Wyoming. The look of wealth remained, the appearance of power. His gray eyes glittered, deadly.

He stared down at Longarm, who was slumped on the bed. "You knew I'd figure it out, didn't you, Long?" he said.

"Oh, I was sure you would, Blackwelder. Now if you'll just tell me *what* you've figured out."

"You're in no situation to be smart with me, Long." Job Blackwelder jerked his head toward the hired gun. "It's because of you that I've hired Mr. Hagadorn here. You've met Enoch, haven't you?"

Longarm stood up. He was by far the tallest man in the room, but the other two men were powerful in their own ways. Blackwelder ruled through money and influence; Hagadorn dominated his world through the terror of his gun. Longarm said, "You and I could have talked without Hagadorn, Blackwelder."

Blackwelder's smile was cold. "Oh, no. It's gone long

past the stage for talk, Long. You should have talked that night back at Clump. You should have told me the truth then. And you should have had sense enough to stay out of my country after you'd lied to me."

Longarm's voice hardened. "Did I lie to you, Blackwelder?"

"All government people lie. They look you right in the face and lie. Anybody that's ever talked to a tax collector knows that. Ain't that right, Enoch?"

"If you say so, Mr. Blackwelder."

Blackwelder smiled sourly. "I say so, Enoch. And you're right. Out here in Bear Paw country, when I say something, that makes it so. I tried to warn you, Long, as well as I could, not to trail me out here. Well, you came snooping around, and now you face your come-uppance."

"I told you I was looking for people destroying government property."

"Yes. Something about cutting Western Union wires. That's rather flagrant lying, seems to me. You and I— we know what you're after, don't we?"

Longarm imitated Hagadorn's servile tone precisely. "If you say so, Mr. Blackwelder."

Enoch Hagadorn drew a deep breath, swelling up with rage. Blackwelder gestured him quiet. "You'll have your time with him, Enoch. I want to hear him say it first."

Longarm felt a jolt of discovery. Whether he knew or suspected any damaging truth about Blackwelder or not was not important. Blackwelder was driven by a guilty conscience. Whatever crime lay in his past, it had festered until it controlled him. He owned the world and he couldn't sleep!

Longarm drew a deep breath. He was not dealing with facts or reason here; he was at war with a guilty conscience in a man almost fifty years old. A guilty conscience that had eroded away all logic, all common sense. It was as if he were caught in a deadly poker game with aces showing against him. He decided to raise the ante, even though it was his life at stake.

He gazed at Job's gray face first, and then at Enoch.

He shrugged and walked to the barred front windows. Outside, the sun blazed on the barren yard and the wastes beyond it. Logan's rich carriage stood with a span of sleek Morgan horses in the traces; Logan was nowhere in sight. He turned back to face Blackwelder, and said in a casual tone, "Oh, that. We've known about that for a long time, Job."

Blackwelder winced. "Have you? Or have you known only since you were drawn into that investigation in Denver?"

Longarm almost staggered. Denver! Alicia Payson! The digging up of the empty grave! The two gunslicks sent to eliminate him! Alicia's disappearance! Suddenly he realized he was staring at Floyd Gunnison, in the flesh.

What was it Alicia had first said? She had sensed Floyd Gunnison's presence in Denver. She knew he was still alive. What she had not been able to find out was that he had lived twenty years under an alias, hiding the truth of a criminal past under a cloak of respectability as a rancher.

He sweetened the pot, raising the ante, teasing Blackwelder's guilty conscience. "If you're that smart, Blackwelder, you ought to know that investigating old crimes is not my job. They'll be after you. I'm still out here looking for people cutting Western Union wires."

"Don't lie to me anymore. It was you digging into old records, old newspaper files. Did you think a man like Plitt Shawlene wouldn't tell me who was doing that? You dug up that grave out in Auraria—"

"You mean that *empty* grave, Job?"

Blackwelder's voice rattled against the walls. "A grave that lay unmolested for twenty years. All of a sudden you want me to believe you dug it up, but have no interest in me. Well, I don't buy that, Long."

"I'm only one deputy U.S. marshal. It'll get expensive as hell killing every one of us they send out this way, Job."

"You let me worry about that. I'm gambling that you aren't on this thing as a U.S. marshal, but that you're moonlighting, trying to make yourself a dishonest buck. All right. How much? What do you want?"

"You think you can pay some money and get away with it, Job?"

"Yes." Blackwelder said with assurance. "I've paid money for twenty years. I came out here as a rancher, so I could live well on the money I had."

"The money you killed for," Longarm corrected him.

"But I became even more successful as a rancher than I had ever been in silver mining. I married a wonderful, decent woman. I had a son. I've kept him out of here this morning because what we have to talk about, he need not know. Nobody needs to know but you and me and Enoch."

"You trust a scavenger like Hagadorn?"

"You worry about me too much, Long. Enoch is smart enough to know he can do this job for me and live well for the rest of his life. Or he can try to cross me and hide like a rat in a hole, as long as he lives. Ain't that right, Enoch?"

"If you say so, Mr. Blackwelder," Longarm answered for the gunslick. Both men strode angrily forward two steps before they hesitated.

"So now it's in the open, Long, right out where you and me can see it. No more lies about cutting Western Union lines. When I heard you were in Claim Jump, hell, I knew why you were there. Think you can bleed me white, Long? Hell, I've fired men smarter than you before breakfast."

"Let's admit you've been smart enough to get away with murder for twenty years, Job—or Floyd, or whoever in hell you are." Longarm saw Blackwelder's face go deathly pale at that name. "Now you're being dumb, killing a U.S. marshal."

"Nobody knows you're here, Longarm. And if you try to escape while I'm in Claim Jump today, and somebody has to kill you, who's going to know it but the buzzards that pick your bones?"

"Even providing yourself an alibi, eh, Floyd?"

"My name is Blackwelder!"

"Never get within fifteen miles of actual violence anymore, eh, Gunnison?"

Blackwelder stood stiffly, fists clenched at his sides. "Were you really stupid enough to believe I would *pay* you to keep quiet, Long? Bullets are a hell of a lot cheaper than blackmail, eh, Enoch?"

Hagadorn almost answered before he bit his lip, catching himself in time. . . .

Chapter 18

Longarm stood at the barred windows and watched Job Blackwelder ride away in a sleek surrey driven by a Mexican and followed by a half-dozen cowhands.

Longarm grinned sourly. This was known as buying an alibi. No matter what happened, no one could involve Job Blackwelder in the death of a U.S. marshal. Blackwelder would be miles from any scene of violence, surrounded by witnesses.

He saw Logan Blackwelder and Enoch Hagadorn standing together in the barren ranchyard, watching the older Blackwelder leave with his small army. When Blackwelder was out of the last gate on the lane, Logan turned and glanced up toward the third floor. Longarm stepped back from the window.

He prowled the room until he heard boots on the stairs. The footsteps stopped outside his door. The door was unlocked and Logan walked in, followed by Enoch.

Logan closed the door, locked it, and pocketed the key. He grinned coldly at Longarm. "Hear you made the old man mad, Longarm. You ought to have better sense than to do that."

"You ought to have better sense than to believe everything you hear, kid," Longarm said. He walked to the window and stood gazing down into the sunstruck yard.

Hagadorn said, "Shut your mouth, law-dog. Nothing you say is going to help you."

Longarm shrugged. "You think he's never going to know the truth, Enoch, even as stupid as he is?"

Logan went livid with rage. "Who you calling stupid,

215

lawman? You're the one in this trap, ain't that right, Mr. Hagadorn?"

"We'll take care of the son of a bitch, kid."

"Pa left word," Logan said. "Mr. Hagadorn and me are to guard you and not let you get away, but we got a better idea, don't we, Mr. Hagadorn?"

"That's right, kid."

Longarm said, "Did you tell Mr. Hagadorn about Curly Tom Lane, Logan?"

Logan's mouth twisted. "What about Curly Tom, law-dog?"

"You ought to tell Mr. Hagadorn about how dangerous it is to get mixed up with you and your old man. Curly Tom wanted to talk to me—on that train—didn't he? He knew he was in over his head, and he wanted to talk to me. Only you and your old man had to keep him from talking to anybody, didn't you? Did you push Curly Tom off that train, Logan?"

"Shut up," Logan said. "Curly Tom was a cowardly fool. Mr. Hagadorn is smart. A hell of a lot smarter than you are, Longarm."

Longarm pretended to survey Hagadorn closely. "He doesn't look too smart to me. It ain't smart ever to do another man's dirty work, Hagadorn. You do another man's killing, you may end up paying for his crimes."

"Keep your mouth shut," Logan warned Longarm.

Enoch Hagadorn smiled coolly, enjoying himself. "It's all right, kid. The lawman is trying to rile us up. He knows the truth."

"What truth is that, Hagadorn?" Longarm said.

"That doing other men's killing is my profession, Longarm. Just as you kill for the government. We're not all that different. Murder is murder. Waving a flag over murder don't make it anything more than murder."

"Say, that's damn clever thinking, Mr. Hagadorn." Logan shook his head, awed.

"Yeah," Longarm laughed. "It's that kind of thinking that's got him where he is today, kid."

Hagadorn flushed slightly, but remained cool. "I seem to be in better shape than you, Longarm. I'm sitting clean and pretty. From where I stand, you're in one hellish spot."

Logan laughed. "Yeah. That's right, Mr. Hagadorn. You want to tell him?"

"Tell him what, kid?"

"Hell, our plan for him, Mr. Hagadorn." Logan laughed and faced Longarm across the room. "Pa said you weren't to be allowed near a gun. No weapons for you, Longarm. He really hates your guts. He wants to see you dead."

"The worst way," Longarm agreed.

"But Mr. Hagadorn don't see it quite that way. Mr. Hagadorn says if you die without a weapon in your hand, it reflects bad on him. When you die, Mr. Hagadorn wants you to know you died at the hands of a better man than you, Longarm."

Longarm leaned against the window, frowning. "I don't believe this. You're saying, Hagadorn, that you're going against orders? You're going to face me—with a gun?"

"That's right, law-dog. Your own gun. Show him, kid."

Logan pulled Longarm's Colt from his belt and hefted it in his palm. "Here it is, Longarm, your own weapon. Hell, that's the way Mr. Hagadorn wants it."

"I could tell you a lot of things wrong with that gun, Longarm," Hagadorn said. He patted his own holstered gun. "Just a straight .45 caliber, that's the gun. But I won't waste your time. Tell you what we're going to do. Your gun's there on the foot of the bed. We're going to let you pick it up. Put it in your holster. You outshoot me, Longarm, you walk out of here."

Logan placed the gun on the foot of the bed and backed away from it.

Longarm didn't move. He remained half-seated against the barred window, studying them. He said, his voice cold and low, "You might have the kid suckered into thinking you're a big man, Hagadorn, but we both know you haven't got the guts to face me with a loaded gun in my hand. Is that the catch, Hagadorn? You asking me to pick up an empty gun?"

Before the enraged Hagadorn could answer, Logan yelled at him, voice quavering, "What you mean? Mr. Hagadorn could blow you to hell ten times out of ten—"

"Only one time counts, kid," Longarm said. "And that's the one time your big-time killer hasn't got the guts to face."

Enoch Hagadorn's face was red to the roots of his silky hair. His hands trembled at his sides. But again, before he could control his savage emotions enough to answer, Logan answered for him.

"There's a bullet in your gun, damn you!" Logan raged. "I didn't want to put a bullet in there. But Mr. Hagadorn wanted it. Mr. Hagadorn put a bullet in there for you, Longarm."

Longarm went on leaning against the window. He spoke in a soft, taunting tone. "Mr. Hagadorn's biggest mistake. Maybe his last one."

"Pick up the gun, Longarm." Hagadorn's voice was ice cold, but his rage quavered beneath it.

Longarm grinned coldly. "What's your hurry to die, Mr. Hagadorn? If there is a bullet in that gun and I ever pick it up, you're a dead man."

Hagadorn shuddered visibly, but when he spoke, his voice was under control. "There's a bullet in it, lawman. Show him, kid. Go on, show him."

"Sure, Mr. Hagadorn." Watching Longarm warily, Logan went to the bed and took up the Colt .44-40. He broke it open. "There's the bullet, Longarm. Ready to fire. Just like Mr. Hagadorn said."

"That's right," Hagadorn said. "Only it's not such a good gun for this kind of work, Longarm . . . not the best."

Logan laughed and closed the cartridge chamber. He hefted the heavy weapon one more time and then laid it on the bed again.

"Too heavy for a fast draw, huh, Mr. Hagadorn?" Logan said.

"That's right, kid."

"Not for a *man*," Longarm said in a soft voice. He stood up, hearing that sharp intake of Hagadorn's

218

breath that was like the frantic singing of a rattler. He turned his back and stared through the bars.

"What you looking for out there, law-dog?" Hagadorn said. "You might as well turn around and pick up that gun. That's your only chance. There's just one way out of here—over my dead body."

"Yeah," Logan whispered, in an ecstasy of awe and admiration. "That's all you got to do. Pick up that gun and face Mr. Hagadorn. You live—you walk out. Over his body. That's the only way." He laughed, trembling with anticipation.

Longarm leaned over, bracing himself on the windowsill. His hand closed over the concealed derringer. He palmed it and turned slowly. "Any way I can, eh?" he said.

Something flickered in Hagadorn's pale eyes. He gasped, the loudest sound in the room, and slapped at the gun in his holster. His fist closed over the grips and he was drawing as Longarm walked toward him.

Longarm extended the derringer in his fist and squeezed the trigger. The bullet struck Hagadorn in the chest. He stared at Longarm, eyes anguished. "You son of a bitch," he said.

He stumbled, then folded to his knees and finally crumpled to the floor. Stunned with disbelief, Logan stood staring at his fallen idol. When he looked up, Longarm had the derringer fixed on him. His mouth sagged open. He kept shaking his head, his hand trembling near his gun.

"Don't make any stupid moves, kid," Longarm said. "This is a double-barrel. If a bullet from it killed Hagadorn, it ought to blow you to hell."

Logan looked as if he might vomit. He could only nod his head.

"Turn around, kid," Longarm said.

Logan nodded, laughing strangely, trembling.

"Put your arms against the wall. Palms flat."

Logan nodded again and obeyed. Longarm stepped closer to him. He removed the gun from Logan's holster, keeping the muzzle of the derringer prodding the youth in the back. Logan trembled but did not move. Longarm searched him quickly and deftly, but found no other weapons.

"I can help you get away," Logan whispered, barely able to speak.

"Sorry, kid. I don't need your help. Hate to do this. It's going to hurt me worse than it does you." He struck young Blackwelder with his own gun, behind his ear. Logan crumpled to the floor and lay still.

Longarm slipped Logan's gun into his belt. Then he knelt beside the prostrate boy and took the door key from his pocket. He thrust his own gun into its holster, snapped the derringer back on its gold-washed chain, pocketed it. He started from the room, then came back and took Hagadorn's gun. "For luck, Hagadorn," he said. "You know how it is. Sometimes you just can't have too many guns."

He delayed one more moment, checking the room. Satisfied, he unlocked the door, pulled it ajar less than an inch, and surveyed the hallway. It was empty. Logan and Hagadorn had come up here holding all the aces, supremely confident, cocky. They had not brought back-ups.

Longarm exhaled heavily, sidled through the door, and closed it behind him. He locked the door and pocketed the key. Then, grinning wolfishly, he took the key Emma Frye had given him from his pocket. Holding it, he crossed the hall and pushed the key into the lock.

He turned the lock and thrust the door open.

Even before he spoke, Alicia leaped up from the bed, crying out, "Longarm! Oh, thank God, Longarm."

"There you go," he said, as the blind girl threw herself into his arms. "Doing it again."

"Knowing you were here?" she cried, kissing him frantically. "Oh, I knew you were here. I knew last night."

"You smelled me," he said.

She laughed, her battered face wreathed with happiness. "Who cares?" she cried. "I knew! I knew, Longarm, I knew!"

With his arm about her, holding Hagadorn's loaded

gun in his right fist, Longarm led Alicia cautiously down the stairwell to the second floor.

He felt a flush of rage through his body. Alicia looked as if they'd been using her for a punching bag. He hoped they would meet somebody who would try to stop them. Anybody.

At the foot of the stairs, Longarm paused and searched the second-floor corridor. It lay silent and vaguely lighted by the sun through curtained windows. Far down the hallway, a Mexican maid, carrying pillows, emerged from the door of a bedroom. When she saw Longarm and Alicia, she stepped quickly back into the room and closed the door.

His arm about Alicia, Longarm hurried along the shadowed hallway to the wide, curved staircase. He saw no one in the foyer below. He guided Alicia downward.

As they descended, Emma Frye appeared from the parlor. Her eyes were filled with tears. She said, "Oh, thank God, Mr. Longarm." She wept suddenly. "God bless you."

"God bless you too, Mrs. Frye," Longarm said.

She ran ahead of them and opened the front door. "There are armed men out there at the bunkhouse," she said. "Logan's carriage is there. I hope you can make it. I pray you can make it."

Longarm nodded, swung Alicia up in his arms, and ran across the wide porch. He went down the steps and placed Alicia inside the runabout, then ran around the vehicle.

Behind him, Mrs. Frye screamed, "Look out!"

He fell against the side of the carriage as a man with a rifle fired from the side of the house. The bullet struck the dirt at Longarm's feet. Before the man could raise the rifle again, Longarm fired. The man yelled, dropped the gun, and lunged into the cover of the house.

Longarm swung up onto the seat of the buggy and laid the whip across the backs of the horses. The carriage lunged forward, racing across the yard toward the lane.

"Are you all right?" Alicia called, clinging to the seat.

"Sure. Hell, he was scareder than I was," Longarm said.

The rifleman fired again from the corner of the house. Other men spilled out of the bunkhouse.

Longarm caught Alicia by the shoulders and pulled her head down in his lap as the gunmen fired. "Oh, Longarm! Now?" she said.

He laughed, firing at the men running into the yard, not hoping to hit anybody, but just trying to make them think. Then somebody realized that if Longarm was free, the boss's beloved son was in that house—and none of them wanted to be at Snake Head Ranch when Job Blackwelder returned, if his son were harmed.

Longarm raced through the first gate and looked back. Then he spoke to Alicia. "We've bought some time, honey."

Alicia was clinging to him, her face buried in his lap. As they slowed and went out the second gate, she looked up, her pale eyes brimming with tears. "I know I'm all right again now," she said. "I'm with you."

"Wish I had your faith," he said. "We got Snake Head men behind us and Snake Head men in front of us—and every one of 'em wants us dead."

"You'd have my faith," she said, clinging to him, "if you knew you as well as I do."

They'd gone less than a mile when Longarm saw the blossoming of dust behind them. It was as if he could see Logan, revived, half-crazed over the death of his idol, wild with fear of his father when Job learned that Longarm had escaped, riding like a madman at the head of the gunslicks from Snake Head Ranch.

"They're back there," he said softly.

She sat up, but pressed her hip close against his, as if she drew confidence from touching him. She clung to his leg against the rattling and swaying of the buggy on the flint-hard trace.

"They'll try to kill us," she said. "I wondered why they didn't kill *me*. At first, Floyd Gunnison didn't believe I was really Alicia Payson. He was convinced I was dead. Somebody had made him believe I was dead twenty years ago, and he had lived with that belief for twenty years. It was hard to let go, even when he knew I was Alicia. They brought me out on that train—in their private car."

"With Emma Frye as your maid and guard. I was on that train."

"I know."

"I was as convinced as Floyd was. He believed you were dead. Well, even when Curly Tom Lane was killed for trying to talk to me, I believed Blackwelder was what the world believed he was—a rancher as rich as Croesus."

"I was afraid they would kill me when we first got back to this ranch," Alicia said. "They knew everything about me that they needed to know. They knew who I was. They knew we had tried to find them. They knew we had dug up that empty grave. Now I know why Floyd waited. He wanted you here too. He wanted to kill us both, to know we were both dead—in a nice neat package—then he'd be safe again."

"He'll never be safe," Longarm said. "His guilty conscience is eating him up. He's his own worst enemy."

"Not as long as I'm alive," Alicia said.

Ahead, Longarm saw a hard-packed road. Last night, with Logan driving, they'd swung left off it, into the Snake Head Ranch lane. That meant Claim Jump was to the right. But so were Job Blackwelder and his riders. Blackwelder was nailing down his alibi. He would know nothing about the death of a U.S. marshal or a blind girl, if anyone ever discovered their bodies. He would have witnesses.

At first, Claim Jump seemed denied to them. They would run into Blackwelder, and they were already outnumbered by Snake Head ranchmen. But in Claim Jump there were people. If he could get Alicia among witnesses, he could maybe save her life. But he could well meet Blackwelder's men this side of the boom-town.

To the left lay the open basin country and the Mormon farms, and beyond them the digger Indians and desolation. He shivered, considering the alternatives. There was not a lot to choose.

Long before he was ready, the trail loomed before him. To the right lay Claim Jump, witnesses, and Blackwelder and his guns. To the left lay a trail that would peter out in enemy territory and waterless desolation. Alicia needed people; she needed more help than he could give her, no matter what she believed. He swung the runabout hard to the right, holding her tightly against him.

He glanced back along the lane toward the ranch. That dust cloud was growing larger, coming nearer. No matter how beautiful, strong, and gallant these Morgan horses were, they were carriage horses, and they were pulling a vehicle and two people. The horsemen were clearly gaining on them.

He laughed in irony. "Don't look back," he told Alicia.

She clung to him. "I can't," she said.

He stared ahead, wondering how many miles it was to Claim Jump, how many miles these beautiful horses could keep up this pace. They galloped, their magnificent heads high, their manes like sails unfurled in the wind, ears pricked tall, muscles and tendons straining, giving everything they had.

He saw another cloud of dust ahead. There was no way of knowing it marked Job Blackwelder and his riders returning from Claim Jump. But Longarm *knew*. Job Blackwelder lived with a guilty conscience eating away his sanity. He was on his way back to Snake Head to learn what he had to know before he could breathe in peace—that Longarm and Alicia Payson were dead.

"What's the matter?" Alicia said. "You're all tense."

"I get like that when I go without coffee."

"They're ahead of us too," she said.

"Jesus, I'm glad you can't see," he said.

Longarm stared at the mushrooming dust on the road ahead. A glance over his shoulder showed him that Logan's riders were almost at the cutoff. They could not turn back and make a run into the basin. Going off this trail into the wasteland was just delaying the inevitable and buying them nothing.

They needed a place to hide; they needed people; they needed witnesses. Blackwelder wanted them dead, but not enough to kill them before witnesses.

As if in answer to his unspoken prayer, Longarm saw a sign nailed to a weather-battered, bullet-pocked two-by-four: *Shaftsville Mine.*

Longarm laughed aloud. Shaftsville Silver Mine. That was where Hollinsworth had said he had been the day he met Longarm and the former Purity Garrison on the plains. That meant people: miners, workers, office people, animal tenders.

He pulled hard to the right and the horses responded. The road into the foothills was almost as hard-packed and well used as the main trace to Claim Jump.

"There's a mine up here," he told Alicia, laughing. "We're going to make it. You're going to be all right."

The road narrowed, winding upward through rock outcroppings. They met no one leaving the mine site. Longarm strained, listening, but there were no sounds coming down from the mine. He noted in passing that the Western Union lines climbed this ridge and crossed it.

Suddenly the road ended at a locked wooden gate. Beyond it he could see weatherbeaten buildings, but no signs of humanity.

The sign on the gate was not new. It was gaping with bullet holes and the paint was mostly sand-blasted away, but the words left no doubt: *"Shaftsville Silver Mine. Closed. Private Property. Keep Out."*

Shaftsville was an abandoned mine, and they had sped upward into a cul-de-sac. Longarm pulled up and sat, dust clouding across him, breathless, beaten, unable to speak.

Chapter 19

Alicia's voice reached down inside Longarm and yanked him back from despair. It was not himself he was troubled about, beyond any man's natural disinclination to die violently before his time; it was Alicia. He had brought her into this trap, a lane surrounded by high rock outcroppings and ending at a locked gate outside an abandoned silver mine. The bravery in her voice was exactly what he needed to spur him to make one final effort. "Longarm," she said, "we're still all right. We're together. They haven't got us yet."

He laughed suddenly and drew her hard against him. For one long breath in eternity she clung to him.

Longarm looked around, searching for a way out, even a goat path into those rocks. There was nothing. The high fence, topped with barbed wire, climbed and scrambled up into the rocks and stunted pinyon. Behind him the two plumes of dust melded and became one, blown toward them on the mine road.

Making up his mind, he leaped from the buggy, grabbed the horses by the checkreins and turned them in the narrow roadway. When the animals were finally headed down the trail, he reached up, caught Alicia under the arms, and swung her down beside him.

He estimated as well as he could when the riders would reach the place where the mine road narrowed to a cart path between the outcroppings. Trailing the reins loosely over the splashboard, Longarm took the buggy whip from its socket. Then he struck the horses, yelling, "Get out of here!"

The horses lurched forward. Finding no restraining hands on the reins, they raced forward, going swiftly down the trail, the light runabout bouncing wildly behind them.

He watched them for less than two seconds, the thought spilling through his mind that he'd like to see Blackwelder's riders when those runaway horses bore down on them in a narrow path walled in by boulders, and with nowhere to go.

He lifted Alicia in his arms and swung her over the locked gate. She caught the crossbars and let herself down. Longarm grinned at her self-sufficiency. He climbed the gate and swung down inside the mining property beside her.

Taking Alicia's hand, Longarm strode at a half-trot along the mine road. It turned and twisted upward at a sharp angle alongside a sheer precipice falling from a plateau perhaps a hundred feet above them.

The tortuous road wound through rocks and boulders, coming out at last atop the butte where the main structures of the mining company had been constructed —and abandoned.

There was an eerie sense of silence about the deserted grounds. Narrow-gauge tracks led into the mine entrance far across the plateau in the hip of the high-jutting ridge. Weeds grew between the ties. The rails themselves were rusted from disuse.

Hardly aware that he spoke, so deep in thought was he, Longarm muttered, "Damn."

"What's wrong, Longarm?" Alicia asked.

He laughed, driving the thought from his mind. "Nothing. I was just thinking about a son of a bitch who lied to me."

"Another one?"

He nodded. "Another one. Only this one lied to me about this place—and God only knows how many other things."

"What does it look like?" she said. "Are there any places to hide?"

"There are nothing *but* places to hide," he told her. "But we need a good one. There must be at least twelve gunmen back there looking for us."

As they strode across the flat top of the butte, he

227

described the silver-mining operation to her, the road that wound past the office shacks, barns, corrals, smithy, car sheds, explosives shack, mine entrance, and across the butte, far around the hillside, and back down to the gate. A few water-starved junipers and dusty cottonwoods offered the only shade.

He drew little consolation or encouragement from what he saw in this abandoned mine site. Discouraged men had closed it down, a dead and empty prospect, and returned it to the lizards and the rats and the sagebrush.

Longarm paused in the middle of the mine property and gazed down toward the gate. He could not see the gate from up here, but he could see the wisps of dust rising from its direction. Then a gunshot cracked and Alicia gripped his arm tautly. "Longarm?"

"The Blackwelders are unlocking the gate," he said, "the Blackwelder way."

The sound of gunfire rattled upward and echoed back from the rocks.

Longarm took Logan Blackwelder's gun from his belt, checked the cartridge chamber, and found it fully loaded. He pressed it into Alicia's hand. "Use it," he told her, kissing her lightly, "on anybody who comes toward you—and doesn't smell like me."

Above the soughing wind they heard rapid hooves approaching up the narrow roadway. Beyond, along the road out, Longarm discovered another dust cloud, but he drew little hope from it. They would have to fight their way out.

He looked around one more time, then caught Alicia's hand and ran along the narrow-gauge track toward the mine entrance. A rusted ore car had been abandoned near the mouth of the dark tunnel. Longarm put his shoulder against it and rolled it into the cave entrance so that the opening was almost blocked. Their pursuers could still come in after them, but this car would slow them down.

"We'll go inside the tunnel," he said. "We'll make them come and get us. We can see them come in the mine doorway—and they won't be able to see us."

Alicia only nodded, clinging tightly to his hand.

Holding Alicia closely against him, Longarm sidled past the ore car into the mine. Inside, the darkness loomed like some bottomless pit. The broken rails were his only hope for following the tunnel deeper underground.

For the moment he crouched behind the car, with Alicia at his shoulder, and watched where the road came up onto the top of the butte.

Blackwelder's open surrey was the first vehicle to swing into view. It was followed by armed men on horseback.

Longarm spotted Logan. He wore a pistol in his holster and carried a rifle. His head was bandaged, and the bandage was bloody. Longarm could see that Logan wasn't thinking about pain; the younger Blackwelder was obsessed with vengeance.

Job Blackwelder gestured his driver to pull his rig in near the explosives shack, under the meager shade of a cottonwood, and leaped down from the carriage. He stood at the brink of the shade, deploying his men in all directions.

Longarm's hand itched on his pistol grips. He had a clear view of Blackwelder, likely the best he would get. Instinct warned him to shoot Blackwelder now; to wait would be to court total disaster.

He hesitated. He had more than his own life to consider. He wanted to get Alicia out of here alive. It seemed to him that he had to have a smarter play than simply to gun down the rancher. Even if that stopped those gunmen for a moment, that was all the time it would buy, and it would tell them where he and Alicia were hiding.

He watched those cowmen swing down from their horses and follow Blackwelder's directions, warily checking every hiding place outside the mine. This told Longarm that Blackwelder was certain he and Alicia had run into the mine. Blackwelder was only moving cautiously. Longarm had escaped him once when he had left the job to underlings. It was going to be done right this time. Before they approached the mine, Black-

229

welder would be satisfied that Longarm and Alicia were not hiding, looking for a chance to steal horses and run again. Blackwelder meant to do it himself this time.

A pistol shot rang out from near the barns.

Blackwelder wheeled around. His great voice boomed across the clearing. "What was that?"

"Sidewinder," a man yelled back. "Almost stepped on the damn thing."

Somewhere a bugle sounded.

It was as if a vision of avenging angels had appeared suddenly to the Blackwelder riders. The two Black-welders led the race to the brink of the precipitous side of the butte. They stood, staring downward in stunned silence.

The bugle blared louder, clearer. Alicia whispered, "What's that, Longarm?"

"That may be known in history as a latter-day miracle, sweetheart. That's the cavalry. From Fort Bloody Run. It's Captain Felder Kennecut and a platoon of his finest."

"What are they doing here?"

He laughed again, shaking with laughter. "They're looking for me. Kennecut's got a man-sized hate on for me, and he means to take me back to stand trial for jailbreak and helping a fugitive to escape."

He watched Blackwelder's men retreat in confusion from the edge of the cliff.

Watching them, Longarm felt rising hope. "We know Captain Kennecut is looking for me. But Blackwelder's men don't. A guilty conscience brought them up here, and a guilty conscience may save us yet. If Blackwelder thinks they're after him, he'll have two choices—run or fight."

Blackwelder was yelling at his men, but they were no longer listening. His voice was the loudest sound in the area, overriding the blaring of the bugle and the thunder of cavalry hooves up the winding cart path.

They leaped into their saddles and rode out across the butte to the exit trail on the other side. They weren't going to wait to ask questions. They were out to murder, and they could easily believe the army was on their trail. No matter how soon reason prevailed, it would be too late. Longarm could place Alicia in Kennecut's protection, which was like putting her in her mother's arms.

By the time the army crested the top of the butte, Blackwelder's men were racing for the far downslope. Dust clouded everywhere. Through it, Longarm saw Blackwelder's surrey swaying and bouncing as the Mexican driver whipped the horses.

Hunkered down beside the ore car, Longarm watched the company of Bloody Run soldiers thunder in pursuit of the fugitive riders. The soldiers' action arose from natural military instinct: if the quarry runs, chase it.

Longarm watched Captain Felder Kennecut riding at the head of the troop. He rode rigidly in his saddle, his heat rash forgotten. He extended his saber over his horse's head, yelling, "Charge, men! Charge!"

The guidon passed next, and the rest of the company raced after it. The soldiers crossed the top of the butte and headed down the far trail. The dust smoked up and filtered away on the wind down from the hill.

Longarm edged forward, whispering to Alicia to stay where she was.

As he straightened next to the ore car, a gun cracked from the direction of the explosives shed.

Longarm lunged back into the mine entrance. Crouching, he watched Job Blackwelder, alone, hatless, gun in hand, running toward the mine entrance. He fired again, low. Bullets struck the metal car and whined off in several directions.

"Get back," Longarm told Alicia.

They retreated along the mine tunnel, following the tracks. Almost at once they were immersed in total darkness.

Alicia whispered, "Take my hand."

Longarm clutched her hand, following her in the stygian darkness.

Alicia seemed not to hesitate. Longarm swore under his breath in awe. Alicia could "see." Her sharply honed senses worked for her in the darkness.

231

"Long!" Blackwelder's voice echoed and thundered inside the tunnel. "You and the girl. You might as well give up. You'll never get out of here alive. I'll never let you get out alive."

Defiantly, without any real hope, Longarm fired toward the voice. Blackwelder laughed and fired twice in rapid succession. The bullets ricocheted crazily in the tunnel.

Alicia kept moving deeper into the cavern. Completely and helplessly blind, Longarm followed her, stumbling in the dark.

"I hear you in there, Long!" Blackwelder yelled. "I'm coming for you, Long. I'm coming for you!"

Longarm heard the sound of stumbling steps behind them, and fired again toward the sound.

Blackwelder laughed and fired back, but he remained where he was.

Longarm tried to remember how many times he had fired his Colt. He carried only five loads, always keeping an empty chamber under the hammer.

Longarm suddenly realized that Alicia had released his hand. He reached out in the darkness, with the sickening sensation that if he moved, he would plunge into bottomless depths.

He could not find her. In panic, he crawled first one way and then the other along the tracks. It was as if she had disappeared.

Suddenly, ten feet behind him toward the entrance, a gun detonated. In the flare of light, he recognized Alicia. She was crouched, he saw in that split second, holding the gun out in front of her.

She fired again. Farther along the tunnel, Longarm heard a sudden gasp. He knew Blackwelder was hit. Alicia had "seen" him in the dark. She sensed his presence, knew exactly where he was.

She fired one more time, and then the gun in Blackwelder's hand erupted. The big rancher fired into the muzzle flash of Alicia's gun.

Blackwelder's first shot found its mark, and Longarm heard Alicia cry out. Blackwelder fired again. It was as if Longarm could sense the bullet's impact in Alicia's body. She did not make a sound.

Blackwelder's third shot dug into the dirt of the mine tunnel.

Raging, Longarm crouched and fired toward that yellow blossom of flame. His gun clicked on an empty chamber. He shoved the pistol into his holster and yanked Enoch Hagadorn's gun from his belt.

Pressed against the wall, Longarm sprayed fire toward the place where Blackwelder's gunfire had erupted. When Hagadorn's gun was empty, Longarm threw it from him. He remained braced against the wall, a support timber biting into his back. There was no movement from Blackwelder, no sound.

After a moment, Longarm crawled along the tunnel until he found Alicia. She was sprawled out, facedown, between the narrow-gauge tracks.

"Alicia," he said.

She did not answer. There was no movement from the place where Blackwelder had been firing at them.

Suddenly, Longarm could no longer endure the oppressive blackness. He felt smothered, unable to breath in the unrelieved darkness. His hands groped around until he found a stick of wood.

Fingers trembling, he lit a match and held it against the dry wood. The stick caught and flared, sending fingers of orange light through the blackness.

Longarm saw Blackwelder slumped against a tunnel support. His eyes were open, staring in death. He had lost his gun.

Raging, Longarm hurled the sputtering torch at the dead man. The wood struck the body and flared out, plunging the tunnel once more into total blackness.

Longarm knelt beside Alicia and lifted her in his arms. Her head flopped back. He groaned low in his throat. He pulled her to him and cradled her in his arms. There was no pulse, no breath. She was dead.

His eyes burned with tears; his throat felt tight. He kept telling himself that Alicia had accomplished what she wanted most in life. She had avenged her father's

233

death, her own lifetime of blindness. She had found her hated enemy in the dark, and she had killed him.

For a long time, Longarm did not move. He hunkered there in the darkness, holding her lifeless body in his arms.

Chapter 20

"Longarm!"

The voice outside the mine clawed at Longarm, yanking him back to reality. He sat a moment longer, then placed Alicia's body tenderly against the tunnel wall. He moved slowly toward the mine entrance, trying to place that voice in his mind. Logan Blackwelder? Felder Kennecut? Nolan Garrison?

Within the shadows of the entrance, Longarm hesitated, searching the grounds outside. He saw Eastlake Hollinsworth's carriage, with the sign on the side: *"Read the Claim Jump LEGALIZER and Go to Bed at Night with Nothing on Your Mind."*

The horse stood, drooping, in the shafts. The canvas-topped buggy was empty. For a moment the stillness stretched across the tableland.

He saw their shadows first—truncated, dark forms on the sun-baked ground. Then he saw Hollinsworth, pressed against the wall of the explosives shack. He was holding a handgun tautly at his side as he waited, his gaze fixed on the mine entrance. Behind him stood Setao, pinned to the hot boards of the shack by Hollinsworth's restraining arm across her.

Hollinsworth was watching the mine entrance as a cat watches a mouse hole, but he hadn't yet glimpsed Longarm in the deep shadows.

Hollinsworth yelled again. "You in there, Longarm? You all right, Longarm? I've come to help you, Longarm."

Longarm stared at Hollinsworth. He was no longer wearing the leg cast. Hell, it didn't matter. By now Longarm knew the leg cast had been another of

Hollinsworth's lies. Maybe everything the big man had said to him was a lie. It had begun when he told Longarm and Purity that he had come from the Shaftsville Mine, where a robbery was in progress. Shaftsville had been closed for months, maybe for more than a year. But he'd known a stranger wouldn't know that. Maybe he had been up here in the mining property. The Western Union lines crossed here, and it was a good, empty place in which to cut them.

When Setao had told Longarm in jail that Eastlake had hurt his leg, he had realized that the cast was a lie. Eastlake had worn the cast to throw any suspicion off him. And that varnished, clublike, single crutch: If a man secured a knife to it and stood up on a carriage seat, he could snap the taut telegraph lines quickly and easily. The portly publisher had apparently broken one crutch; that explained the strangely finished and polished club Purity had handed Longarm to kill the rattler that day in the desert when they had met Eastlake for the first time.

He had begun to doubt Eastlake when the publisher said he'd visited Plitt Shawlene in Denver, yet hadn't known Trixie Mondale. At that time, Plitt was with Trixie every waking moment, and anyone visiting Plitt would have to be aware of Trixie. No, the lie was an alibi for the wire-cutting across Nevada at Elko; that cut was a red herring to lead investigators away from the Claim Jump area where most of the cuts were made.

He knew suddenly that Sheriff Wyatt Peale had been dead already when he saw him sitting in that chair in Eastlake's office. He could only speculate as to what had happened between them, but the facts supported his theory: Peale and Hollinsworth had had a falling-out. Peale was scared, or greedy. Peale was going to squeal on Hollinsworth to the U.S. marshal. Eastlake had killed Peale to silence him, and removed the body, maybe forcing Setao to help him. That explained why she'd been seen with a man leaning on her, his arm about her, that night. Eastlake had left the body in the alley and then tried to kill Longarm. When he missed, he ran, and actually turned his ankle in the mud, trying to get away.

And why had he done all this? Because he had been involved in a gold-fraud scheme in South America. He knew how long these strategems would work. He'd known the U.S. marshals were coming. He was ready for them, but he was greedy. If he could get rid of Longarm as well as Peale, there was time for another score before he had to run. So far, he had cleared millions by having advance knowledge about silver prices, when the markets to the east could not get them because the wires were down.

All of this flashed through Longarm's mind in the space of a taut breath. He had been on his way to talk to Hollinsworth the night Logan and Hagadorn had jumped him.

"You there, Longarm?" Hollinsworth yelled again. "I've come to help you, Longarm."

Longarm retreated behind the ore car. He patted the gun in his holster, realizing it was empty. He backed deeper into the tunnel. Alicia had used Logan's gun. There might be a couple of bullets left in it—if he could find it. She had dropped it when Blackwelder shot her the second time.

And Blackwelder's gun. It was back there somewhere around the rancher's body.

Feeling the darkness envelop him, Longarm felt his way along the tunnel. When he bumped Blackwelder's body with his boot, he knelt and groped around in the darkness, unable to find the gun.

Longarm caught the rancher and pulled his body over on the tracks, searching around the upright against which Blackwelder had fallen.

Dying, Blackwelder must have tossed the gun from him. Longarm could hear Hollinsworth approaching the mine entrance.

Deciding to gamble, Longarm pressed as close behind the four-by-four upright as he could get, and struck a match. The flame showed Blackwelder sprawled across the tracks in death, the gun nowhere in sight.

From the entrance of the mineshaft, Hollinsworth fired toward the flicker of matchlight. Longarm doused the flame and sank as far behind the support as he could.

He heard Hollinsworth laugh, that big belly-shaking sound. "You in there, Longarm? Come on out. You're beginning to try my patience after you've already tried everything else, as the madam said to the deadbeat customer who refused to pay her. You like that, Longarm? Got a thousand of them . . ." He fired again. "Hear how I talked my wife into marrying me, Longarm? I took her out to the barn and she listened to my bull. . . . I told her, 'Sure, there are four times as many men as women in the nuthouse—but who puts them there?' "

Hollinsworth leaned around the ore car and fired again, the bullet screaming in the tunnel.

Longarm grinned coldly. He was unarmed, but Hollinsworth didn't know that. And Hollinsworth was having trouble keeping his own courage up. He kept talking to hide his own growing panic from himself.

"Come on out, Longarm," he yelled.

"You already tried to kill me in that alley, Hollinsworth."

Hollinsworth laughed loudly. "Nothing personal, Longarm. You just got in my way."

"You'll have to come in and get me, Hollinsworth."

Hollinsworth laughed. "You'd like that, wouldn't you, Marshal? You think you're going to take me in on some piddling wire-cutting charge. Hell, Longarm, I've got all the money in the world—and more waiting in the banks at Denver by the time the silver exchanges close tonight. Sorry, but I can't let you spoil that, Longarm. I worked too hard. I waited too long."

"I'm taking you in, Hollinsworth. Nothing personal."

Hollinsworth laughed. "You're my kind of man, Longarm. You got a sense of humor." He fired, the bullet whistling along the dark tracks. "But you ain't taking me nowhere. Anyhow, wire-cutting is something you'd have to prove. And you might suspect, Longarm—you might even know—but you'd never even get to court. You have no proof."

He fired again, and then he was silent. Longarm knew he was reloading. After a moment, Hollinsworth yelled, "Setao! Setao, damn you! The dynamite! Bring me the dynamite!"

"Won't work, Hollinsworth. That's the worst groaner of all. You want me, come and get me. And I'm not going to try to arrest you for cutting those Western Union wires—even though we both know you did it."

"No deals, Longarm. You're too dangerous. I can't let you live. Lot of money at stake."

"No. I'm going to take you in, Hollinsworth. Not for wire-cutting that I can't prove, but for a crime I *can* prove, with a witness who has only to appear—dead or alive—to testify against you."

Hollinsworth laughed and fired again into the darkness. "More jokes, Longarm?"

"No jokes, Hollinsworth. Nothing personal. I'm charging you with statutory rape."

"Statutory rape?" Hollinsworth exploded into laughter. "Man! It's almost a sin to shoot a man with your sense of humor."

"Statutory rape—against a ward of the United States government, Hollinsworth."

"What the hell are you talking about?"

"About you. About Setao. She told me. You ran away with her from an Indian reservation. If you ran away, you never got the Indian agent's approval of your marriage. Even if you married Setao, Hollinsworth, you're still guilty of a federal offense."

"Hell, Longarm, I've known about that law for years. Nobody ever enforces it."

"Two people do, Hollinsworth. Captain Kennecut and me. Nothing personal, Hollinsworth. You lay down that gun. It'll make it a hell of a lot easier on you."

Hollinsworth laughed. "All you got to do is arrest me now, lawman. Come on out, and I'll blow you and your outmoded law to hell." He lifted his voice again. "Goddamn it, Setao, I told you! Bring me that frigging dynamite!"

Longarm looked up. He saw a flickering in the darkness and realized that the ore car was being shoved forward. Suddenly Hollinsworth grunted fiercely and shoved the car with all his strength. He stood laughing as the ore car sped down the track.

Longarm pressed in against the wall behind the support. There was not room for that wide-bellied car to pass without carrying him with it.

Drawing in his arms, Longarm bumped the derringer in his vest pocket. His heart lurched. One shot left. But he had to survive first.

He could see it, flickering in the blackness. It accelerated, rattlingly along the narrow tracks. And then, only a few feet from him, the car wheels struck something and the car derailed and crunched into the tunnel wall.

Blackwelder's body had braked the car.

Hollinsworth was laughing above him, near the mouth of the tunnel. "You still there, Longarm? Still going to take me in?" He roared with laughter.

Longarm hesitated no longer. Palming the derringer, he slithered on his belly, snakelike, along the tracks.

He saw Hollinsworth retreating slowly toward the mouth of the tunnel, the light behind him. Suddenly Hollinsworth decided his mission was accomplished. He laughed, throwing his head back. "So long, Longarm," he called cheerfully. "See you in hell . . . no hard feelings."

Longarm came up to his knees and then sprinted forward as Hollinsworth yelled again for Setao and the dynamite.

Hollinsworth heard Longarm behind him. He jerked his gun up and spun around.

Only a few feet from the bulky man framed against the sunlit entranceway, Longarm fired the last shot in his derringer.

He heard the impact of the bullet in the big man's stout belly. Hollinsworth tried to bring his gun up, and could not. His knees sagged. As he fell, he turned his head, yelling. "Setao, the dynamite, you damned red whore!"

Hollinsworth was on his knees. He dropped the gun

and clutched at his belly. He toppled forward as Longarm ran past him.

Longarm ran out of the tunnel, abruptly bat-blind in the blazing sunlight. He saw a streak of shadow as Setao ran toward him, her arm cocked over her head.

"Setao! No!" he yelled. "You don't have to do anything he tells you anymore. Never again. Don't throw it, Setao!"

His vision cleared enough to see her throw the sticks of dynamite with all her strength into the mouth of the tunnel.

He grabbed her wrist and raced toward the brink of the precipice. The explosion behind them sent them hurtling over the side of the butte and down the steep incline. It sealed the mouth of the tunnel. It shook rocks and boulders loose in the hill, sending an avalanche down across the ridge.

Longarm went rolling, falling, sprawling down the side of the incline. Rocks bounced and danced around his head.

He heard Setao screaming something as they toppled. He never did know whether she was talking to him, to herself, to Eastlake Hollinsworth, or to the gods of her people.

Longarm struck against a boulder and it broke his fall. Rocks, debris, and Setao struck hard against him. They lay for a moment entangled, battered by falling objects.

Around them the world blazed from the explosions, and high over everything—trees, boulders—flames shot skyward, licking at the sun and cascading down in showers of sparks.

"The world really moved that time, Mother," Longarm sighed fervently.

"Yes," Setao said. She nodded. "Yes. I moved it."

SPECIAL PREVIEW

Here are the opening scenes
from

LONGARM ON THE BIG MUDDY

twenty-ninth in the bold
LONGARM series from Jove

Chapter 1

It was early in the morning on the Fourth of July when Longarm saved the orphans from Vice-President Schuyler Colfax of these United States.

Old Schuyler wasn't really the vice-president anymore, and he had no way of knowing a streetcar load of orphans was on its way to a picnic in Cheeseman Park that morning. But while he'd been in office, he'd managed to get one of Denver's main thoroughfares named after himself, and that was where the trouble started.

Colfax Avenue ran east and west, and because Schuyler Colfax had been the most crooked vice-president in U.S. history, his admirers in Denver had tried to make up for it by laying out the avenue they named after him as straight as possible. So when it got to the steepest hill in Denver, Colfax Avenue just went straight up the slope and to hell with the horses. Denver didn't have cable cars like San Francisco. When the horsedrawn streetcars came to Capitol Hill, they just had to do their best. When they were headed east with a heavy load, the passengers got out and walked up the long grade. On the way west, everybody just hung on and prayed that the brakes would hold.

Longarm wasn't thinking about any of this as he turned the corner of Lincoln and Colfax to walk downhill that morning. He was too close to the office to ride a streetcar and too mad at his boss, Chief Marshal Billy Vail, to consider the past crimes of higher public officials. Here it was, a public holiday, and he'd just left the bed of a right friendly schoolmarm because the infernal U.S. marshal he worked for had decreed that the office would be open until noon.

Longarm legged it down Colfax slow and moody, looking for something to kick. It was shady under the cottonwood trees along the red sandstone walk, but it was shaping up to be a hot day, and it was already too damned noisy. Folks in Denver didn't shirk the celebration of the Glorious Fourth. They'd been shooting off firecrackers and worse since about the middle of June. As he headed down toward the Federal Building, it sounded sort of like he was marching to Shiloh again. The small stuff crackled like small arms all around, and every few minutes some idiot lit a quarter-stick of dynamite that rattled windows for blocks. Folks were still talking about that cowhand who'd blown his head off the other night in front of the Silver Dollar. So as Longarm approached the corner of Colfax and Broadway at the bottom of the slope, he didn't pay any mind to the crackle of minor explosions out of sight around the corner.

At the same time, a streetcar filled with kids passed him, going the other way. He wouldn't have paid that any mind, either, if some little son of a bitch hadn't thrown a well-aimed torpedo at him.

Longarm cursed and sidestepped as the tiny bomb went off right where he'd been about to put his booted foot. He turned to glower at the kids on the streetcar as one of the little bastards threw another one at the only handy target and a sweet little girl stuck her tongue out at him. He figured it was likely against the law to shoot back at them. The twin blasts had spooked the team of horses, so the streetcar moved up the slope too fast for them to toss anything else his way. He grimaced and turned away to resume his lackluster stroll to the office. At that moment, a trio of men wearing trail riders' outfits tore around the corner, running like hell. Longarm frowned but got out of their way as he saw that they seemed to be chasing the streetcar. He shrugged and took a few more steps before a man in the blue uniform of the Denver Police Department staggered around the corner, a billy club in one hand and a

245

revolver in the other. Longarm just had time to notice that the copper had been hit and was bleeding all down one side when a shot rang out from behind him and the copper went down with a bullet in the chest.

Longarm crabbed sideways as he reached across his belly, drew his own double-action .44, and got a cottonwood trunk between himself and the streetcar the three men had boarded on the fly. He knew he'd made the right move when a bullet thudded into the tree at the level of his own heart.

Risking a quick peek around the trunk, he saw that he couldn't fire at the cloud of gunsmoke hanging between him and a streetcar filled with kids, and pulled his face back just as another round spanged into the trunk to tear a divot of bark out and scream its way off in the general direction of the Rocky Mountains. He glanced at the gunned-down copper and saw that trying to aid him would be pointless as well as suicidal. Either the copper was dead, or he liked staring up at the sun with his eyes wide open.

Longarm saw that there were buildings to his left and the open grounds of the terraced state house park to his right. On the far side of the Capitol grounds he spotted some other blue uniforms legging it up the hill to try and head the streetcar off on the far side. Longarm performed some mental trigonometry and decided they were just going to miss their connection. The outlaws had obviously commandeered the streetcar, and once they made the top of the slope, they'd be able to whip the team into a run.

Two more coppers came around the corner. One ran to the man down in the street. The other pointed his revolver thoughtfully at Longarm, who yelled, "I'm law! U.S. deputy!"

He saw that the one bending over the dead man was still alive, so he figured the streetcar had to be beyond pistol range by now. He shot a look up the slope, saw that he was right, and asked the copper who joined him behind the tree what in thunder was going on.

The Denver lawman said, "Bank robbery, around the corner on Broadway."

"Jesus H. Christ, they expected to escape by *streetcar*?"

"Oh, some kid with a roman candle spooked their mounts while they was inside, holding up the bank. We've been having a right interesting running fight, up to now. The goddamned fireworks going off all around sort of complicates things. Most times, when folks hear gunfire, they get out of the way, but——"

"Say no more, old son, I get the picture. Cover me while I catch a streetcar, will you?"

"You're crazy! I can't fire into all them passengers!"

"Aim *high*, damn it!" growled Longarm as, not waiting for an answer, he broke cover. The angle of the curbside trees helped for the first few yards. He knew, as he legged it up the slope the way he'd just come, that if he couldn't see the ass end of the streetcar, it couldn't see him, so he ran as fast as he was able in his low-heeled army riding boots. The team drawing the heavy load up the hill couldn't begin to move as fast, so he started to gain. Then, as he closed the gap, the end of the car began to wink at him between the stout tree-trunks, and some rascal began to pepper him as he dashed from tree to tree. The copper down the slope was sending fire over the domed roof of the car, and that helped throw the gunman's aim off: The kids screaming all around him might have made him nervous too. Longarm would have started tossing kids off about now, had he been in the other's shoes. But the son of a bitch knew no decent cuss was about to fire at a target surrounded by kids, screaming or not. As he broke cover, Longarm saw that the roughly dressed outlaw had picked up a little girl and was shielding his worthless hide behind her ribbons and bows as he sent shots alternately at Longarm and the coppers down the slope.

Longarm dashed across the walk to a brownstone stoop as he saw that it was a standoff for the moment. He didn't dare move in closer. He gauged the range and made it to another tree, farther up, as the gunman missed him on the fly again. They were almost to the top of the slope. Capitol Hill wasn't a true hill. It was the edge of a flat-topped mesa that ran way the hell

247

east, beyond the city limits, so any minute he could expect the commandeered streetcar to take off at a greater speed than any man on foot could manage. It was annoying as hell, but Longarm was stuck for a better play, even though he knew he wasn't getting anywhere with this one.

Then the outlaws made a series of stupid moves.

The first one was that the man on the rear platform dropped the little girl and elbowed his way deeper into the passengers. Longarm had no idea why, but he ran like hell, ignoring the stitch in his side as he gained on the streetcar, grabbed the edge of the rear guardrail with his free hand, and got both feet on the protruding lower edge of the rear platform.

As he started to haul himself up and over the guardrail, the heavy car came to a halt, then started rolling slowly back down the hill!

Longarm cursed, holstered his .44, and grabbed for the brake crank at his end of the car. He'd watched them work these things up and down the hill often enough to know that one crewman walked behind the car on the downslope, braking the wheels with this son-of-a-bitch crank, which usually seemed work for *other* folks!

He thought he might be slowing the car down a mite, as the brake handle got painfully hot in his palm and squealed like a sow giving birth to a litter of broken beer bottles. But, while it might have run away faster without him on the brake, it was still headed down Colfax a hell of a lot faster than the Good Lord—and the turn at the bottom—had ever intended.

A red-headed kid stuck his head out to yell, "Those rascals shot the driver and unhitched the team to light out bareback!"

Longarm wondered what else was new. There wasn't a damned thing he could do about it, as far as he could see.

Then, as they screamed across Lincoln and started down the steeper slope beyond, he saw that there was. The improvising outlaws had apparently run into other lawmen, to the east. The three of them were tear-assing off across the terraced lawn of the state house. Two men were aboard one draft horse, and the other was on the remaining dapple gray. Both brutes were still harnessed together and making a little trouble for the riders.

It wasn't too clear where the outlaws meant to go, if they'd planned that far ahead. The erstwhile streetcar horses were running downhill, almost parallel to the runaway car. Longarm could see that his efforts with the brake had done some good. The runaway team was gaining. So he let go of the hot and likely useless brake handle, drew his gun again, and started firing.

He aimed at the near horse, of course, but his round carried a trifle high and knocked the rider on the off-horse clear. This seemed to discourage the two who were left. They rolled off, and after they'd slid and tumbled a spell in the grass, Longarm saw that they were rising with their hands up and that the two coppers he'd left at the bottom of the slope were moving in to take them.

By this time the streetcar had almost made the bottom of the hill too, and it was still moving fast. As it approached the intersection of Colfax and Broadway, Longarm hauled himself up into the car and yelled, "Everybody *down!*" as he dropped behind the bulkhead.

Nobody else paid much mind. They were all screaming and staring wide-eyed as the streetcar slammed into the big brewery wagon that Longarm had seen they were going to hit.

Everybody on board went down *then*, all right! The runaway streetcar came to a halt, still upright on the tracks, as the brewery wagon absorbed its momentum with a horrendous wet explosion that sent suds and barrel staves four stories high and a half-block in every direction!

Longarm peered gingerly over the edge of the platform as beer dripped off the brim of his Stetson and everything else in sight. The brewery teamster was wardancing in the middle of a very sudsy street, while his

Percherons loped off in the general direction of Cheyenne.

Longarm turned to see if any other passengers were still alive. The noisy kids had been stunned to momentary silence, and it was hard to tell the girls from the boys, with everyone covered with foam like that.

The crash and all the preceding commotion had attracted folks from near and far. A man in business dress and a derby ran over to the outraged brewery driver, slipped in the suds, grabbed the already-soaked driver, and they went down together, cussing fit to bust. Longarm saw more coppers coming from the direction of City Hall, across Broadway. They were smart enough to circle wide of the beer slick as they headed his way. Longarm rose and made his way forward through the kids to where two beer-soaked women knelt over a foam- and blood-covered man down in the suds between the seats. Longarm's pants were already soaked through, so he dropped to one knee and placed a wet hand against the streetcar driver's wet throat. "I'm alive, damn your eyes," the man said. "Where the hell is Wabash?"

"Don't know," Longarm replied. "Where are you hit, and who's Wabash?"

"I'm creased under the floating ribs, but I don't suspicion I'm hulled. Bullet knocked all the wind outten me and I felt like I was dead for a spell, but it's starting to smart, so I'm likely going to get up mad as hell in a minute. Wabash is supposed to be my brakeman."

Longarm looked around. The suds were sort of thick in places, but he didn't see enough foam anywhere to cover a body. The kid who'd been tossing torpedoes at innocent pedestrians volunteered, "I saw a man in streetcar duds jump off and run like hell when them jaspers come aboard with guns."

One of the two women said, "Roscoe, you mustn't use such language!" So Longarm looked at her. She and the fatter gal with her were wearing outfits like the Harvey Girls who served vittles for the Atchison, Topeka & Santa Fe, but he doubted they were waitresses. The gal who'd corrected Roscoe sighed at him through the foam on her face and explained, "Roscoe and these other children are from the Arvada Orphan Asylum. This other matron is Miss Hewitt and I am Morgana Floyd."

"I don't know how we'll ever be able to thank you for saving us, sir," the fat one said.

Even a fat lady covered with beer deserved common courtesy, so Longarm said, "Just doing my job, ma'am. My handle is Custis Long and I'm a deputy U.S. marshal."

Roscoe's eyes widened and his jaw dropped. "Hot damn! You're the one they call Longarm! I seen you on Larimer Street the other day, talkin' to one of them fancy ladies from the Silver Dollar!"

Morgana Floyd gasped, "Roscoe! I've a good mind to wash your sassy mouth out with soap and water!"

But Longarm said, "I'd start by taking away his fireworks before they dry out again, ma'am. He's already foamed up enough."

The fat gal laughed. But Morgana said, "Oh, Lord, we are all messed up. What on earth *is* this foamy goo?"

Longarm frowned as he inhaled more malt and hops, but she seemed serious. As the bubbles began to burst, he could see that she was a right pretty little thing, and the soaking-wet, black bodice of her matron's uniform promised some fortunate man in the future a mighty nice honeymoon—he doubted that there was any other way to undress a grown-up woman who didn't know what beer smelled like. He smiled benignly at her. "We hit a brewery wagon, ma'am. I'd say it was mostly lager with a little ale."

"Oh, no, we *can't* be drenched with Demon Rum!"

"No, ma'am, it's only beer, and as you can see, it's going flat and drying fast. It's a warm day and we're a mile above sea level, so—"

"Oh, heavens, we're going to have to take these children back to the orphanage and get them out of these ruined clothes," Morgana cut in.

"Aw, hell," Roscoe said disappointedly. "What about our picnic?"

"I'm sure we'll be dried out long before we can get all the way back across town, dear heart," the portly matron observed to her companion.

"There you go, ladies. It don't matter whether you head home or go on to the picnic grounds," Longarm said. "You'll all be dried out in about an hour anyway." He frowned at Roscoe and growled severely, "Empty your pockets, outlaw. I'm disarming you in the name of the law."

"I've only got one torpedo and some durned old ladyfingers," Roscoe protested.

Longarm relented slightly. "Well, I'll let you keep the ladyfingers if you promise to shoot 'em off after you get to the park. But I'm going to have to take that torpedo off you. Those things are dangerous even when a kid has sense."

Grudgingly, Roscoe handed over the almost dry torpedo as a copper came aboard to investigate the situation. Longarm identified himself and asked the copper to get a doc for the wounded man. The copper said he would, and went on, "I might've known that was you under all them suds, Longarm. That was some mighty fancy shooting you just did. I'd have aimed for one of the horses, but I must say you took all the fight out of them bank robbers when they saw you could nail a man in the ear at that range."

Longarm just shrugged modestly. He saw no need to correct a fellow peace officer with ladies present.

More policemen and some civilians were gathering around the stranded streetcar now, so Longarm turned back to Morgana (who was getting better and better looking as she dried out), and said, "We'll have us another teamster, and I see they've rounded up the draft horses over yonder, ma'am. I was on my way to my office, but if you want, I'd be proud to see you all out safely to the picnic grounds. I mean, it's my duty to protect women and children and—"

"Don't be absurd!" the woman snapped. "I said we had to change all our clothes. Dry or not, I'm not about to be seen in public smelling of an alcoholic beverage!"

The fat girl met Longarm's eye and sighed, "She's probably right, and she *is* in charge."

So Longarm tipped his hat politely and got off the streetcar while he was still ahead.

Life was like that, he told himself, as he headed officeward through the gathering crowd. The pretty one had been too prissy for a grown man to tarry with, and the good sport had been fat. But what the hell, the short adventure had given him a good excuse for checking in late, and how many papers could Billy Vail make a man fill out between now and noon?

He got to the corner near the Federal Building and took out his pocket watch. He was still unreasonably early, and it was only fair that a hero ought to be allowed to steady his nerves and dry out a mite more before he slipped into harness. So Longarm headed for the nearest saloon as he pondered just where he'd most enjoy tossing the torpedo in his pocket after he'd dried it out and wet his whistle.

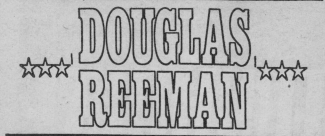